DOLORES

DOLORES

BY

IVY COMPTON-BURNETT

With an Introduction by
CHARLES BURKHART

William Blackwood & Sons Ltd
Edinburgh and London

William Blackwood & Sons Ltd
45 George Street
Edinburgh EH2 2JA

First published in 1911

First impression printed at the Press of the Publisher.
Second impression printed offset by Lindsay & Co. Ltd,
Blackfriars Street, Edinburgh.

ISBN: 0 85158 104 8

INTRODUCTION

THE first and till now the only edition of *Dolores* was published by Blackwoods in 1911. It sold well, and was promptly forgotten ; apparently even its author did not want to remember it, since she did not publish another novel until 1925, nor did she include *Dolores*, the first of her twenty novels,. in later lists of her publications. But now that her career of sixty years is ended, and her long achievement more and more acclaimed, *Dolores*, standing at that remote beginning, is curiously reborn. When a writer is alive, his works tend to be regarded one by one, as they appear ; when he is dead, they tend to be seen as the whole they have become. The genesis of genius attracts a natural speculation. If the author of *Dolores* preferred to forget it, her readers will not. When a writer dies, he loses his privacy, all but his essential, his irremediable privacy ; and critics, disciples, the rare book dealer and the bibliographer would not leave him that, if they could help it.

The first edition of *Dolores* (which is now virtually unobtainable) contains in its end pages, in the manner of volumes at that time, a thirty-two page Catalogue of Messrs Blackwood & Sons' Publications. It is interesting reading. Blackwoods was publishing Conrad and Forster ; *The Longest Journey* was in its second impression. But its leading author by far was George Eliot, dead thirty years, one Victorian who still retained her eminence. Of her works Blackwoods offered a New Popular Edition, a Warwick Edition, a Standard Edition, a Cabinet Edition, a Popular Copyright Edition, and a Cheap Edition. There was even a new edition, at 3/6, of *Wise, Witty, and Tender Sayings, in Prose and Verse, selected from the Works of George Eliot.* Among her great female predecessors in the English novel, I. Compton-Burnett is in a general way most like Jane Austen, least like Charlotte Brontë, but the dominant influence on *Dolores* is George Eliot, an influence so pervasive that it extends to characterisation and tone, subject, theme, and even diction.

Perhaps it extends too far or not far enough, because *Dolores* seems both overdone and underdone Eliot. Its story concerns a young Victorian woman, Dolores Hutton, who sacrifices her chances for personal happiness to the larger interest of duty to her family. Its settings are the village of Millfield in Yorkshire, where

Dolores' father, the Reverend Cleveland Hutton,
is rector, and Oxford, where Dolores attends a
woman's college ; the twenty-one chapters of
the novel are fairly evenly divided between
Millfield and Oxford. Its characters are, in
Millfield, the members of the middle-class house-
holds of that village (Hutton ; Blackwood ;
Cassell ; Merton-Vane), and, in Oxford, the
women teachers at Dolores' college, a don or
two, two school companions and friends of
Dolores, and a great but unrecognised dramatist
(his name alone, Sigismund Claverhouse, might
seem to have conferred a certain notoriety).
Its structure is a series of Dolores' dutiful
sacrifices : to begin with, she must reject a
position as teacher in her college upon her
graduation from it to become instead the
governess of a younger stepbrother and step-
sisters. The favourite child of her father the
rector, Dolores bears patiently the ill will of
her stepmother. When an uncle provides for the
education of her pupils, Dolores is free to return to
Oxford and to Claverhouse, whom she loves and
reveres. Unfortunately Claverhouse has fallen
in love with Dolores' shallow and pretty friend
Perdita, and it becomes Dolores' task to help
bring about this marriage. It is brought about,
but after nine months Perdita Claverhouse dies
in childbirth, and Dolores returns to her role
of spiritual companion and amanuensis to

Sigismund, whose eyesight is failing, and who has begun to reciprocate her love. Frustration, however, is the rule : her stepmother dies, and Dolores must return to Millfield to preside over her lonely father's house. She does so, for the next five years. She rejects an Oxford don ('Soulsby') who has long admired her when she discovers that her younger sister Sophia is in love with him. It is once again a question of their father the rector's needs, and Dolores easily arranges that Soulsby marry Sophia instead of herself, herself continuing the martyr role of father companion. On a brief visit to Oxford, Dolores is re-united with Claverhouse, near-blind and near death. In a climax of self-abnegation Dolores comes back to her father, to find, ironically, that he is about to marry for the third time and no longer needs her. The irony is compounded in that Claverhouse, whom she is now free to join, dies during her brief absence from him. She ends as teacher in the women's college.

Presumably, for the rest of her life, she will be a dutiful teacher. Duty is a keyword in George Eliot's novels, and it is here ; sometimes, as the preceding synopsis has shown, assuming the classical form of duty versus love. The sense of duty that inspires the highminded Dorothea Brooke, the heroine of *Middlemarch*, is the same sort of obligation felt by Dolores

Hutton. They are related in other ways. The young Dorothea's marriage to the middle-aged pedant Casaubon, whose magnum opus is to be a *Key to All Mythologies*, resembles Dolores' devotion to Claverhouse, who is much older than she, and whose dramas, as they are once or twice described, sound similarly vast. Unfortunately neither Dolores' nobility nor Claverhouse's dramas are questioned ironically as their counterparts in *Middlemarch* are. Dorothea's sense of duty is presented as both noble and absurd. Dolores' is only noble. And thus becomes, too insisted-upon as it is, absurd inadvertently. What ironies in Dolores there are, are amateur, discrete, and heavy observations of discrepancies, while those in *Middlemarch* seem like the inevitable products of a grave, austere, and philosophic vision.

There are in *Dolores* a range of social comment, an attention to class differences, and an emphasis on setting that will not be met with again in the following nineteen novels. They show that the author of *Dolores* was conversant with the typical scope and the areas of comment of Eliot and the other Victorians. Specifically Eliotean is an insistence upon the importance of ' low ' or obscure destinies, on the heroism of the unheroic. Such ' ideas ', the cast of intellectualism to *Dolores*, are rare or missing in the later nineteen.

There are other Eliot echoes. The addresses

to the reader, of which there are many, reproduce
the tone of Eliot's addresses, weightily humorous,
portentous, finger-wagging. Didactic throughout, the author of *Dolores* tells us very early
that ' Dolores ' means ' sorrows ' (for duty is
sacrifice and suffering), reminds us much later
that the heroine's life has been sorrowful, and
even supplies a happier-natured friend named
Felicia to drive the point home. George Eliot
almost never wrote a light or supple phrase,
and, knowing Dame Ivy's later style, one finds
astonishing the sentences like polysyllabic pud-
dings in *Dolores*. The following can serve as
example for those Eliot-derived habits of style
just mentioned :

> Now, as a person of observation, and
> knowledge of human nature in its subtler
> aspects, for example, as acted upon by
> difference in religious views and sameness
> of blood, are you disposed to dark surmise
> on the relations of the houses of Blackwood
> and Hutton ; or wondering how long it had
> been since relations between them existed ?
> In this thing you may take heart. Their
> ground of intercourse never presented clefts
> on its surface, though the ensuing stratum
> was at times volcanic. As far as the masters
> of the families went, the intercourse was so
> entirely on the surface, that this covered
> eruptiveness did not affect it. (Chapter II.)

What *Dolores* lacks that George Eliot's novels,
even her first ones, pre-eminently have, is the
richness of detail, the patient construction of
effect blended with exploratory pause, the ample
and leisurely pace so characteristic of the
Victorians, who so frequently complained of
the increased tempo of modern life. But
Dolores was written in the twentieth century,
and no matter how it leans backward to adopt
the stances of an earlier fiction, its subject is
too big for its length. Some chapters read like
outlines for chapters. There are many undevel-
oped characters, truncated scenes, phrases which
intimate issues that a paragraph should expound.
The effect is that of a remarkable intelligence
exercised perversely and uncomfortably. Dame
Ivy's imagination did not respond to the philo-
sophical, the sociological, the theological ; but
her admiration for George Eliot led her to adopt
just those biases, and she could flesh them out
only meagerly.

There are other aspects of *Dolores*, besides its
being so marked as influenced, that indicate its
interesting immaturity. It seems that the author
did not know what kind of novel she wanted to
write, and the fact that, on her own evidence,
her brother had some share in the composition
of the work, may further have clouded her aim.
Dolores is intermittently a Bildungsroman, a
domestic drama, a comedy of manners, and,

if one judged only by the first three chapters,
a religious novel, of Church versus Chapel. It is
a mélange ·of moods as well as of modes ; passages of alert bright comedy are side by side
with the meditative, the dour, the lugubrious.
The character of Dolores is presented with more-
than-Victorian sentimentality ; she suffers, and
suffers, and suffers.   The young Compton-
Burnett often describes where it would be more
effective to dramatise, and she will talk a character out of existence where he should be talking
himself into it.   In Chapter I especially, there are
excessively long descriptions of several quite
minor characters.   Surely the most bizarre
element in the compound of *Dolores* is the
Gothicism of the Claverhouse family, wizened
ninety-year-old Janet Claverhouse and her
deformed son, the genius Sigismund.   Their
macabre daily life, as described in Chapter V,
makes them the oddest household in twenty
novels devoted to the eccentricities of families.

What the beginning author has to find is his
unique tone.   Once he knows what he sounds
like, the rest follows.   To begin as a writer is
to get in touch with one's self, to learn what
is one's own most truthful and natural voice.
The uncertainties listed in the last paragraph
are peripheral matters compared with the uncertainties of tone.   Several styles, in addition
to the Eliot imitations already noted, jostle one

another in the pages of *Dolores*—the jaunty, the glum, the intense, the urbane, the impressive. There are many bad sentences like the following :

> But as the days passed, they carried with them that which was of them. (Note the five pronouns. Chapter IX.) . . . Dolores' time was her own from dawn to dusk. Her purpose was not of the things to which Dolores was easily blind. (This means that Dolores knew her purpose. Chapter VII.)
> But there was no place in Dolores' soul, for remorse for that which was wrought with pain for the sake of conscience. (Three ' for's '. Chapter XI.)
> He [the Very Revd. James Hutton] was yet in the prime of his pomposity and portliness, his fondness for kindly patronage, and his contentment with himself and his ecclesiastical condition. (Alliteration is used heavily throughout *Dolores*. Chapter VII.)

There are unconvincing verbal tics used to identify a character (Mr Blackwood, Mrs Merton-Vane, Soulsby). And there is much else one could say about the abstract, the pretentious, the wordy, the opaque. But what is curiously impressive, in fact the glory of these errors, is the determination, the energy, the psychic vigour they show.

In the long run, the sixty years' run, she did

not settle for any received style, any received
notion.   She found her own voice by abandon-
ing the voices of the past, the revered dead
masters of dead prose.   In *Dolores* she tested
them.   Fourteen years later, in *Pastors and
Masters*, she had fully attained her own, if
still shaky, tone.   In the nineteen novels subsequent to *Dolores* George Eliot is mentioned
once ; a ridiculous and self-loving lady, Gertrude
Doubleday   in   *Manservant   and   Maidservant*,
fancies and encourages a resemblance between
herself and the great Victorian, and serves tea
under her portrait.

Comedy is the purge for the pretences of
Dolores,   for   the   verbose   and   the   quasi-
philosophic ;   comedy   is   the   mode   adopted
for the later nineteen.   It has already asserted
itself in *Dolores* (and this may be what, in
Dolores, finally interests us most) : no novel
with a character named Perdita Claverhouse
can be entirely glum.   In the satire of highminded gentlemen like Mr Blackwood and Dr
Cassell ;   in   the   verbal   wars   between   the   two
sisters Mrs Hutton and Mrs Blackwood, acid
antagonists ;   in   the   aggressive   witty   candour
of Elsa Blackwood or the smoother more absurd
wit of Felicia Murray—in these the comedy of
the future is predicted.   Mr Blackwood is a
first run-through of the ninny type, like Peter
Bateman in *Brothers and Sisters* ; Sigismund

Claverhouse is the first of countless writers, culminating in Hereward Egerton in the nineteenth novel, *A God and his Gifts* ; Elsa and Felicia are prototypes of the truth-speaking sophisticates who will offer their witty opposition to family tyrants in every subsequent work.

There are other minor foreshadowings, situational devices that will be used dozens of times, such as servants listening at keyholes (Julia, the serving woman of the Claverhouses) or fateful discovered documents (Perdita's tragic diary of her marriage, read after her death by her husband). But it is the comedy that counts. The proportion of melodrama to comedy in *Dolores* is, perhaps, three to one ; in the later novels, this proportion is reversed and increased —for one page of heavy drama bristling with rhetoric there are ten or twenty where wit dominates. Not that the two elements are so sharply demarcated as this would sound : nonetheless the supreme moments in the novels are those when everything stops and pure comedy reigns.

It begins in *Dolores*, markedly with the chorus of schoolmistresses, whose wit must surely be Dame Ivy's own, unaided by her brother or anyone else. One cannot claim for the schoolmistresses the comic quality of, for example, the exchanges between Mortimer Lamb and the butler Bullivant in *Manservant and Maidservant*

or the luncheon party in *Elders and Betters*.   But
one can claim a good deal.   Here is the end of
Dolores :

"You are experienced in people's manners
of offering their hands, then, Miss Cliff ? "
said Miss Greenlow, in tones of polite
comment.

"Ah !   The cat is out of the bag," said
Miss Dorington.

"No," said Miss Cliff, with easy laughter.
"I have no right to speak as one having
authority."

"Ah !   That is all very well now," said
Miss Dorington.   "You certainly spoke in
an unguarded moment with no uncertain
sound."

"How many of us have that right, I
wonder," said Miss Lemaître.

"I suspect Miss Adam," said Miss
Greenlow, shaking her head.

"Miss Adam, you are a marked character,"
said Miss Cliff.

"Clearly we are right, Miss Lemaître,"
said Miss Greenlow ; as Miss Adam yielded
without great unwillingness to the impulse
to look conscious.

"Anyhow we are rude," said Miss
Dorrington genially.

"Oh, we can surely talk to young people,
as old women may," said Miss Cliff.

" If youth is the qualification, Miss Hutton is the fittest mark for our elderly interest," said Miss Lemaître.

" Miss Hutton, can you meet our eyes ? " said Miss Adam, not without suggestion that this was beyond herself.

" Oh, we will acquit Miss Hutton. She is the most sensible of us all," said Miss Cliff.

It is appropriate that this is the end of the novel. It is as if here, after the flounderings, the true voice has been found. It is this same voice which will be heard fourteen years later in *Pastors and Masters* and, developed, perfected, throughout the remarkable novels that follow.

Charles Burkhart

DOLORES.

————

CHAPTER I.

It is a daily thing: a silent, unvisited church-yard; bordering the garden of the parsonage; and holding a church whose age and interest spare our words; a few tombs fenced from their fellows, and marking generations of the family held as great; others naming primitive lives that grew and waned by the spot which har-bours their silence; and at some moment of its lying in sight an open grave with its mourners.

An open grave with its mourners. It is a daily thing, but not to be denied our heed. Let us mark the figure foremost in the sombre throng, that clerical figure of heavy build and with bent head. That is the Reverend Cleve-land Hutton, the vicar of the parish.

He is not very worthy of our words, the Reverend Cleveland Hutton. He is perhaps less worthy than his parish would have held, and his appearance tends to suggest. The heaviness of build, which was interpreted in the light of feminine fondness for the cloth as a sign of mental and moral profundity, was on other interpretations simply heaviness. The expanse of his brow was due in smaller measure to developement of the brain beneath, than recession of the hair above. The unusual length of his hinder locks, though a feature which, as he was aware, has been in some cases an attribute of genius, was in his own to be referred, simply, to his directions to his barber. Even his Christian name, though to the rustic portion of the village it was an illustration of his removal from things common amongst remaining mankind, had been given him for no better reason than that it was his mother's maiden surname—a reason which even to his mother seemed to have appeared sufficient only in the case of a younger son, since his elder brother was known to his family as James. In his clerical character also he was one of many. He had discharged the duties of a curate till he was thirty-five; and his recent appointment to this country living, which he had himself been heard to allude to as his first step up the ladder of preferment, was likely to be his final one; and was due not less to the fact that his mother's cousin was connected with its patron, than to the force of his personality, or the repute of the pamphlet he had published.

No; there was nothing in the Rev. Cleveland Hutton to mark him a man apart. But it does not follow there was nothing about him to be written or read. Our deepest experience is not less deep, that it is common to our race; and the heart of the Rev. Cleveland Hutton was not less wrung, as he watched the ebbing of the life that was to him of price, and wrestled in remembrance of the forgotten wrongs of tone and word, which even the supreme agony of remorse could not make as if they had not been, that it was an ordinary human heart, which had beaten for thirty-eight years in obedience to ordinary human daily things. It was a strong still face, from which he tore his eyes, turning again that its picture might defy the years with different days. There had been a strong, woman's heart to cleave to his own, through the struggles of the lingering unbeneficed time, the loss of his first-born, and other things finding a place in his ordinary human lot. Standing by the open grave, dreading for the numbness of grief to pass, and leave him the facing of the future that was dark, he was as fitting a mark for compassion as if his name were to live.

Nor was compassion withheld. The mourners behind him are standing with lips set firm and with bowed heads. They are not his relatives:

for the Reverend Cleveland Hutton had a knack of becoming estranged from his kin. He had at times met occasion to borrow from them, or coercion to allow them to borrow from him, and had not met the rarer experience of averting regrettable results. The only member of his family present was his elder brother, the Reverend James Hutton; who, never holding business dealings with relatives on principle, did not find himself disqualified for conducting the burial service. They are all of the district's familiar dwellers; and they will serve, if patience can be held through seeming wandering, as an example of the power of this passage of the ordinary human lot upon the ordinary human heart.

If you had entered this straggling village, at the time—somewhere in the latter half of the nineteenth century—when its parsonage was the home of the Reverend Cleveland Hutton, you would have thought it well provided in the matter of its spiritual needs. It contained, besides its church of passable antiquity and interest, a Wesleyan chapel without such qualities, and a wooden building in a field; which from having been the barn of a now obsolete farmhouse, had come to be a sort of meeting-place at general disposal for religious ends. But it does not follow, because a place is well provided in the matter of religion, that it is equally furnished in such matters as charity and tolerance. It might rather seem that Providence felt good equipment under both these heads an extravagant moral dower for a single spot, and was at some pains to avoid it. Bearing this in mind; and summoning thither our experience of ordinary human nature as wrought upon by minor religious disagreements, and of districts with a church with traditions in favour of a high ritual, an old-fashioned Wesleyan chapel, and such a peopling that every working man is an accounted unit in each congregation; let us turn our eyes on the figure behind the Reverend Cleveland Hutton. It is a figure similar in height and garb, but with a subtle suggestion of difference.

That is the minister of the Wesleyan Chapel.

Look next at the mourner behind the Wesleyan minister — that broad-shouldered man with the air of the prosperous country gentleman. That is Mr Blackwood; who for some time has been a prominent figure of the neighbourhood; having found in it some years ago a roomy house at a reduced rent, and within easy distance of facilities for Wesleyan worship—adaptable conditions to his large family, straitened income, and the branch of dissent in which both he and his wife had received their nurture. Of his appearance there is little to be told beyond what is said. Mrs Blackwood was of the opinion that he looked like a member of parliament; and he could himself testify that on several occasions in the

train he had been taken for one. The sena-
torial suggestion about him had the excuse that
this had once been his destiny. Family losses
following his early marriage had cancelled the
prospect; and Mr Blackwood, who had seconded
with much compliance his parents' assumption of
his insight into national conditions, recognised in
a similar spirit that misfortune had averted the
career for which he was moulded ; and surrendered
himself with what was felt a rather fine suppres-
sion of repining to the obscure but untaxing
career of a country gentleman. This life was
diversified by experience of more arduous nature.
Mrs Blackwood was unable to be reconciled
to the anomaly of public qualities withdrawn
from the general advantage; and having strong
feelings upon temperance and the deplorable significance of the spread of Roman Catholicism,
was wont to urge him to the use of his accepted
rhetorical gifts, upon which her views had an
unwonted concurrence with those of relatives-in-
law. Further losses in substance having lessened
facilities for country pleasures, he had greater
resource to declamatory interests. Habit begot
inclination ; and brought into outline opinions in
which he had acquiesced, in the same manner as
in his own deliberative fitness ; and the addressing
of " meetings," political, religious, and temperance,
came to be the main interest of his leisure—in
other words, of his life. Temperance and religion

encroached upon politics, as being less exacting
mentally, and better adapted to the rather
emotional and fervid discourse in which he felt
his talents to lie; and at the time when this
story opens he was recognised in Millfield as an
amateur gentleman-evangelist, prepared to exercise his oratorical powers for the intangible
advantage of his kind; in the chapel, the open
air, or the building in the field; and whether
at the request of the Wesleyan minister or in
response to his own heart's prompting. This
course of experience, involving the mingling with
people of a lower social and mental level on a
footing at once of pre-eminence and genial assumption of equality, had not been without effect upon
him; and in many respects he was altered from
the days when he was designed for a member of
parliament. His manner had developed in the
direction of freedom rather than polish, and the
air of the open-handed country squire was lessening. His greeting to cottagers had grown from
his former "Good day," to a "Well, friend, how
goes the world with you and yours?" or "Well,
Rogers, I shall expect to see you at the meeting
on Tuesday next." He was rather over-prone to
enter into talk, with a view to turning it to
temperance or religion, with strangers in the
train; and his arguments to prove to the Reverend
Cleveland Hutton that a high ritual really involved idolatry, were marked by more sincerity

and emphasis than delicacy. But there was much that was gentle and genial about Mr Blackwood. Any labouring man of the district, even if he was a churchman, and could not but regard the Reverend Cleveland Hutton as the standing example of what human nature might attain, would have told you that he was " a real gentleman." If he confounded the enjoyment of platform prominence with zeal for the souls of his fellows, and the emotions inspired by the sound of his own voice with the enthusiasm of inspiration, the confounding was innocent and honest : and to-day he forgot to view the Reverend Cleveland Hutton through the darkling haze cast by his high ritual, and stood simply with bowed head, and a heart that was full for his brother.

Let us next observe the mourner behind Mr Blackwood, who is also broad-shouldered, and also one of the familiar figures of the neighbourhood's gentry. That is Dr Cassell, the physician of the village and the district. On casting on him the first comprehensive glance of a stranger, you would hardly take him for a doctor. The indefinable air of the physician was wanting. His close-cropped hair and beard, his rubicund cheeks, and the general trend of his outward personality suggest the man of bnsiness. But he had as great a right to meet you on a physician's standing as the most professional-looking of his brethren ; for he was a physician

not merely by virtue of choice and training, but
by nature. As a boy of sixteen he had set a
bone under the guidance of his instinct; and in
the period to which he referred as "my commercial life"—in which, to divulge a fact which
tended to escape himself, his influence on trade
had been wielded indirectly through the faculties
called into use by errands and accounts—his
kindly amateur skill had won him some lasting
gratitude. On his transition from commercial
life to his present estate of prosperous country
practitioner, though a part of his career as much
as any other to his credit, he was not accustomed to dwell. His degrees were American;
and his following of the text-books of an English medical course was marked by no pedantic
devotion to the letter. His practical healing, it
may be said, was not greatly less, that it was
achieved under the direction of nature rather
than of text-books.

But he was not a man to be carried away
by modern tendency to narrowness; and medicine
was not the only subject in which he felt interest. He delighted in gathering knowledge
under any head; preferring it in promiscuous
fragments complete in themselves, and adapted
for retailing—a process in which his delight
was keener. His ideas of knowledge, and the
traits which marked his imbibing it, though it
can hardly be claimed for him that they were

peculiar to himself, were not those common amongst gentlemen with degrees. If he wished to connect some ideas with a well-known name, which to him was merely a name—and there were a good many well-known names standing to him in this which he naturally felt a somewhat bald relation—he would commit to memory some anecdotes of the owner's history, in preference to perusing any part of his works. He never alluded to the fact that he did not read imaginative literature, perhaps hardly realised he did not read it; but he avoided it by instinct, as barren of material suited for transmission in pithy fragments, and hence in all senses barren. He was, in a word, a "self-educated man" in the fullest sense of that subtle term. He was regarded in Millfield as a person of infinitely broad information, capable of pouring forth erudition upon any subject at a moment's notice— a view accepted without question by Mr Blackwood, but not accepted at all by the Reverend Cleveland Hutton; who had himself obtained a second-class in classics at Oxford, and who had once, in talking with his wife, gone so far as to observe that Cassell was an illiterate, canting fool.

The reason of the first of the epithets selected by Mr Hutton we have perhaps learnt enough of Dr Cassell to gather. The second leads us to consider him under a final head. He was a man whose personality had many sides; and in addition to his medical and encyclopædic pre-eminence, he was the third of the trio of local religious leaders, of which the Reverend Cleveland Hutton and Mr Blackwood were the first and second. In the religious accommodation of the district he was not so fortunate as his colleagues; for he was neither a member of the Establishment nor of the Wesleyan body. What he was, it is a less simple matter to make clear; and resort must be had to his own account of his abstract experience. He was accustomed to begin from the point where, at the age of twenty - seven, he had been converted, and to pass to a stage at which he had become a Plymouth Brother. From this body, for some scruple of conscience upon which he was vague, he had later seceded, though he always retained a tenderness for it, referring to its members collectively as "the brethren"; and at the time when this story opens, he had reached, at the age of thirty - nine, the emancipated stage of holding worship with his wife in his dining-room. His religious attitude was simpler, and may be given with more exactness, than might be presumed from the trouble of meeting its needs. The teachings of the Bible, interpreted according to the letter and without the commentator's aid,—he thought the tendency to put the word of man before that of divine revelation

one of the gravest signs of the times,—formed
the larger part; and the remainder consisted of
an antipathy to Roman Catholicism. The doctor's
horror of Roman Catholicism is entitled to a
word. It was not an everyday, easy horror. It
had a subtlety and force of its own. Moham-
medans, Buddhists, and worshippers of wood and
stone were in his eyes simply mistaken races;
obstinately mistaken perhaps, and inexplicably
ungracious in their reception of evangelising
offices; but nevertheless brother-men, unfortunate in knowledge and environment, and very fit
objects for missionary effort. To members of
the Romish Church his attitude was one of utter
condemnation; which never faltered to the extent
of weakly admitting reason in the place of dog-
matism; and which extended to any truckling
or pandering in the shape of over-broad views
upon religious tolerance, or high ritual on the
part of clergymen; and even caused him to look
askance at the little gold cross which dangled
on the waistcoat of the Reverend Cleveland
Hutton. That his intercourse with Mr Hutton
was confined to his medical capacity it is hardly
needful to state; but there had been an occasion on which he felt urged to transcend the
professional boundary, and send the latter an
anonymous postcard — we must remember in
judging him that his early experience had not
been that which is usual to professional gentle-

men,—asking him what justification he had, even granted that he felt entire indifference on his own ultimate and infinite prospects, for extending this callousness to those of others.

Dr Cassell's claim to be held a religious leader rested on his willingness—more exactly, perhaps, eagerness—to "speak" on religious subjects in the building in the field, whenever occasion demanded, or, with further concession to exactitude, permitted; to as large an audience as previous notices on its walls, and hints offered in person on professional rounds could gather. This leaning was a natural strain on his amity with Mr Blackwood; and might have put an end to it, had it rested on foundations whose undermining was possible. Happily it did not. Mr Blackwood and Dr Cassell stood in an indissoluble relation. Each was the other's chief repository for his recurring effluence of thought and opinion. Each had the same views upon Roman Catholicism — though Mr Blackwood could not but regard his friend as somewhat lacking in the gift of charity in his attitude to definite persons of this persuasion;—and the same fondness for repeating them, and resignation in hearing them repeated. Moreover, Mr Blackwood found a revelling-ground for his controversial talents in the winning of Dr Cassell to enthusiasm for Temperance; for which the latter's tolerant sympathy was prevented from

taking a fervid form by the relation of wine to
his personal habits. He also combated his tendency to be what he considered somewhat narrow
and over-literal, and regardless of the bearing
of the context in his interpretation of isolated
texts—not that Mr Blackwood had leanings to
the over-broad in such matters, or ever faltered
in his position as regards the higher criticism.
Dr Cassell on his part found his neighbour
a faithful believer in himself as a qualified re-
tailer of tit-bits of knowledge; appreciative of
their interest, and never acquainted with them
beforehand, and, if not an eager, a resigned and
considerately responsive auditor of anecdotes.

The other local families of not ungentle blood
were chiefly members of the church; holding the
relation of friendship only to Mr Hutton, merely
of patients to Dr Cassell, and hardly any relation
to Mr Blackwood; to whose mind in their turn
they had a negligible bearing on things in their
practical aspect, since such was the extent of
their connection with the meeting-house and the
chapel. Mr Hutton was held by most of them
in strong esteem; Mr Blackwood in half con-
temptuous disregard; and Dr Cassell in views
so various, that the best to be done is to quote
two typical comments uttered one morning within
an hour of each other,—a gentleman observing,
that any skill Cassell might have in physic was
balanced by his unprofessional trick of obtruding

his grandmother's notions; and a lady, that "the doctor" was such a dear friend and counsellor—really as good as a physician and a clergyman put together.

Now the moment may be meet for a word of warning given in kindness, lest there occur any waste of superior sentiment. Upon Mr Blackwood and Dr Cassell would be wasted both the disdain of philosophy and the indulgence of charity. They would have been as proof against the one as oblivious of the other. Let us think of them, simply, that they are of a race which has lived straightly and is dying hard; and whose death, if it marks a progressive step in our vulgar dogmatics, must rob our kind—if not of its most beneficent—of its most ingenuous and blithe. For it were idle to try and bring home with what exquisite innocent experience they would mount the extemporised platform in the building in the field—the subtle delectation involved in the staying of the cravings of the inward self, in its rarest and happiest union, with a sense of suppressing, and being known to suppress that self in disinterested effort; or to scan the present or past for men of gentler domestic living, and doings more cleanly and kind. Let us follow them down the country road as far as their ways are the same: for the burial service has come to its close; its rustic attendants are dispersing in gossiping groups;

and the Reverend Cleveland Hutton and the
Reverend James Hutton are walking up the
path that leads from the churchyard to the
parsonage.

"Poor Hutton!" said Mr Blackwood, in the
loud emphatic voice which he employed when
he felt he was giving the gist of a matter—
"poor Hutton! This has been about as great
a blow to him as any he could have had. We
shall see him altered, I expect—I expect we
shall see him altered."

"Yes," said Dr Cassell, who did not excel in
conversational parts, unless they were employed
in an amiably didactic direction—"yes, yes, that
is so. That can hardly be otherwise."

"Well," continued Mr Blackwood in the same
tone, "a funeral is a solemn thing—a solemn
thing. Whatever our religion is, and whatever
opinions we have on other subjects, that is the
same for us all. A funeral is a universally
solemn thing."

"Curiously enough," said Dr Cassell, coming
to a pause in the road, as was his wont when in
the grip of the didactic spirit; and employing his
didactic tone, which was marked by pauses
tending to occur at unnatural junctures, and
had a peculiar, neutral sound as if he had withdrawn his own personality from it; "curiously
enough, it is not *universally* solemn. Among
some early races—I do not recollect at this

moment exactly to what nations they belonged
—it is, or rather it was, the custom to rejoice
over death and to mourn at birth. It would
seem rather—dissentient with our notions, would
it not?"

"Ah," said Mr Blackwood, walking on, "there
is a great deal of truth underlying that notion—
a great deal of truth, I daresay. Those old
ancients could have taught us a great deal—
there's no doubt of that. When we mourn at
death, we mourn for ourselves — there is no
getting out of that. But still a funeral is a
solemn thing in every way—at any rate for
those who are left behind to see it; there is
no getting out of that either."

"I fancy there have been—on some occasions
—episodes to relieve the solemnity," said Dr
Cassell, coming to a pause, in which his friend
complied this time with less alacrity; and
summoning a twinkle to his eyes; his com-
punction on yielding to levity drowned in the
flood of his ideas. "A country parson was
once—leaving the churchyard, after burying one
of the villagers;—and--meeting another at the
gate, observed: 'Well, Johnson, so Roberts is
no longer amongst us — has joined the great
majority, eh?' and was somewhat startled at
receiving the reply: 'Oh, I don't know about
that, sir. He was a good sort of man, wasn't
he, as far as anybody could judge?'"

Mr Blackwood laughed with good-natured heartiness, though not with full approval; for he happened to be an exception to the rule that enthusiasm for religious subjects is coupled with a tendency to pleasantry upon them. Dr Cassell walked on, trying to repress a twitch about his mouth, under a sense of having in the last minutes done himself justice.

"Well, Doctor," resumed Mr Blackwood after a minute's silence—he always addressed Dr Cassell emphatically as "Doctor," and the Reverend Cleveland Hutton as "Vicar"—"are you coming to support us at the temperance meeting next Wednesday? I am engaged to speak, you know. It was very much against *my* will, I am sure; but people seemed to desire that I should; and I could not refuse my services to such a cause, so I shall just do my best—and make a terrible hash of the business into the bargain, I daresay." Mr Blackwood paused, awaiting contradiction of the conclusion of his speech, rather than an answer to its opening question; but Dr Cassell chose to give the latter.

"No, I think not," he replied—"I think not."

"Well, but come now, Doctor," said Mr Blackwood in loud, genial tones, laying a stress upon occasional words, as was his custom in argument. "You can't *deny* that the cause of *Temperance* is one of the *finest causes* in the country.

There's no possibility of expressing in words the harm that the *drink* does to the nation; and as for the harm it does to individuals—well, there is no need to tell a *man* of *your* knowledge of life that."

"Perhaps not," said Dr Cassell, unable but to recognise something in this ending which did not call for the throwing of doubt; "but one cannot always judge—of the right and wrong of principles—by the amount of apparent good or harm resulting from them."

"Oh, come now, Doctor," said Mr Blackwood, not choosing to adopt a philosophic standpoint, "you have to look at these things *practically.* The amount of *practical* benefit done by the fighting of the drink is *enormous.* Why, only last week, when I was visiting the place where I used to live, and where I used to give a weekly address on Temperance, an old fellow came up to me—an old Irish fellow, I think he was—a working man, and a *fine-looking* old fellow too; and he said: 'Well, sir,' he said, 'I have to thank *you* for something—if you call the saving of myself and my wife and the whole of my family from *ruin* something. I went once or twice to your addresses,' he said, 'and I *assure you* that I was a different *man* from that time.'" Mr Blackwood brought the fist of one hand down upon the palm of the other. "I can tell you the old fellow was *grateful,* and it did me *good* to hear him; it did that, upon my word. It was encouraging—very encouraging—I can tell you."

"Talking of the drink in connection with Irishmen," said Dr Cassell, coming to a pause; and interposing quickly without regard to congratulations; "have you heard of the Irishman in the barn and his bottle of whisky?"

"No," said Mr Blackwood, rather weakly, as he also stopped.

"There were two Irishmen sleeping in a barn," said Dr Cassell, "who had laid in a bottle of whisky for their joint refreshment; and one of them, waking up—found the bottle empty, and began to—remonstrate with his comrade upon —what he assumed to be his greed. 'Shure, Pat,' said the other, 'it was me own share at the bottom of the bottle, and I was obliged to pour away yours to get to it.'"

Dr Cassell laughed heartily; and finding that his last pause had occurred at his own gate, shook hands with Mr Blackwood and walked up his garden-path, finding it needful to suppress some chuckling as he went.

Mrs Cassell came to meet him as he crossed the hall — a slender, comely woman, with a manner that was slightly mincing and slightly effusive, and seemed to involve continual effort. Dr Cassell laid his hand on her shoulder as he passed in silence to his study. He was an excellent and affectionate husband, but disposed to a tacit manner of domestic intercourse. It was not his way to broach his intellectual stores except for outsiders; and Mrs Cassell, who was an excellent and affectionate wife, wary on the points on which he was sensitive, was less in need of compassion than many supposed, judging from the strained expression of interest, which coincided on her face with the didactic spirit in her spouse. It might hardly be thought on a casual view of Mrs Cassell, that she was the woman to make a congenial and useful wife for the doctor. She was content that the mysteries of medical science should remain to her mysteries. She took scanty pleasure in general information, or for that matter in information of particular kinds; and she was little better versed in housewifely arts than he was himself. But the doctor, like some other gentlemen meeting acquaintance on a standing consistently intellectual, was not unwilling to show himself adaptable, and to deviate somewhat from his recognised line in his domestic sphere. He was not, moreover, without suspicion of the effect which might be wrought on an attitude of un-questioning belief towards himself, by a sense of being capable of sharing his mental experi-ence; and he was rather averse than otherwise —vaguely acted upon, perhaps, by a sense of his "commercial life"— to seeing gentlewomen

employed in domestic usefulness; and not seldom
found occasion to observe on his rounds that his
wife "took no interest in household matters."
What kind of matters Mrs Cassell *did* take
interest in, it will hardly be worth our while
to decide; since neither her husband nor her
friends — not one of whom had defined ideas
about them — found their intercourse with her
hampered by this vagueness. It may merely be
added that her religious history had coincided
almost exactly — and since her marriage quite
exactly—with Dr Cassell's; and that whatever
we may think of her in her conjugal character,
the truest tribute of wifehood was her own, in
that never in the eleven years of their childless union had Dr Cassell felt himself other
than blessed.

Another gentleman who held this fortunate
view of his domestic experience was our other
acquaintance, Mr Blackwood. On walking up
his own garden - path, a less trim path than
Dr Cassell's—for Mr Blackwood's union, though
having the point we have noticed in common
with the doctor's, had been by no means childless, — and perceiving through the open door
the figure of his wife, clad in a pinafore, passing to and fro between the dining - room and
the kitchen, he told himself that nobody could
wish to see a prettier picture, and hastened
in to tell Mrs Blackwood the same.

"Well, my *darling*," he said with stress of utterance—he generally addressed his wife and daughters in emphatic terms of tenderness; and the practice had become so habitual that its fulfilment was often mechanical — "and what do you mean by trotting about, dressed up in that gown that makes you look so young and pretty, and pretending it's a pinafore? What do you mean by it, eh?"

Mrs Blackwood, whose brightness of temperament and wifely affection were prone to meet the too frequent fate of excellent qualities, and be disguised by superficial peevishness, hardly felt this a fitting comment upon uncongenial exertion, and continued trotting and made no response.

"Why, my *love*," said Mr Blackwood with loud solicitude, "have you been running about, and working yourself to death, so that you haven't a word for your husband? Come— leave all that alone for this afternoon, and let me hear something pretty."

Mrs Blackwood disappeared into the kitchen without replying; laid away the pinafore in one of the drawers of the dresser; and returned to the dining-room with a smile of welcome for her husband.

She was a small, sharp-featured woman, with an energy of manner and movement which belied a delicate form, and hair whose early grey-

ness made a comelier background for her pale,
fair cheeks than their one-time duskier framing.
She was a woman of some quickness of feeling
and intelligence, and some lack of depth in
both ; with a reverence for intellect and desire
to be held intellectual. Her confidence in
her right to such a repute had resulted in
a tendency to talk for the display of the wide-
ness of her reading and knowledge—of neither
of which this predication could be made—in a
spirit of exaltation above mere exactness, which
her family's unsceptical attitude had not tended
to counteract ; and a proneness to exaggerate,
which Mr Blackwood would combat with play-
ful affection, incurring considerable peevishness.
Her zeal for religion and temperance did not
fall short of her husband's ; was indeed, as we
have seen, the parent source from which the
stream of his enthusiasm flowed. It was by no
means an unheard-of thing, for her to "speak"
herself upon one subject or the other ; and in
the building in the field she was a highly-
thought-of character. In former days, before
variation of income in inverse proportion to
children had driven them to the large house
with the small rent at Millfield, and before the
art of oratory had become Mr Blackwood's
second nature—it had been rather foreign to
his first nature—it had been her custom to
assist him in the preparing of his speeches,

and even to coach him in their delivery; for
she had a natural bent towards declamation;
and in her earlier married life had belonged
to a debating society, and on one occasion pro-
posed the motion and carried it with much
distinction. The effects of this life upon her
were in the same direction as upon her husband.
The disposition to talk for the display of information had grown—though it happened that
the information had not sustained a similar
process. She had developed a tendency to raise
her voice and gesticulate in argument; and on
subjects on which her opinions were strong, to
assume to her auditors a relation didactic
rather than conversational. When she met Dr
Cassell, with whom she had stock points of
difference, she would take up a discussion where
it was left, without heed to things intervening,
and without ascertaining whether he desired its
resumption. The views of her in Millfield varied
with their holders even more than such views
are wont. The general rustic opinion of her
was as an affable and clever lady, but calling
for less respect—at any rate less outward show
of it—than one whose husband did not descend
to geniality with cottagers. The teetotallers who
formed her especial following, being mostly of
her own or husband's conversion, subjoined—
even if they were churchgoers, and could not
but recognise her secondary quality to Mrs

Hutton—some enthusiastic reverence ; and the
liquid-needers of the other school a slighter proportion of defiance. The factions of church people
and Wesleyans—to take the religious attitude
as unwrought upon by secular influence—had re-
spectively a tendency to shake their heads over
the spiritual darkness she shared with her husband, and an esteem for her as a union of the
graces of womanhood with a masculine capacity
for the demands of public life. Dr Cassell
thought her a woman of conspicuous intellect ;
and was in no degree troubled on the score of
masculine dignity in meeting her in argument
on equal terms. Mr Hutton did not part her
in his mind from her husband. He regarded
the two as a couple of gentle-people by birth,
pursuing as their ruling object the conversion
of themselves to the other human order, and
looked on this line of effort in the natural
attitude of a ritualistic clergyman born in the
earlier half of the nineteenth century, and holding a classical degree and conservative opinions.
He did not fail to resent their assumption of
religious authority ; but hardly felt upon it with
the bitterness which might be feared ; for he
was endowed with somewhat phlegmatic sen-
sibilities ; and, moreover, held the view that
the preferment of a powerful divine rested on
diplomatic dealings with his bishop, rather than
his standing in the country parish, which was

yielding him its tithes for the time in return for spiritual watchfulness.

"Well," said Mr Blackwood, as he seated himself in one of the easy-chairs by his dining-room fireplace, and turned his face to his wife, who had taken the other, "a funeral is a solemn thing. I don't know of anything that upsets and *unmans* me in the same way. As I said to Cassell when we were coming along, whatever religion we have, and whatever opinions we have on anything else, a funeral is the same for us all."

"Yes," said Mrs Blackwood, in her rather high-pitched, but sufficiently pleasing tones; "it makes us realise that we are all pilgrims on the same journey. In whatever direction our paths in life are set, we must all come to the river at last."

"Poor Hutton!" returned Mr Blackwood, leaning back in his chair and twisting his moustache. "Poor Hutton! His will be a lonely life enough after this, I am afraid—a lonely life enough; at least until little Dolores is old enough to fill her mother's place. It went to my heart to see him to-day—I can tell you that it did. He looked ten years older, and entirely broken down."

"And the poor children too—it goes to my heart to think of them," said Mrs Blackwood, wiping from her eyes the tears that were always

responsive to her will. " Poor little girl and
boy !—to lose their mother just when they are
beginning to need her."

" Yes, yes, we can't understand these things,"
said Mr Blackwood ; " we can't understand them.
We can only cling to our faith, and believe that
everything is ordained for the best."

" Did you say you walked home with Dr
Cassell, dear ? " said Mrs Blackwood after a
minute's pause, not finding any hitch in the
transition to easier feeling.

" Yes, we walked together as far as his house,"
said Mr Blackwood, falling in with the change
without reluctance ; " and I made another attempt
—though a very feeble attempt, I admit—to
enlist him on the side of *Temperance.* He would
make a valuable recruit—a valuable recruit." Mr
Blackwood lingered on this expression as though
content with it. " The influence he would
have about the neighbourhood would be immense."

" I don't think he would have as much influence as you have, dear," said Mrs Blackwood,
with the note of peevishness which was prone
to creep into her voice. " You have such a
wonderful talent for gaining influence over
people. I have never seen it in the same way
in anybody else. It is a real gift. I am sure
no one else would have a chance of succeeding
where you have failed." Mrs Blackwood's con-

jugal and maternal jealousy had gone beyond the stage in which it is a pardonable attribute of wifehood and motherhood.

"Ah, I don't know about that," said Mr Blackwood; "I don't know about that, my darling. One can only do one's best; and I don't suppose for a minute that *my* best is anything to boast of. But I think I may say that for the cause of *Temperance* I have done it. I think I *may* say that."

"I am sure you may," said Mrs Blackwood, with soothed appreciation.

It is perceived that Mr and Mrs Blackwood have put from their minds the trouble at the parsonage, with the easy sinking of compassion in the opposite emotion reflexively applied, which may be observed a power common to people stirred towards their fellows' "conversion," and ordinary, unevangelistic human kind. But the trouble in the parsonage lay not less heavily, as it stood in its sad sameness with the years in which the presence lost to it had ordered its life. The gabled house was the same; the broad path leading to the highroad was the same; the narrow path leading to the churchyard, the single oak on the lawn, the autumn-tinted creeper swathing the house in crimson wrappings—they were all the same. Even the scene in the porch was one which its rustic woodwork had often witnessed. The Reverend Cleveland

Hutton and the Reverend James Hutton were taking farewell of each other.

It was an old experience to the Reverend Cleveland—this standing on his threshold in an early hour of the evening, and giving God-speed to his brother, the no less Reverend James. His living was at such a distance from his brother's, as to bring it about that their dealings were conducted through frequent visits of a few hours' length. This system of fellowship was fortunate in regard not merely to the distance; for the feelings between them happened to be those which before and since their time have existed between brothers and sisters in their maturer years; and consisted of a moderately strong mutual regard, and a tendency—also mutual, but rather more than moderately strong—to continual petty irritation; affections to which frequency of intercourse and its speedy ending were fitted.

So strong was the sense of doing simply what was wonted, that the Reverend Cleveland crossed his hall with his consciousness deadened to his grief, and merely oppressed by a vague knowledge of a burden. With the opening of the door of his study, there even came a shadow of the old relief, which was accustomed to mark his return to his wife from the fraternal farewell—generally with the purpose of disburthening his mind of its pent-up comment on the various dispensable qualities of the Reverend James. The next moment, with the sense of the difference carried to-day in his brother's companionship, there came the rush of understanding—the first true knowledge that the responding face was gone, that the listening ear was gone; that through all the stretch of years before him, with all their days and weeks and hours, he must speak and move with words and movements which were hollow forms to his thought. For it is a heavy time when the buoyant spirit is bowed, and cries against its own delusion, that it will wake to the same wrestling upon all its days. The time is not fit to return to watch its working, until it meets the reactive power that bears it through its history.

The Reverend Cleveland Hutton girded himself in the spirit and faced his lot. They lay before him—the darkened years, empty of the presence of Dolores. Well, he would struggle through them as Dolores would have had him struggle. He would rise each day with the resolve to live its hours as a tribute to her; he would enter each year with the resolve to live its days as a tribute to her. In that future time—poor Cleveland Hutton! there was a part of him which his sorrow had left untouched,— when he should have dedicated a pamphlet to his bishop—after, of course, he had written it; and preferment should have resulted from it,

or rather from its dedication ; and he should look
from an elevation in the Establishment upon the
Reverend James presiding yet over the spiritual
interests of a country parish—a prospect in
which he felt a strong fraternal confidence and
a stronger fraternal satisfaction,—he would look
back on all he had excellently done, and feel
that the having lived the years as though
Dolores were at his side, almost brought Dolores
back to him.

And the heritage she deemed as greatest—
the opening lives she had nurtured—here indeed
was a daily thing to be done—the bringing her
lisping son to fairness of manhood, and the honouring his mother in his words and deeds. . . .
And the nine-year-old Dolores, with her mother's
voice, and her mother's face, and her fitting part
in her mother's name of sorrows !—he bowed his
head over a breast that heaved ; it was yet too
soon for the comfort that but proved his loss.

CHAPTER II.

THE parsonage lies the same in autumn sunshine. The creeper on the porch is the same in autumn blushing. The oak on the grass stands the same in stirring silence.

But the oak stands the same after its acorns are strewn for many seasons.

Were the tombs so many in the churchyard when last you saw it?—were the familiar ones so grey and lichen-grown? Was the moss so close on the wall which marks its bound? Was the creeper on the porch of the parsonage framing its windows with many-tinted falls? From porch to sill, and from sill to casement, it has crept through its ten years' journey.

A figure is walking through the churchyard towards the parsonage. A glance is knowledge. It is the figure of the Reverend Cleveland Hutton.

Perhaps it causes surprise that he should still be expending on the village of Millfield his ecclesiastical qualities, when it is remembered that he held the steps to preferment in his

C

hands, in his literary and dedicatory powers. It certainly caused himself surprise ; not to speak of bitterness of spirit, and a tendency towards the heretical opinion—more worthy, as it is very justly observed, of a Dissenter—that the Establishment was no better than ordinary, unestablished institutions, in its blundering location of its dignities. And from certain points of view it can hardly seem judicious in Providence, and that foremost of her handmaids, the Establishment, to neglect the advance of a reverend gentleman who has written three pamphlets and dedicated two to his bishop, and not failed to write to the latter on each of the last occasions to request his permission to evince his regard in this manner. It seems so less, when she elevates to a deanery his brother, who has merely printed a booklet entitled "Some Simple Sermons on Great Subjects"—of which attributes, only the former, as the Reverend Cleveland had observed, was to be referred to himself in his creative rather than selective aspect, that is, the aspect in which he was rightly assumed to consider himself revealed—without dedicating it to any one. The folly is clearer, when the former brother has five children and the latter none ; though it should perhaps be said in justice to Providence, that study of her dealings suggests, that possession of children appears to her compensation for lack of possession in other respects.

The Reverend Cleveland's somewhat morose
and heavy countenance was more morose than
usual, as he wended his way up the sloping path
through the churchyard to the parsonage. He
was returning from seeing off at the station his
brother, the Very Reverend James—a courtesy
rendered compulsory by the rarity of meeting resulting from the removal to the deanery. He was
also suffering the emotions following the fraternal
office of intimating to the latter, that he was aware
of the source of the chief ideas in his booklet—
some volumes which had been at their joint disposal in boyhood — without reward in signs of
incision in the armour of gracious complacence,
protecting a very reverend gentleman, taking
leave of his barely reverend brother.

But there creeps a change to his face, as he
passes to the side of the churchyard which skirts
the parsonage garden, and creeps at a moment
when change is meet. Yes; it lies in his sight—
the tombstone whose writing opens memory's
floodgates—" In remembrance of Dolores, beloved
wife of Cleveland Hutton, Vicar of this Parish,
who died in the thirty-sixth year of her age."

But do we forget what was said of the Reverend Cleveland Hutton? He is not a man apart.
Do we pity a sorrow hard in time - begotten
silence? Let us mark his eyes—the eyes of one
fearful of breaking memory's sleep. Some random
words recur; and your thought is a thought you

will not voice. But it is a thought which carries truth. There is another mistress at the parsonage.

No; let us check the words which tremble on our lips. Let us not say them. Let us not say, "Poor human love, that it can lightly bury its dead!" Let us hold our peace, and pass on.

Mr Hutton unlatched the gate which led to his garden from the churchyard, and walked up the gravel path to the parsonage. The voice of Mrs Hutton, who stood on the steps awaiting him—a mellowed, mature voice; for the Reverend Cleveland was not a man to succumb with improvidence to earlier maidenhood—greeted him as he came within hearing.

" Well, dear, so you have parted from the Dean? How do you support the thought of six months in the darkness of his absence? You seem to be bearing up fairly well. Did you ever see such popish pomposity? I wonder what would be the result if they made him a bishop?"

The Reverend Cleveland made no reply for a moment. He was not averse to laughing at his very reverend brother; but contingencies are sometimes broached, which hardly call for sanction even in jest.

"I cannot see—from what I can gather from James—that a dean's life is any more arduous or responsible than an ordinary vicar's," he observed, with an accent of bitterness, as he walked into his study.

"Well, I certainly never saw James looking in better condition," said Mrs Hutton; "not that his appearance has ever suggested his wearing himself out with toil." The Reverend Cleveland readily saw his brother's ampleness of frame a ground for smiling. "I wonder if he will use his leisure to write another booklet. Perhaps this time it will be 'Great Sermons on Simple Subjects.'" The Very Reverend James's isolated literary effort was a recognised subject in Millfield Parsonage for spare ironic talent.

"I can hardly imagine James writing anything great," said Mr Hutton, yielding to some crudeness in fraternal comment.

"Ah, my dear, you never *imagined* him a dean until you saw him one," said Mrs Hutton.

"He did not make himself a dean," said Mr Hutton, deprecating the judgment of the actual agents implied.

"Well—peace be to him—and to ourselves, for the time," said Mrs Hutton. "I have had enough of him for one day. I wonder what he would feel if he could hear us. I should think his left ear must be burning."

"Oh, I have never known James anything but sublimely complacent," said Mr Hutton, indicating the unlikelihood of his brother's suffering this discomfort; and speaking as though he considered a tendency to discontent some moral tribute — a view which would have added to his own self-regard.

Mrs Hutton laughed; and walking to the window, began to watch her children in the garden —two little daughters at play under the eye of a nurse, and a baby boy, to whose mind there seemed nothing wanting in the exercise of staggering as a source of indefinite amusement; from time to time bestowing some advice, voiced with rather unnecessary sharpness, upon the nurse's handling of her charge. The Reverend Cleveland took up his pen, and drew some sermon paper towards him with some austerity of mien.

Sophia Hutton was a woman of five- or six-and-forty, with the manner of carrying years which shows maturity a seemlier thing than youth. When there was added to this gift a generous dower of brunette comeliness and a gentle dignity of bearing, she appeared to the Reverend Cleveland—in the fuller bloom of ten years earlier—a fitting mistress for the stately home which preferment was to bring. For this she seemed to herself no less a fitting mistress; but confinement to a home for which she was less adapted had cost her feelings milder conflict. There was a certain discernment in her survey of things, which saved her a too disturbing perplexity on the Bishop's philosophy in viewing the Reverend Cleveland in a merely beneficed

condition. Moreover, the maidenhood attending
an imperious youth having outlasted the youth,
she did not compare the lot of mistress of a
sufficient household only with that of the mistress of a stately one, but also with a lot where
mistresship played no part. The attractions of
linking her portion with the Reverend Cleveland's had not been enhanced in her eyes by
the son and daughter by an earlier marriage.
The father, whose home she ordered, had himself taken a second wife; and though her late
esteem of stepmothers had not been flatter-
ing to the class, she found that their sway
appeared less repellent regarded as wielded than
obeyed.

As you watch her, do you mark the something
of tone and gesture which touches some familiar
chord—such a chord as is touched when, after
the remembrance of your friend is dim, you come
upon his son grown to a similar manhood? Listen
to her tones, as she leans from the window with
some words to her children on her lips—to that
note which holds a latent peevishness as though
in wait for a purpose. Yes, it is Mrs Blackwood
to whom she is bound by the bond of kin. Ten
years earlier, in the days ensuing on bereavement, when the heart is grateful for pitiful
human fellowship, and human fellowship is kind,
the Reverend Cleveland had passed some time
with his good-hearted and genial, if dissenting

and emphatic, neighbour. He had met Sophia,
the elder sister of his wife, and had induced her
to assume the lost relation to himself. In this
step she was influenced partly by reasons given,
and partly by a genuine, if not a fervid, affection and esteem for the Reverend Cleveland
Hutton.

The resemblance between Mrs Blackwood and
Mrs Hutton went deeper than what is meant
by " a strong family likeness;" and consists of
a film of suggestions insistent on the stranger's
eyes, but unheeded by those which have long
seen it transparent. They were sisters in the
fullest sense — clearly of the same stock and
strain. They were, in a word, in that stage of
affinity where, with human creatures as with
other complex things, contact is another word
for clashing. For it happens with character as
colours, that, though different examples may
make a grateful whole, two shades of the same
are likely in touching to offend. Mrs Hutton
had the quickness of feeling and intelligence
which marked Mrs Blackwood, and greater depth
in both; though hardly sufficient to warrant her
contempt of her sister's shallowness. Mrs Blackwood's tendency to jealousy and peevishness had
also its place in her sister, and was also rooted
to further depth; though under this head the
latter did not insist upon the difference. The
strain of kindliness which nature had implanted

in both—perhaps with a firmer and more generous
hand in Mrs Hutton—had grown in Mrs Blackwood under the influence of Mr Blackwood, and
her own endeavour to live her religion in her
dealings, into a consistent effort to attain to
charity which might almost claim the name. In
Mrs Hutton it had found itself in conflict with
a talent for hitting on the foibles of her kind
with a causticity which passed for wit, and a
mingling of wit itself; had found the struggle
for supremacy vain ; and now held to a suppressed
existence. Mrs Hutton had a greater dignity
of presence and a truer culture than Mrs Blackwood, and did not fail to recognise the latter's
deficiency ; not seldom entertaining the Reverend
Cleveland by mimicry of her sister " speaking "
at a temperance meeting, or talking for display
with gesticulation.

Now, as a person of observation, and knowledge
of human nature in its subtler aspects, for example,
as acted upon by difference in religious views and
sameness of blood, are you disposed to dark sur-
mise on the relations of the houses of Blackwood
and Hutton ; or wondering how long it had been
since relations between them existed ? In this
thing you may take heart. Their ground of
intercourse never presented clefts on its surface,
though the ensuing stratum was at times vol-
canic. As far as the masters of the families
went, the intercourse was so entirely on the

surface, that this covered eruptiveness did not affect it. Mr Blackwood combated Mr Hutton's leanings to ritual, and urged him to stronger influence on the side of temperance, in unfaltering defiance of years and lack of result, affording to himself enjoyment unutterable, and only moderate annoyance to the latter, whose feelings were not so impervious to blunting influence. He regarded his mission as a high and significant one, and reported the degree of his success to the doctor in a serious spirit. The Reverend Cleveland enjoyed at his pleasure his neighbour's masculine fellowship; and maintained towards him an easy goodwill; whose basis in his view of himself as a man of erudition of the more abstruse and higher order, as opposed to the doctor's practical knowledge, did not render it strong to the inconvenient extent of showing him an unsuitable subject for Mrs Hutton's mimicry.

Of the intercourse between Mrs Hutton and Mrs Blackwood an equally easy account can hardly be given. The local view of them was as an affectionate pair of sisters; and it was a current remark how "nice" it was, that they should spend their married life so near each other. But their intercourse was not confined to the safe, if easily exhaustible, sphere of the surface; and in its more perilous province sustained upheavals which would have threatened the exposed exterior, had not they been of that subtle kind to which open notice is forbidden. For example, when they met one day in the village, they expressed content that their ways coincided, and in making their farewells showed a cordial affection, which, however rarefied, was not in the least degree transparent. But if we suppose it *was* transparent, our knowledge will go further; for in a very few minutes the jar had come, the note of discord been struck. It was Mrs Blackwood who struck it. She neglected to show enthusiasm over an account by Mrs Hutton of a eulogy in a church paper of one of the Reverend Cleveland's pamphlets; and when Mrs Hutton was goaded to exaggerate the terms, made it known that she had read the paragraph, and corrected her sister's version. This was more than could be supported by flesh and blood—from flesh and blood of kindred substance; and hence the sisters' dialogue was charged with hidden currents. It became a series of thrusts with verbal weapons seemingly innocent, but carrying each its poisoned point. Before they parted, Mrs Hutton had observed with candour and humility, that she recognised now how bigoted she had once been in her views upon Wesleyanism, and of how much higher a type church-people really were; and that intercourse with a university man made one so different, that it was quite an effort to associate with people of another order. Mrs Blackwood had let fall the casual opinions, that no woman who did not marry before thirty knew marriage in its truest sense; and that Dolores was clearly a great comfort to her father — of course she brought back the old days to him.

The old days! They were old indeed to Dolores; when her early memories were stirred by the signs that they were present with another than those who had known them. But she hardly saw her lot as holding ground for sorrowing, or rebelled against its barrenness of fellowship, and constraint before the watchful eyes for food for jealousy. It was not her way to pass sentence on men and women. Her sense of kinship with her kind was deep to pain; holding her shrinking from judgment, and pitiful of the much that embittered even the gladsome portion. She saw it her part to ease the burdens her stepmother bore with the hardness of rebellion; setting this before her as a duty; which, if it called for her highest effort, neither tried her past her strength, nor merited esteem of self in its doing. For the keynote of Dolores' nature — as it had been of her mother's before her—was instinctive loyalty of service to that rigorous lofty thing, to which we give duty as a name; a stern, devoted service, to duty interpreted as that which was the best which conditions could demand; an unfaltering, unquestioning, it may soon be said, unreasoning service, which showed her in a crisis no place for conflict or conscious sacrifice, but simply laid a course before her as that which was due from herself to her kind. Thus she was equal to the hardness of watching her stepmother's days and her own through her stepmother's eyes, and of accepting her father's formal dealings as the best for the saving of them all.

For the Reverend Cleveland had learned the dread of domestic friction, and the moulding of his doings for his wife's witnessing of them. It was a lesson which nine years earlier he would not have confessed the power to learn. Unthought-of conditions bring out unthought-of powers; and he took what his lot gave him, forbearing to throw away what it yielded in vain struggling for what was denied. But let it not be thought that his wife was a virago or termagant, or that he was not the master of his home. Mrs Hutton was merely an irritable, jealous, sensitive woman; and none knew better that her husband's home was a sphere where the latter was master. A ponderous, remote man, mentally and bodily disposed to heaviness, he lived his domestic routine in a manner which told little in covering much. He showed himself blind to things that awakened his resentment, but experienced more than his family guessed. From time to time he would combat the domestic spirit in days which the household dreaded in accord, and which it was an unspoken family law that no one should heed. He would openly seek the companionship of Dolores — who, living in the emotions under which he sustained, and his wife submitted to, this subtly militant temper, was by far the saddest sufferer,—would even speak of his earlier wedded experience ; not referring to the change in his course, but intending it to carry its lesson. Mrs Hutton regarded these periods as the standing trial of her lot; and lived them with a sense of rebuke, and a keener sense of perplexity ; not perceiving that the smothered smouldering of months had simply reached ignition point and broken into flames. It is a proof that her husband's was the really dominant spirit, that she was docile while they endured, and less prone for some time after to peevish jealousy.

The eldest son of the parsonage — Dolores' companion in the life that was woven only in name with the others of the same scene—was a lesser cause of discord. Mrs Hutton was one of the women, to whom masculine failings have a strong excuse in being masculine ; and as far as his relations with his father went, there was little to awaken jealousy in a breast where it was the most overbearing of inmates. Mr Hutton was not in the least disposed to an over-genial view of a lusty young piece of male flesh under his roof, growing into added lustiness in depend-

ence on his daily efforts. He was rather addicted
to comment on the necessity of putting youthful
opportunities to the utmost profit, as young men
were not to be supported by their fathers all
their lives. The son was a self-absorbed, silent
lad, old for his seventeen years; with an easily
kindled zeal for the excellent; and a fainter
something of Dolores' instinct of fellowship with
thinking things, which had led him to fix his
ambitions on teaching. He had a straitened lot.
His days were spent at a school in a neighbouring town, and his evenings in pacing the lanes
with a book. He regarded his father and stepmother with one of those minglings of feeling
which grow from family communion—alternating
between affection and resentful dislike. He took
scanty notice of the little half-brother and sisters,
and reserved what his nature held for Dolores,
under whose eye he was approaching an upright
and reason-governed manhood.

A favourable time for a glimpse of the brother
and sister is a midsummer evening of the year,
whose autumn saw things as they are shown
with the Hutton family. It was the day of
Dolores' final coming from school; and the trap
which formed the provision of its kind at the
parsonage had been driven to meet her by her
brother; the father's tutored domestic instinct
precluding any form of personal eagerness on
his daughter's return to his roof. She was to

pass the summer at the parsonage, and enter
in the autumn a college for women. She
seconded her stepmother's view that her future
support should not be expected of her father,
and was to be fitted for the teaching to which
she looked forward with her brother. We may
watch her, as she walks up the country road—
a tall, rather gaunt-looking woman — for the
nameless suggestions of girlhood had lingered
but a little while with Dolores,— angular and
large of limb ; with a plainness of dress that
almost spoke of heedlessness, and a carriage not
without dignity in its easy energy of motion.
Her face is turned to her brother's, lit up with
humour and life ; a face with a healthful sallow-
ness of skin, exaggerated aquiline features, and
grey eyes innocent of beauty of lash or colour,
looking under nervous eyebrows, and a forehead
already showing its furrows. She was fresh
from the modern public school, where as student
and student - teacher she had grown from the
early maturity of the girl of thirteen to tolerant
womanhood. It had been a helpful sphere for
her early needs—rich in fellowship, in nurture
for the charity which mellowed her nature's
primary sternness. It was not without cost
that she put away what it gave, as childish
things, and crossed its bound with her face held
to the future.

With her face held thus, she greeted her

brother with the humorous affection of their
long comradeship; uttered no word of the day
as lived by herself; and lent her ear to his tale
of the home routine; showing his father's and
stepmother's lots as they were to themselves,
and summoning an eagerness for his boyish hopes
which should prove that there was one who cared
for them greatly. For Dolores in her dealings
with others suppressed any pain that was her
own; and had only cheer for the creatures she
saw as having no need of further saddening.
Her brother found that she filled the wants
of his life; and in giving his troubles of the
present and hopes for the future to her keeping,
hardly knew that her present and future were
things of which he heard little; or that her life
held its own crushed sorrows, and duties that
were hard and binding.

"I told father I had made up my mind to
teach," he said, as they paused in the hedge-
bound road for the trap to pass; "but he does
not try to understand the meaning the decision
has for me. He remarked that he supposed it
was a passable choice, as I had no desire for the
Church, and no aptitude for law or medicine.
It seems the thing to talk about teaching as a
work for feeble youths, who have no chance of
another livelihood."

"Yes, I believe it does," said Dolores, with a
sound of laughter in her full-toned, rather im-

D

pressive voice; "and I daresay, as many do it,
father has put it fitly—the best thing for people
with no aptitude for the Church or law or
medicine. But you choose it as it is in itself."

"It is a comfort to hear a sane remark," said
Bertram. "The talk that goes on at home,
Dolores! It is invariably bounded by the doings
and misdoings of the parish, or of Uncle James—
misdoings in the latter case. And the mater is
for ever put out about some little trifling thing
that cannot possibly matter. We never have
a day of peace."

"Her married life has hardly been all she
expected, I am afraid," said Dolores. "She is
fretted by little things, that cannot be avoided
any more than they can seem to be worth worry-
ing about. How are the children, Bertram?"

"Oh—well, I suppose," said Bertram. "Evelyn is fretful as usual; and Sophy waits on her
as usual; and we have begun to call the baby
Cleveland. The mater says it is time he was
called by his name. I believe it is a source of
satisfaction to her that it is he and not I who
is named after father.

"Poor baby Cleveland!" said Dolores. "I
am sure we need not grudge him his name,
especially as it was given him after you had
had the chance of it. Look, Bertram, here is
the very person for us embryo teachers to meet.
We cannot fail to be wiser five minutes hence."

"And wiser still ten minutes hence," muttered Bertram, as the gate of the cornfield clicked; and Dr Cassell—greyer, stouter, and ruddier, but otherwise unaltered for the further years of dispensing medical, scriptural, and general matter —stepped into the highroad.

"How do you do, Miss Dolores? So your last session at school has come to an end. I must congratulate you upon your latest success."

"Dolores, I had forgotten your scholarship," said Bertram.

"Ah, we don't keep pleasant things in our minds so long as unpleasant," said Dr Cassell. "And this is a very pleasant thing, I hear, Miss Dolores. Your college course — or the larger part of it—provided for! You are to be congratulated."

"She is indeed," said Bertram. "The scholarship carries a lot besides its money value. We are all very proud of her."

"It is nothing to be proud of, unless hard work is a cause for pride," said Dolores. "It is simply the necessary means to a necessary end."

"It may be as well not to feel proud of it as a success," said Dr Cassell, making a gesture with his hand. "There is never likely—as far as I have had opportunities of judging; and I think my opportunities have been as extensive

as those of most—to be too much humility in
the world. But satisfaction in the gaining of
knowledge is a different feeling." The doctor
came to a pause; and Dolores and Bertram
allowed their eyes to meet as they followed
his example. "A young man once observed to a
great preacher, that God had no need of human
knowledge. 'Sir,' was the reply, 'He has still
less need of human ignorance.'" The doctor
walked on, seeing the vanity of attempting to
enhance the given effect; but after a few steps
paused again.

"You are richer—in the possession of brains
and knowledge—than in the possession of anything else—with the exception of the true religion—on earth. A certain great musician—I
think it was Beethoven — had a — somewhat
worldly—brother; who one day sent him a card
inscribed with the words, 'Johann von Beethoven'—I am sure now that the musician was
Beethoven—'landowner.' In reply, the great
man sent his own card, bearing as a retort the
inscription, 'Ludwig von Beethoven, brain
owner.' Dr Cassell laughed, but made no
movement forward, and after a minute resumed.
"Talking of musicians," he said, "that is a
strange story of how Mozart spent his last
days in composing the Requiem he believed to
be his own. You both know it, I suppose?"

"Yes," said Bertram, detecting the note of

wistfulness, and perceiving that Dolores was disposed to indulgence. "There is a book about the musicians at home, and we are all well up in them."

"Ah! I see," said Dr Cassell, as he shook hands and turned on his way.

"Dolores, your scholarship has become such a standing cause for rejoicing that I did not think of speaking about it," said Bertram. "Father is very proud of you in his heart—though, of course, he is not allowed to show it. Studying and teaching at the same time, and competing with people who are only studying, means more than any one thinks who is not initiated."

"Oh, no, dear, it has not meant much," said Dolores, smiling at the face beside her — a younger copy of her own, with a softening which left its claim to comeliness. "Nobody is quite without gifts, and mine have gone in one direction. Besides, I was working for my own sake. I am going to college for my own future, and I should not feel justified in going without lightening the expense for father."

"I do not see why you should be expected to qualify to teach at all," said Bertram. "Neither of the little girls is to do anything of the sort. I don't think the mater comes out well in this matter. For it is all her doing at the bottom, of course."

"Oh, I look forward to teaching," said Dolores.

"I take the same view of it as you do. And I am not studying against the grain."

"If you were, you would be not the less expected to do it," said Bertram. "It is not right that the mater should lead father to make differences between his children. You cannot but see that yourself, Dolores, with your stern views of justice."

"Oh, we must not look at things only with justice," said Dolores. "It must be hard for a woman who—like other women—wishes to be first with her husband, and to see his interest centred on her children, to have two children who are strangers in her home; preventing her eldest child from being his first, and taking the precedence of the older ones. I think it is natural she should want to be rid of the eldest, almost more so if she is a daughter, and may seem to compete with herself."

"Well, that is putting things from the stepmother's view with a vengeance," said Bertram. "How about the stepchildren? If father had not married again, think how different your life would have been. You would have been everything to him. You must know that you are still his favourite child in his heart. But the more you are away, the less it will be so, Dolores. 'Out of sight, out of mind' is a maxim which applies entirely to father."

Dolores was silent, walking at a quickened

pace. Her lot held its own pain; which was
not less sharp that she uttered no word of it.
When she spoke, her voice had its usual vigorous
tones.

"It does not do to think of what might have
been. We must admit that father has found
happiness in his second marriage, and it is that
we have to think of. It was his own life he was
concerned with when he married again. It was
no right of mine to be everything to him. We
have always had from him a father's affection
and a father's duty. More than that we have
no reason to expect."

"If *I* have always had a father's affection,"
said Bertram, "I should not say that affection
was a strong point with fathers."

Dolores was silent; and no more was said till
they walked up the garden of the parsonage.

"Well, Dolores," said Mrs Hutton, coming into
the porch; "I am glad to see you at home again.
You must be tired after your long journey.
Children, came and say 'how do you do' to
Dolores."

The two little sisters—Sophia, a noble-looking
girl of eight, and Evelyn, a fragile little damsel
two years younger—obeyed with an eagerness
which brought a chill into Mrs Hutton's mellow
tones.

"Come, there is no need to be boisterous. Do
not be rough, Sophy. Bertram, there is no

occasion to stand in the middle of the hall, leaving no passage for any one. Your father is in his study, Dolores, if you would like to see him."

"Well, my daughter," said the Reverend Cleveland, stepping from this sanctuary in response to the sounds that reached him, and speaking with a touch of emotion in his tones, "so you have left your school-days behind you. Well, it is a chapter of your life past; so things go by one by one till everything is behind. But I think you may look back on them as a chapter well lived——"

"Come, Cleveland, let some of us move out of the hall," said Mrs Hutton. "I daresay Dolores would prefer some tea after her journey to listening to such a mixture of metaphors. Who ever heard of any one's school-days being a chapter — and a chapter well *lived*, too? Come, children, run into the dining-room."

Poor Mr Hutton, checked in the rather morose philosophising natural to him as a vehicle of fatherly greeting, bestowed upon his daughter a conventional paternal embrace, and followed his family in silence.

"The news of your scholarship gave me the greatest pleasure, my daughter," he presently said, with the formal precision which marked his dealings with Dolores. "Its proof of perseverence and ability is as gratifying as its substantial aid. I am glad to be assured of your fitness for the work you have chosen. Convinced of your power to succeed, I could wish you nothing better." Mr Hutton had a way of making public defence of his sanction of his daughter's earning her bread.

Mrs Hutton gave a quick glance at her husband, and opened her lips ; but closed them again, and busied herself with the wants of her children.

" Dolores is the cleverest person in the house, isn't she ? " said Sophia, fixing her eyes gravely on Dolores' face, as if appreciation were a serious matter.

" She has had the most advantages," said Mrs Hutton.

" We met Dr Cassell on our way from the station," said Dolores, " and heard two entirely fresh anecdotes. His memory is bottomless."

" Did he congratulate you on your scholarship ? " said the Reverend Cleveland, who, as a university gentleman of clerical calling, took a somewhat exaggerated view of the moment of matters academic.

" Yes, it was he who reminded me of it," said Bertram. " But he does not follow that sort of thing. His ideas of education are very queer. However, he assured her she was richer in the possession of knowledge than of anything else on earth."

"Well, well, he might be further wrong there, my daughter," said Mr Hutton.

"My dear Cleveland," said Mrs Hutton, "we all know that Dolores is your daughter. You need not remind us of it again."

Mr Hutton did not glance at his wife, or give any sign of hearing her words. He fell into silence.

"Father always calls Dolores that, doesn't he?" said Sophia, who was subject to the tendency of early days to cast every other remark in the form of a question.

"No, no, of course not; only sometimes," said Mrs Hutton. "All fathers call their daughters that sometimes—after they are grown up."

"Has this scholarship been gained by a pupil at your school before, Dolores?" said Mr Hutton.

"Oh, pray do not let us talk about the same thing for the whole of tea - time," said Mrs Hutton. "I am sure we are all very glad that Dolores has made the most of her advantages, and so gained other advantages for herself. But we need not confine our conversation to it entirely. It is such a very dull subject for the children."

Dolores coloured and made no response to her father.

"Has the scholarship been gained by a pupil

from your school before, my daughter?" said the Reverend Cleveland, repeating his question as though he supposed she had not heard it.

Mrs Hutton, whose instinct seldom failed her where her husband was concerned, appeared to be absorbed in presiding at the urn, while Dolores made a brief reply; and the Reverend Cleveland broached another subject, as though no inkling of the jar had reached him.

"By the way, my dear, I met your sister and brother-in-law this morning; and we are to spend the evening with them on Wednesday. Cassell is to be there, and Mrs Merton-Vane, and the new Wesleyan minister; so we shall be quite a party. A queer enough party in all conscience; but one cannot pick and choose one's company in a village. I thought it best to accept. That was right, I suppose?"

"Yes; Carrie would be vexed if we refused. She always wants to show us off to the Wesleyan ministers. Dissenters are proud of being related to church-people, just as the Americans are the nation who set most value on a title," said Mrs Hutton, who was no longer hampered by her native sectarianism.

There was a general laugh; and for the next few minutes Mrs Hutton was sprightly and talkative.

"I suppose that Bertram and I must go on

foot and leave the trap to you ladies, so that you can keep your furbelows in order?" said the Reverend Cleveland, with a laboured effort to maintain the geniality of his daughter's home-coming.

Bertram smiled and agreed, but Mrs Hutton was silent. The knowledge that Bertram and Dolores were included in her sister's hospitality killed any pleasure in her thoughts of it. Her husband confined his formality with his eldest daughter to his own home; and she saw the evening resolve itself into hours of humiliation under her sister's eyes.

" I cannot think," she observed to her husband when they were alone later, " why Carrie cannot ever ask us to her house without Dolores and Bertram. They are no imaginable relation of hers."

The Reverend Cleveland was silent. Silence was neither taxing nor self-committing. He often availed himself of it.

" It is such a very peculiar thing," continued Mrs Hutton, not soothed by this unreadiness of response. " It seems as if my path is to be con-tinually dogged by my stepchildren. Any one would think that it was you and not I who was related to Caroline."

Mr Hutton rose and moved towards the door. He was not a man of recreant spirit any more than he was a man of words; but there were matters where his powers of endurance were minimised.

"Well, well, I expect she means it for the best," he said. "I daresay they think that, as you have the stepchildren, it would not help your position to refuse to recognise them'

62

CHAPTER III.

"WELL, *Vicar!*" said Mr Blackwood, with
genial emphasis, as he welcomed Mr Hutton
into his drawing-room. "I am *glad* to see you
one of our party again. Well, Bertram, you are
growing a fine, strapping young fellow. I declare
you will soon have left your father behind you.
I declare that he will, Vicar—I declare that he
will."

Mr Hutton shook hands with his host, gave
a covered glance at the Wesleyan minister,
observed to Dr Cassell that the evening was
dry, and fell into silence; feeling that the
initiative due from an ordained Churchman in
Dissenting company was at an end.

"Now, *Vicar*," said Mr Blackwood loudly, in
the tone of one proceeding to the main business,
"let me introduce you to Mr *Billing;* who for
the next three years will be amongst us as our
minister; and, I hope—am sure, indeed, if he is
minded as we are—as our friend. Now, one of
the advantages we Wesleyans have over you

Church of England people "— Mr Blackwood's utterance of the last words implied that he did not see himself what especial significance they carried—" is that we have the services—and the friendship—of a different member of our body every three years; instead of being tied to one man all our lives, whether we like him or no. Mr Billing,—Mr Hutton, my brother-in-law—at least, I suppose he is my brother-in-law. I am not well up in these marriage relationships. At any rate our wives are sisters. I can tell you that for a certainty."

Mr Billing, a wholesome little man of forty, with smooth, red cheeks and twinkling little eyes, excellent both as a man and a Methodist, as his fathers had been before him, but falling short of them in not being excellent as a grocer as well, offered a tentative hand to the member of the body his host referred to with this measure of tact; and underwent increase of humility rather than the opposite process in goodwill, as the latter bent his head with entire remoteness of expression.

" Now, this is what I *like* to see ! " exclaimed Mr Blackwood, who was untroubled by exaggerated keenness of perception. " I *like* to see people of different sects mingling together, and associating in a friendly way with one another. It is *my* belief that that is how it was intended to be. I confess that I am a thorough *Wesleyan*, born and bred, myself; but that does not prevent my being able to see, and be *glad* of what is good in other sects. What do you say, doctor?"

"Yes—yes, certainly," said Dr Cassell, in a parenthetical tone, without raising his head.

"Yes, yes, that is the attitude," said Mr Billing, with a quick and rather indistinct utterance, which gave an idea of hurrying that its want of culture might be missed; "that is the attitude we should strive to get at. I trust—I think we are given grounds for hoping—that the day will come when it is the universal attitude. I think— it is thought, you know—that we are to judge that from the prophets."

"'If a man hath all things else, and hath not charity, it *profiteth* him nothing,'" said Dr Cassell, with deliberate distinctness and a smile.

Mr Billing gave the doctor a glance of some esteem, and laughed, saying, "Yes, exactly." Mr Blackwood, who was addicted to inattentiveness, made no response: and the Reverend Cleveland followed the latter example; an effort to attain an expression of utter disregard resulting in one of the same degree of disgust.

After a minute's silence, during which Mr Billing fidgeted amiably, half turning to one and another as though desirous of talk but unprovided with a topic, the door opened to admit the ladies—Mrs Cassell, Mrs Blackwood, and Mrs Hutton; followed by Dolores and the three eldest children of Mr and Mrs Blackwood. Behind came Mrs Merton-Vane, the wife of the agent of the local nobleman — a comely, kindly, foolish matron, whose foremost quality was a persistence in appending her husband's Christian namē by a hyphen to his surname, and regarding his post as agent to a nobleman as establishing his own family as noble. She had chosen to sweep alone into the view of Mr Hutton, whose acceptance of dissenting hospitality was her reason for doing the same.

Mrs Blackwood turned her attention to the introductions to Mr Billing; reserving for him the chief of her cordiality ; and looking annoyed by the air assumed towards him by her eldest daughter — a dainty, naughty maiden a little younger than Dolores ; who turned away after a careless bow and began to chatter with a favourite's audacity to the Reverend Cleveland. Herbert, a quiet-mannered youth of seventeen, shook hands, and stood aside talking to Dolores and Bertram. Lettice, a stolid - looking girl with a sweet expression, remained with her eyes fixed on his face, while her mother entered into talk.

"I did so enjoy your sermon on Sunday, Mr Billing, and so did my husband. I was so struck by parts of it, that I came straight home and made some notes of them. You know I sometimes speak myself on these subjects in my humble way; and I found your sermon was so very suggestive."

" Indeed, indeed, was that so ? " said Mr Billing, jumping slightly in his seat, as was his wont when he was nervous or grateful. " I—I am glad, Mrs Blackwood."

" How ve-ry nice for you to hear Mr Bil-ling ! " said Mrs Merton-Vane, who had a trick of pronouncing occasional words with a break in the middle, to the accompaniment of an inclination of her head. " How ve-ry nice ! "

" Yes, indeed it was," said Mrs Blackwood, in her high - pitched, somewhat strained tones. " We all enjoyed it so very much, did we not, Lettice ? "

" Yes, indeed we did," said Lettice. " And I am sure we shall enjoy many others from Mr Billing no less."

" Well, well, I hope so —with the higher help," said Mr Billing, dropping his voice at the last words, and making, we will suppose, some transition in their application.

" I was so much struck by the simile at the end of it," continued Mrs Blackwood. " It is such a beautiful idea—that every good action leaves its light behind—'a light that shall never be quenched.' You know there is something of the same idea in Shakespeare ; when Portia says that, just as the light shines from a window on the darkness of the night, ' so shines a good deed

in a wicked world.' You know the passage, Mr
Billing ? "

" Yes, I believe I have come across it," said Mr
Billing—" that is, I do not think it strikes me as
—as being new to me."

" But I think we may accord Mr Billing the
tribute of originality," said Lettice, whom her
family considered intellectual. " His idea and
that of Shakespeare are quite different."

" Yes—I do not think they are the same," said
Mr Billing, turning slightly red, and looking
down.

" It is when Portia and her maid are returning
from the trial of Antonio," continued Mrs Blackwood; " and Portia sees the light of her own
windows from the road. What a fine play it is,
is it not, Mr Billing ? I think it is quite one of
Shakespeare's finest."

" Yes—indeed—do you ? " said Mr Billing. " I
am not a great reader of Shakespeare myself, I
am afraid."

" It — is — strange," interposed Dr Cassell,
" how extremely little is known of Shakespeare—
as a man. I believe that almost the only auth-
entic story about his youth is—that he was on
one occasion taken up for poaching."

" Others abide our question. Thou art free,"
quoted the Reverend Cleveland in an undertone ;
as if, though not caring to join in the talk, he did
not grudge it a subdued note of culture.

"That is such a sweet po-em, Mr Hutton," said Mrs Merton-Vane. "I used to be so fond of poetry when I was a gi-rl. But that is a long while ago now."

"Well, my *darling*," said Mr Blackwood to his wife, "suppose we go in to supper, and postpone any further talk till our guests have had some refreshment."

"Or are having some," put in Dr Cassell, with a smile.

"Yes, let us, mother," said Elsa, who enjoyed saying things to draw attention. "You can sit by Mr Billing, and indulge in physical and spiritual sustenance at the same time."

"What, de-ar?" said Mrs Merton-Vane, with amiable perplexity.

Mrs Blackwood gave her daughter a glance of disapproval, as she led the way into the dining-room. Elsa had been indulged in childhood by parents exulting in her looks and her spirit; but of late had evinced some unfilial independence, and partiality for worldly things; in contrast to Lettice, who had already been converted, and had even given an account of this process in herself as testimony at a meeting.

"Well, now, Mr *Billing*," said Mr Blackwood, in one of his pauses in carving; which tended to occur rather frequently; his attention not being easily detained by unevangelistic duties;

"I hope that you are of the same mind as my wife and myself upon the *Drink* question. You will never find wine or spirits upon *our* table. I hope that you and I are agreed on *that* subject, at any rate."

"Yes, indeed, Mr Blackwood," said Mr Billing; "yes, indeed. It has been a matter of great thankfulness to me, to find how much good work has been done in that direction in this neighbourhood—and done by your agency, if I understand aright. It is my opinion that there would be very little wrong with our old country, if we could get rid of the drink."

"Hear, hear!" said Mr Blackwood, laying down the carving knife and fork. "That is the sort of thing that it does one *good* to listen to."

"Dear Herbert," said Mrs Blackwood, "do think of what you are doing, and attend to the wants of our guests. Mr Billing has not anything yet."

"Oh—no—not at all—no; thank you, thank you, Mr Blackwood," said Mr Billing; jumping in reception of his plate.

"I hope we shall hear you speak on Temperance soon, Mr Billing," said Lettice.

"Oh, there will not be any need, Mr Billing," said Elsa. "Father and mother will take all that off your hands. They get quite jealous of anybody else's speaking on Temperance.

"Elsa, how can you say such things?" said

Mrs Blackwood. "Your father and I do our best for the cause we have so much at heart; but if the work should be taken from us by abler hands than ours, we could do nothing but rejoice."

"Yes, that is it, my darling," said Mr Blackwood. · "You are right, as you always are—as I have found you on every occasion for twenty years."

"How pret-ty it is to hear him!" said Mrs Merton-Vane, looking round the company.

"Herbert, do not be so absurd, dear," said Mrs Blackwood.

"Do you—are you—you are a teetotaler too, I suppose, Mr Hutton?" said Mr Billing, nervously, to the Reverend Cleveland; whom, dissenter on principle though he was, he could not but regard as a weighty personality, and a fit object for affable address, and whose open smile at Elsa's words he had not perceived.

"No," said the Reverend Cleveland without elaboration.

"We can't *all* feel the same about ev-er-y-thing," said Mrs Merton-Vane, inclining her head.

"Ah, well, Mr Billing, we hope to convince the Vicar in time," said Mr Blackwood.

"We—are told," interposed Dr Cassell, "to 'take a little wine for our health's sake, and for our often infirmities.'"

"Oh, but, doctor," said Mrs Blackwood, with eager shrillness, "it is definitely proved that the wine in those days had practically no intoxicating power. We cannot accept such different conditions as parallel. I was reading such an admirable little treatise on the question the other day. It put the different arguments so very powerfully. You would be most interested in it, I am sure, doctor. Would he not, Lettice?"

"Yes, he could not fail to be," said Lettice. "There was so much interesting information in it, besides the treatment of the main question; and that, of course, was exceedingly able."

"I believe," said Dr Cassell, "that there are many different views upon the subject."

"Oh, yes," said Mrs Blackwood, gesticulating slightly with her hand; "but all those were discussed and most convincingly refuted. Nothing was glossed over, or passed by without perfectly fair treatment. I really must find the booklet for you, Dr Cassell. Do not forget to remind me, Lettice, dear."

"Oh, I would not read it, Dr Cassell," said Elsa. "It is only one of mother's tracts."

"Oh, you fun-ny child!" said Mrs Merton-Vane, looking at Mr Hutton.

"But surely," interposed Mrs Cassell in very gentle tones, breaking off her dialogue with Mrs Hutton, to fulfil the duty of seconding her husband; "it is not for us to put our own

interpretation on the words. Surely they should
be enough for us as they stand."

"No, I don't agree with you there, Mrs
Cassell," said Mr Blackwood loudly; "I don't
agree with you. I remain a staunch upholder of
Temperance myself. We Wesleyans don't shrink
from showing our colours for a cause we honestly
have at heart; and I shall never shrink from
showing mine for Temperance. Ah, yes; there
are Wesleyans in every part of the world, showing their colours for what they believe in their
hearts to be right."

"Of course the Wesleyans are the largest
religious body in existence," said Mrs Blackwood,
with detached appreciation of her native sect.

"The largest dissenting body," supplied
the Reverend Cleveland in a casual tone, suggesting an opinion that it was not worth while
to adopt a decisive attitude in his present environment.

"Ye-es," said Mrs Merton-Vane, inclining her
head in rather shocked repudiation of the other
view.

"The largest dissenting body, dear," said Mrs
Hutton, repeating her husband's correction to
her sister with more distinctness.

"No, dear," said Mrs Blackwood, her voice
becoming a little higher pitched; "it is generally
known that no other religious sect can compare
with the Wesleyans in point of numbers."

"Or in point of anything else," said Mr Blackwood — "in point of anything else, my darling."

"My dear Caroline, it stands to reason that one of the dissenting sects could not be larger than the whole of the Established Church," said Mrs Hutton with a little laugh, as though it were hardly needful to state a truth so obvious.

"My dear, it is not a question of its standing to reason," said Mrs Blackwood. "It is a question of what is definitely known and proved. It is an established fact that the Wesleyan body is twenty times as large as any other body."

"Oh, my darling, come, come," said Mr Blackwood. "We all know that the Wesleyans are the largest and the most important body; but *twenty* times as large as any other is putting it rather strong."

"My dear Herbert, I do not know why you should contradict me," said Mrs Blackwood. "I should not speak if I had not my information on dependable authority."

"Oh, well, if you have it on dependable authority, my love, then that is all right," said Mr Blackwood, with tenderness.

"What do you think about it, Miss Hutton? I suppose you know all the arguments on both sides by heart," said Mrs Cassell, with no misgiving on her words as a compliment to Dolores' studious tastes.

"No; it is a branch of statistics in which I am quite unversed," said Dolores, smiling.

"Why, de-ar, I thought you knew ever-ything," said Mrs Merton-Vane.

"Are any of you Wesleyans aware," said Dr Cassell, his tone nòt indicating any great respect for the sect he mentioned, "that you owe your existence—your existence as a religious body—to a mere accident?"

"No, doctor; let us hear the story," said Mr Blackwood, with an easy frankness of falling in with the doctor's plans.

"When John Wesley was six years old," said Dr Cassell, "the rectory where his family lived —Wesley senior was a clergyman, you know—was burned to the ground. Every one in the house had—as it was supposed—been rescued; and the family were watching the gradual—devastation of their abode; when it was discovered that John was missing. He was asleep in an upper room and had been forgotten. After many vain suggestions—of methods of rescue—he was saved by a man's standing on the shoulders of another, and lifting him from the window. Hardly was the rescue accomplished, when the roof fell in. A moment later the founder of the Wesleyans would have been lying crushed beneath a heap of burning chaos."

"Well, doctor, I never heard that before—I never heard that," said Mr Blackwood loudly.

"No-o," said Mrs Merton-Vane, inclining her head with full corroboration of the novelty.

"I think, doctor," said Mrs Blackwood, "that we should say that we owe the existence of our sect to a special intervention of a higher power than ours, rather than to 'a mere accident.'"

"Yes, yes, I think so, indeed," said Mr Billing, slightly shaking his head, and looking at the floor.

"The father of the Wesleys," continued Dr Cassell, "is said to have viewed the—conflagration of his home with perfect calm; observing: 'God has given me all my eight children; I am rich enough.'"

"Ah, indeed!" said Mr Billing.

"Just fancy, if he had been burnt there wouldn't have been any Wesleyans," said Elsa, laughing.

"Elsa, if you must talk so foolishly, you had better not talk at all," said Mrs Blackwood.

"But, mother, it is so amusing to think of you and father without the chance of being Wesleyans," said Elsa, with further laughter, and a knowledge of the direction of Bertram's eyes.

"This escape in childhood made a deep impression upon John Wesley," said Dr Cassell; continuing as if no break had occurred, though with no bitterness to Elsa; and at once attracting Mrs Cassell's gaze. "He always regarded it as a proof of his being destined—for some especial

religious mission. Later in life he inscribed under
a portrait of himself the following words—' Is not
this a brand plucked from the burning?'"

"Oh, I *wish* my hus-band was here," said Mrs
Merton-Vane, showing appreciation.

"Did he indeed—indeed?" said Mr Billing.

"Well, Mr *Billing*, you have a sample of the
doctor's powers of *instruction*," said Mr Blackwood. "I can tell you he is one by himself on
that matter. There's not a subject under the
sun, which he can't *talk* about, and give you any
amount of *information* about, at a moment's
notice. Anecdotes, facts, bits of science—it all
comes as grist to *his* mill; I can tell you that
it does."

"You—er—you have been a great reader?"
said Mr Billing, fidgeting slightly as he addressed
the doctor.

"Yes—well—yes, I think I may say I have
been a reader," said Dr Cassell, making a frank
effort against a smile. "From my boyhood my
tastes have tended in the direction of books rather
than of anything else. I am interested in a great
many subjects. I do not think there is one that
engrosses me to the exclusion of others; though
of course medical matters have absorbed me a
great deal. I think I may say that I am *not*
like the man who was so lost in mathematics,
that he forgot his own name and the date of
his birth."

"I am su-re you are not," said Mrs Merton-Vane.

"So am I," said Mrs Hutton, allowing her eyes to meet her husband's.

"It is strange to think," said Lettice, with rather conscious modesty, "that, had there been no Divine intervention to prevent the death of Wesley in childhood, there would have been such a gap in the evangelization of the world. One is apt to forget, in religious matters as in others, how large a train of events may be attached to a single incident."

"That is just the same as I said, Letty, only put into stilted words," said Elsa.

"You're quite right, you're quite right, Letty, my darling," said Mr Blackwood.

"Yes, it is so in all things," said Mrs Blackwood, in tones of a quality to attract attention. "Suppose Shakespeare, or Browning, or Milton had never been born, or had died in childhood! Think of the immense difference in the world of thought! We hardly realise, when we are being inspired by their finest passages, how trivial an accident might have torn them from us."

"Mother, you never read Shakespeare, or Browning, or Milton," said Elsa. "And if you did, you would not know which were the finest passages."

"My dear Elsa, think what you are saying before you speak. You know quite well that

Milton has always been my favourite poet. I was reading some of 'Paradise Lost' only the other day — the part about Adam and Eve in the Garden of Eden, and comparing it with the corresponding parts of Genesis. How very magnificent some of the passages are, are they not, Mr Billing? The language is so good, and the rhythm is always so accurate. As I was saying to Lettice, Milton's poetry carries so many lessons in it."

"Yes, yes, a great man — Milton," said Mr Billing. "A sincere Christian, in addition to all that brought him worldly fame."

"I really think," continued Mrs Blackwood, "that if I were asked to give the palm to any one poet, I should give it to Milton. His poetry is so suggestive. In every line there is something that transports you at once to the classic days of ancient Greece and Rome. I always feel so much better informed after reading him. I do not think any other poet quite comes up to him in that."

"My dear, you may take the credit to yourself of your view of the vocation of poetry," said Mrs Hutton. "It is entirely your own."

"Oh, you do not follow me, dear," said Mrs Blackwood, in a careless tone, but continuing quickly. "Dolores, you understand what I mean, I am sure. I expect you know Milton nearly by heart, do you not? I knew a great deal when I was your age, I know; and his classical allusions must be so very illuminating to you, with your knowledge of the classical languages and mythology."

"Yes, Dolores is the one for classics," said the Reverend Cleveland. "She is better read in them already than many a lad of her age."

"How nice to be so clev-er, de-ar!" said Mrs Merton-Vane.

"I suppose you and your father are great companions, Miss Hutton?" said Mr Billing, looking with heightened interest at Dolores, and reflecting that she looked just the sort of lady to be the erudite associate of a gentleman.

"Oh, I am away from home a great deal," said Dolores, sparing her stepmother. "When I am at Millfield, my brother and I are a great deal together."

"Oh, my dear, you and your father have always been such great friends," said Mrs Blackwood, not neglecting the opportunity for sisterly revenge. "You have so much in common—so many tastes, and so many memories. I always think he seems quite lost when you are away."

"He must seem rather seldom at disposal then," said Dolores, smiling — not unconscious of Mrs Blackwood's motive. "I am only at home for a third of the year. But I think it is only a matter of seeming. He has become quite used to my being away."

"Cleveland is so very absent-minded," said Mrs Hutton, with a little laugh. "Last summer he told me to ask Dolores for a book nearly a week after she had returned to school. He actually did not know whether she was in the house or not."

"Clev-er people are always a little for-get-ful now and then," said Mrs Merton-Vane, inclining her head towards Dolores in sympathetic explanation.

"Well, my *darling*, if we have all finished, suppose we go into the drawing-room," said Mr Blackwood, loudly addressing his wife. "Open the door, Herbert, my son. Well, *Vicar*, as Mr Billing here is a non-smoker, and the doctor and I are the same, as we need not tell you, perhaps you will become one yourself for this evening, and join the ladies with us at once. I never believe in trying to do without the ladies, do you, Mr Billing? We owe most of what is good in ourselves and everything else to them, you know. What do you say, my love? You agree with me, I am sure."

Mr Blackwood linked his arm in his wife's and led the way from the room. His guests followed; with Mrs Hutton at their head, and brought up by the Reverend Cleveland; who mutely repudiated Mr Billing's surrender of precedence, with an air that seemed to say that personally he found it no gratification to be prominent in this company. In the drawing-room Mrs Blackwood entered at once into talk with Dr Cassell.

" Dr Cassell, I was reading a pamphlet the other day which you would have been so interested in. It was about the Roman Catholics; and it treated the question in the main almost exactly as you do; but with some minor differences, which I really am not sure I do not incline to myself—they were put so very convincingly. I should so like you to read it. It was called 'Roman Catholicism—its Spread and Significance.'"

Dr Cassell leant forward in his chair, and held up one hand.

" It is a subject—Mrs Blackwood—upon which I hardly require to read further treatises. I know it—only too well—under both the heads to which you allude—to which the title of the little work you mention, alluded. I do not think further reading could add to my comprehension of it."

" Ah, Mr Billing, the *doctor* is the man to consult, if you want to know anything about the Roman Catholics," said Mr Blackwood. " *He* is an authority upon them, I can tell you. *He* has studied the question, and no mistake, has the doctor."

" You consider the spread of Roman Catholicism a serious thing?" said Mr Billing, addressing Dr Cassell.

Dr Cassell leant forward, and again raised his hand.

F

"You ask me, Mr Billing—whether I consider —the spread of Roman Catholicism—a *serious* thing. My answer is — that I consider it a *hopeless* thing, a damnable thing, a thing that is sucking the very life-blood of our religion." Dr Cassell held himself for a further moment in his didactic posture, and then leaned back in his chair.

"But do you not think," said Mr Billing, "that the spread of agnosticism and atheism—I fear we must recognise that they are both spreading—is even more serious — more significant of vital danger to the faith?"

"I do *not*," said Dr Cassell, implying a not uncomplacent knowledge that his view was peculiar. "I have met — in the course of my medical experience—as I could not have failed to do—examples of all the three forms of—er— perverted religious conviction; and I am of the opinion — that the Roman Catholic is more— obstinately tenacious of error, and pernicious in influence, than either the atheist or the agnostic. Both the latter are—as a rule more or less amenable to argument, and more or less straightforward and aboveboard in their tactics. But the Catholic—" Dr Cassell broke off and shook his head.

"You have had dealings with them?" said the Reverend Cleveland, his tone accepting this as a matter of course, and therefore implying collapse of the doctor's position if he should be mistaken.

" I will tell you," said Dr Cassell, relapsing into his anecdotal tone, "of an experience I had with one. I was called in to attend a patient — a Catholic—in his last illness; and I found him in a state of great depression about the state he was about to enter; burdened with notions of purgatory, praying to the Virgin, and so forth." The doctor paused to allow this grave evidence to be grasped. " I endeavoured—to bring the light or the true faith to his darkened mind; but—with little success — owing to its prejudiced and— generally unhappy condition. As I was leaving the room, I happened to pause for a moment, holding the door ajar; and I fancied as I stood there—that I heard a faint noise"—the speaker gesticulated slightly with his hand and his tone became mystical—" as of somebody moving quickly away from the door-mat. When I opened the door, I came upon a *priest*—ostensibly coming across the passage. I shall never forget the *appearance* of the man, as he came towards me, with a sort of *leering* smile on his lips—his long, black, gown-sort-of-thing hanging about him, and a crucifix suspended from his neck. I stopped him—I placed myself dead in front of him—and I remember now how his eye quailed beneath mine. 'So,' I said, 'you have added to your list of deadly sins—the sins that have clouded death-beds and damned souls. Go,' I said, 'and dare to contradict a word of mine to that dying man,

as you will answer for it at the judgment.' Would
you believe it, the fellow never even *answered*
me! He calmly walked by me, and into the
sick-room; though, mark you, he did not once
raise his eyes to mine. The next day—no, wait
a minute"—the doctor checked with a motion of
his hand any exclamations on the point of breaking
forth—" I received a message—purporting to be
written by the patient—though I knew he was
too weak to handle a pen—informing me that my
services would not be again required. This message I *ignored;* happening to regard the future of
a soul—as of greater importance than the will of
a priest. I was not allowed—to set my foot
over the threshold. Orders had been given that
I should not be admitted; and my only course
was to leave the priest to his work—doubtless he
wished to get the man's money bequeathed to his
cause. The money I have no doubt was *gained*—
the soul of the man—" The doctor broke off, and
just perceptibly shook his head.

Mr Blackwood twisted his moustache, and
observed without altering his easy posture in his
chair, "Ah! Ah!—an awful thing—the power of
these priests—an awful thing—there's no doubt
of that." Mr Billing dropped his eyes to the
ground, and nodded once or twice, muttering,
" Yes, yes—yes, yes," as though he could well
believe what he heard, but looked upon the
subject as hardly a matter for words. Mr

Hutton raised his eyes and met his wife's, and perceiving an unsteadiness about her lips, dropped them and assumed an equivocal expression; and in a moment addressed the doctor.

"Well, but, Dr Cassell, you could hardly ex pect the priest to feel grateful to you, especially as you worded what you had to say as you did. I daresay he was an honest fellow, doing his best for what he thought to be right, as you were."

"I once knew a Roman Catholic priest, and he was a de-ar man," said Mrs Merton-Vane, with a vague sense of supporting Mr Hutton.

"It was not my object to make him *grateful*. My object was to bring him to a sense of the abominable wickedness of his course. It was the last thing I expected of him—that he should be grateful!" said Dr Cassell, ending with a grim little laugh.

"Well, on what ground do you find fault with him then?" said the Reverend Cleveland. "I hardly follow you."

"I think I may retort," said Dr Cassell, frankly militant, "that I do not follow *you*. I should not myself describe a man, whose habit it is to listen at doors, as 'an honest fellow.'"

"Oh, but," said Mr Hutton, with casual surprise at ignorance of a widespread truth, "the Catholic priests are considered justified in going to any length for the sake of their cause. A breach of morality committed in furtherance or their faith is righteous in their eyes. They would regard it as service for their religion."

"I think that nothing could show more clearly than that — the superiority — of our religion — the religion of the majority of us here," said Dr Cassell, with the quiver in his voice of temper kept when loss of it is to be expected, and a glance at the cross on the breast of Mr Hutton. "It is given to us to know, that it is not lawful to do evil—that good may come."

"Oh, come, Vicar," interposed Mr Blackwood in loud tones; "the doctor is *right*—as *right* as it is possible for a man to be. This spread of the Roman Catholics is an awful thing—an out-and-out *awful* thing—there's no denying that. Of course there may be good people amongst them, mistaken through no fault of their own; we all admit that. But we can't have you talking as if priests and people of that sort ought to be allowed to do their worst without any check. We can't have that."

The Reverend Cleveland just glanced at his host, and then looked out of the window with disengaged contemplativeness, tapping his finger-tips together.

"Now, Mr *Billing*," suddenly observed Mr Blackwood, changing the topic with frankly exclusive regard to his own inclination, "I was glad to hear—from some one or other—that you were a *Liberal*. Now, if there is anything that

makes me feel thoroughly *rubbed up the wrong
way*, it is all this *Toryism* and *Conservatism*, and
all those other "isms," that really mean utter
selfishness, and disregard of all classes but one's
own. If there is anything that makes me feel
drawn towards a man, it is when I hear that he
is a *genuine Liberal*. A grand word that—
Liberal."

"Well, I think I may claim to be genuine;
I do not regard myself as a spurious article," said
Mr Billing, a sense of his effort at humour
prompting him the next moment to turn a little
red, glance at Mr Hutton, and look at his hands.

"Well, I am glad to hear it," said Mr Blackwood. "You and I must have some walks and
talks together."

Mr Billing jumped, and looked towards Dr
Cassell—feeling in the warmth of his emotions
a desire to soothe that wounded gentleman and
draw him again into converse.

"You are a Liberal too, I suppose, Dr
Cassell?"

"No," said Dr Cassell, pausing after this word,
as though hardly able again to evince a generous
loquaciousness; and then leaning towards Mr
Billing, and speaking in hesitating, narrative
tones. "I do not regard myself as belonging
to any particular—political party. I have never
been able to find—justification in the Bible—
for a man's giving of his time and interest to

political matters ; and I withhold mine. It seems
to me that religion is so much the greatest thing
in life, that energy bestowed upon other things
is energy wasted."

"But I meant on which side do you vote?"
said Mr Billing, choosing what he supposed the
most direct way of ridding himself of perplexity.

"I do not vote," said Dr Cassell, pregnantly.

Mr Billing, not being a member of the doctors'
circle at Millfield, looked a little bewildered and
glanced round the company.

"Ah, Mr Billing, now that is a subject upon
which the doctor and I do *not* agree," said Mr
Blackwood loudly, coming to the help of his
guest with the assignment of the local leaders
of thought to their sides. "The doctor, you
know, believes in that theory, that the world will
go on getting *worse and worse*, and all that sort
of thing, until at last it reaches the stage when
the elect are caught up in the air,"—there was
no suggestion of a flippant attitude towards Dr
Cassell's convictions in Mr Blackwood's · tone,
rather the dropping that belongs to sacred reference—"and the world with every one else is left
to the dealings of the Devil, and that sort of
thing—you know those views, of course ; and so
he does not think it worth while to try and make
things better——"

"I do not think it *of any avail*," broke in Dr
Cassell, leaning forward.

"Well, it is all the same in *practice*, doctor," said Mr Blackwood. "And it is *practice* we have to think of. Now, Mr Billing, what *I* believe is, that little by little the whole world will be evangelized, and that the gospel will be preached in every corner of it, as we are told in the Bible. That is what *I* believe; and that is what I think we *ought* to believe. I have no sympathy with this living for *oneself*, and not thinking of one's duty to one's fellow-creatures myself. *I* think——"

"If I had sympathy with that course, I do not think I should give all my spare time to—preaching the gospel to—and otherwise working for the good of — my fellow - creatures," said Dr Cassell; just glancing at Mr Blackwood to make this rather bitterly-voiced observation; and then turning to Mr Billing, as though unable to refrain longer from putting his case for himself. "I regard it as impossible—I think I may say *know* it is impossible, from scriptural sources—to materially benefit the world—in its spiritual aspect—or to arrest its ultimate downfall; beyond endeavouring to—increase the number of the elect by evangelistic work. I think the true Christian should stand apart from the world."

"Ruskin's view — with religion in the place of letters and the arts," said Mr Hutton, in a very low and somewhat caustic tone.

"Well," said Mrs Merton - Vane, with a

mingling of sadness and bitterness, "I am a
Conservative myself, and so is my hus-band.
Our fam-i-lies have been Conservative from the
earliest times. Of course, we both come of such
very old fam-i-lies. Lord Loftus was saying to
me only yesterday, 'My dear Mrs Merton-Vane,
if every one held the opinions of *your husband*,
the world would be a different place.' That is
what he said, Mr Hut-ton."

"But—er—how do you suggest, Dr Cassell,"
said Mr Billing, "that the necessary work in
other matters, the work needful for the welfare
of the nation, should be carried on, if no—er—
righteous person must take part in it? Should
we not all do our duty in the political system
of our country, that the existing scheme may
answer as well as possible? What of the
practical results if everybody stood aside?"

Dr Cassell leaned forward, looking somewhat
ruffled. He had so long interpreted a conversation as a didactic utterance by himself, that
argument on equal terms struck him as deliberate
baiting. "I base," he said, in a tone at once
huffy and impressive, "all my actions and all—
my opinions—as far as in me lies—upon scriptural grounds. The Bible—and nothing but the
Bible—is my authority for them. I am answer-
able to no man for them."

Poor Mr Billing fidgeted, and looked as if he
would like to apologise, if he could call to mind a

definite ground for apology; and was much re-
lieved by an appeal from his hostess.

"Mr Billing, I really cannot agree with Dr
Cassell in his view that Christians should stand
apart from the world. It seems to me that
they ought to mingle in the world, and do their
best to lift it to a higher plane, and hasten the
day when the gospel shall be known amongst
all nations. You know all really great men
have felt in that way. Socrates and Dr Johnson,
and so many people like that, found their
greatest pleasure in mingling with men. You
know, Socrates would have saved his life if he
had consented to go away from Athens—the
city he loved. I think that standing apart
from the world is the very last thing for a
Christian."

Mr Billing looked his appreciation and uncertainty how to express it; and Dr Cassell,
after a moment's pause, leaned forward with a
clearing brow.

"Do you know the reply—Mrs Blackwood—
that Dr Johnson made, on being asked to take
a walk in the country?"

"No, doctor, no; let us hear it," said Mr
Blackwood in an easy tone.

"His reply was," said Dr Cassell, "'Sir,
when you have seen one green field, you have
seen all green fields. Sir, I like to look upon
men. Let us walk down Cheapside.'"

"How very interesting," said Mr Blackwood, "and how like Dr Johnson! I think he would have been such an interesting man to know, do not you, Mr Billing? Boswell's ' Life of Johnson ' is such an illuminating biography—the best biography I have read, I think; and I have always been so fond of biography as a form of literature. Do you not admire it, Mr Billing?"

Mr Billing's honesty was spared by the announcement that the vicarage trap was at the door. The Reverend Cleveland rose without pause, and stood with his eyes on the floor, frankly awaiting his wife's movement for departure. When this was made, he shook hands in silence with his fellow-guests, showing Mrs Cassell and Mrs Merton-Vane some courtliness, and Dr Cassell and Mr Billing some coldness. He then observed to Mrs Blackwood, "We have to thank you for an exceedingly pleasant evening"; and took up his stand near the door, in waiting for the ladies of his family to precede him from the room. Mrs Blackwood escorted her sister and Dolores upstairs; leaving Dr Cassell to enlightenment of Mr Billing, whose attitude did not henceforth waver from the gratefully receptive; and a sisterly talk enlivened the assumption of wrappings.

"So Cleveland and Bertram are going to walk on, dear," said Mrs Blackwood.

"Yes, dear," said Mrs Hutton. "They leave

the trap to us feminine creatures. It does not hold more than two."

"When we lived at Hallington," said Mrs Blackwood, "we had a trap that only had room for one besides the man; and when Herbert and I went out, he used to wait to put me into it before he started himself. He used to say he felt so worried, when he thought of me clambering into it alone in the dark."

"Oh, that was such a dangerous trap," said Mrs Hutton. "It really was hardly safe."

"Oh, no, dear," said Mrs Blackwood; "it could not have been safer; it was only Herbert's nervousness about me."

"Ah, those were your early married days," said Mrs Hutton, adjusting her hood before the glass.

"Oh, but Herbert has not altered in the least since then," said Mrs Blackwood, her voice becoming a little higher pitched. "He fidgets so about me, that sometimes in company he makes me feel quite foolish."

Mrs Hutton pulled out her strings without sign of accepting this statement; and Mrs Blackwood felt urged to its elaboration.

"I always think it is such a wrong theory that husbands are different after they are married. I think that as they begin, so they go on. You see Herbert worries about me just as much as ever; and Cleveland never has been anxious about you, has he? He does not let things like that disturb him."

"My dear Carrie, it is rather absurd to talk about *Herbert's* being worried," said Mrs Hutton. "I do not remember seeing him worried in his life."

"Oh, you do not understand him, dear," said Mrs Blackwood. "He does not show his feelings on the surface. I often think what a sad thing it would have been for him, if he had married some one who did not believe in anything that was not under her eyes. I am so thankful that we were brought together."

"Thankfulness on that point is a needless self-exaction, dear," said Mrs Hutton. "As you were cousins, special providential arrangements to bring you together were not required."

"My dear, our grandparents were second cousins," said Mrs Blackwood. "People connected in that degree very often never meet. I always feel that Herbert and I were given to each other."

"I remember you so well when you were engaged," said Mrs Hutton, with a little laugh.

"I remember it too," said Mrs Blackwood; "and how I used to pity you, for having no chance of getting married, though you were the elder sister. Girls are so amusing in the way they look at things."

"I never can understand how women can

marry boys," said Mrs Hutton, surveying her reflection in the mirror.

" My dear, when a woman marries as young as I did, she naturally marries a young man," said Mrs Blackwood. " Of course a man is getting on in years when he has one life behind him."

" I meant I could not understand a woman's accepting a man younger than herself," said Mrs Hutton ; " as though she would secure a husband at any cost."

" My dear Sophia, Herbert is only a few months younger than I am. He was asking the other day which of us was the elder. The difference is so small, that he never remembers which way it is."

" Is it really so small as that ? " said Mrs Hutton. " It hardly seems possible, does it ? Well, we must be going down, dear. Our men-folk must be nearly home. We have had such a pleasant evening. It has been quite a break for Dolores after her term's work."

In the drawing-room Dr Cassell was found seated on the edge of his chair, and leaning towards Mr Billing, with hand upraised ; his wife's eyes fastened on his face, and the Blackwood family listening in the background—that is to say, Lettice listening ; Elsa exposing his mannerisms with silent mimicry ; and Mr Blackwood twirling his moustache as an effort against

sleepiness.　　Dolores and her stepmother drove
to the parsonage in silence; and parted on the
threshold for the night, the latter to win the
Reverend Cleveland to some difficult mirth, by
her sallies at the expense of her kindred.

CHAPTER IV.

BEFORE you is a room whose innocence of toy or draping holds it with the figures within it in subtle sympathy. Within it are some women who in some way stay your glance; who carry in their bearing some suggested discord with convention—a something of greater than the common earnestness and ease. Those who are laughing give unchecked heart to their laughter. The one who is distributing cups of some beverage, does it as the unobtrusive service of a comrade.

The scene has a meaning which marks it a scene of its day. It is the common room of the teaching staff in a college for women.

The dispenser of the beverage is crossing the room with movements of easy briskness. She is a woman of forty, older at a glance; with a well-cut, dark-skinned face, iron-grey hair whose waving is conquered by its drawing to the knot in the neck, and dark eyes keen under thick, black brows. That is Miss Cliff, the lecturer in English literature.

G

The companion to whom she is handing a cup —the lecturer in classics, Miss Butler,—and who takes it with a word in a vein of pleasantry, is a small, straight woman, a few years younger; whose parted hair leaves the forehead fully shown, and whose hazel eyes have humour in their rapid glancing.

"I cannot but see it as ungenerous to brew the coffee with such skill," she is saying; "in purposed contrast to my concoction of last week."

"A meanly revengeful comment on my general manner of brewing it," said Miss Cliff. "Well, you may put its success down to my being out of practice. It is the only reason I can think of for it."

"I remember the last time you made it," said a genial, guttural voice at the side of Miss Butler —the voice of Miss Dorrington, the lecturer in German, and a strong illustration of the power of moral attractiveness over the physical opposite; which in her case depended on uncouth features, an eruptive skin, and general ungainliness. "It was that week when you kept getting ill, and at the end I had to make it for you."

"Hoist with your own petard?" said Miss Butler, smiling at Miss Cliff.

"I think it is a great accomplishment to make good coffee," said Miss Cliff, in a consciously demure tone; "a very seemly, womanly accomplishment. I cannot feel justified in relaxing my

efforts to acquire it, if you will all be generous.
Cookery, you know, is the greatest attainment
for a woman."

A short, quaint - looking, middle - aged lady,
with a pathetic manner which somehow was
comical in its union with her calling of mathe-
matical teacher, looked up with a slow smile. " I
fear we are but a boorish set, if that be true," she
said.

" Oh, I know it is true, Miss Greenlow," said
Miss Cliff, meeting Miss Butler's eyes. " I read
it in a book, so of course it was true."

" Of course," said Miss Dorrington, in her
breathless guttural, no genial quality unsuggested
in her face and voice.

" Do any of you remember when you first
realised that things in books need not be true? "
said Miss Cliff, with the half - philosophising
interest in her kind, which was one of her char-
acteristics. " Do you remember feeling the
ground you were used to walk upon, slipping from
under your feet, and a mist of scepticism rising
around you? "

A lady who was standing apart came forward
to join in the talk. She was a Frenchwoman,
over fifty, with a sallow, clever face, and sad
brown eyes which lighted with her smile; who
had led a difficult life in the land of her forced
adoption, and lived with its daughters, feeling
that she owed it no gratitude.

"I imagine most of us had that experience at an early stage for such power of metaphor to be born," she said.

"I did not mean the metaphors to be quoted from childish reflections," said Miss Cliff. "I was putting a childish experience into unchildish language. But I remember the experience itself so well. It marks off a chapter in my life for me."

"Yes; we have so much faith as children," said the remaining member of the band. "I daresay we could all mark off the chapters in our lives by loss of faith in something. We have to guard against losing faith in too many things."

The speaker was Miss Adam, the lecturer in history—younger than the others, and young for her youth; with her zeal for the world where she had her life, not untempered by a wistfulness on the world outside, and her faith in the creed of her nurture as untouched by any of the usual shattering forces, as by her special knowledge of its growth.

"It seems we can mark age by steps in scepticism," said Miss Lemaître. "It would be a help to our curiosity on both, to remember they correspond."

"It would be a very good way of guessing people's ages," said Miss Greenlow, with her inappropriate plaintiveness. "We should simply have to start some disputed topics; and having discovered the doubted points, calculate the chapters marked off."

" We shall have to warn people to be wary in conversing with Miss Greenlow," said Miss Cliff.

" She always has told us that all things can be reduced to mathematics, if enough is known about them," said Miss Butler.

" Well, perhaps we are abusing flippancy," said Miss Cliff, observing Miss Adam's silence. " I suppose it is true, after all, that the youngest-natured people are those who keep their beliefs in things; and we should try to keep youthful in nature, I suppose."

" Youthfulness of nature does not depend upon convictions, surely, speaking seriously," said Miss Lemaître. " Convictions are a matter of intellect; and our intellects have little to do with our characters."

" That is a little dogmatic, is it not ? " said Miss Butler, who was not very fond of Miss Lemaître. " Our intellects must influence our ways of looking at things and people, and our apprehension of them."

" Yes, yes ; I think they must," said Miss Cliff; "and our ways of looking at people especially. In our dealings with each other, faith is often another word for charity."

" Yes, very often," said Miss Adam; " and charity for faith."

" That is coming rather near to heresy, I am

afraid," said Miss Lemaître. " Is not the rela-
tive value of those qualities settled for us ? I
am not sure that their interchangeability is
doctrinal."

" No," said Miss Greenlow, shaking her head ;
" it smells badly of schism."

" Miss Adam meant the word ' faith ' to be
understood in a general, not a particular sense,"
said Miss Butler.

" I should not have supposed that any of us
meant anything," said Miss Lemaître.

" It is rather a philosophic subject for so
soon after luncheon," said Miss Dorrington.

" I know that the time of day is said to
breed mental inertia," said Miss Cliff; " but I
am constrained to the dubious course of spending it in reading essays. You must excuse my
desertion of my post : my pupils have increased.
Miss Dorrington, you will succeed me, I am
sure ? "

" Deplorable irregularity on the part of one
in office !" said Miss Butler, as Miss Dorrington
changed her position willingly and clumsily.

" The students are increasing very quickly,"
said Miss Greenlow. " I don't know what the
opponents of women's higher education would
say to it."

" I imagine that class has resigned its delusion,
that anything can be said for its view," said Miss
Butler, with the casual manner which covers

strong feeling; while Miss Cliff, arrested by the subject, paused with her hand on the door.

"Oh no, they cling to it," said Miss Lemaître, carelessly. "I was listening to two old clergymen talking the other day; and they were agreeing that learning unfitted women for the sphere for which they were fitted by nature and their life through the centuries, with all things included—I believe to the corroboration of Genesis."

"It is such a quaint argument—that women must not do a thing, because they have not done it before," said Miss Dorrington, who had yet to take of a subject an other than genial view.

"We are not to try the water till we have learned to swim," Miss Butler said, in a slightly different spirit.

"Oh, well, they were old," said Miss Adam. "People can hardly be expected to give up the notions they were bred up in, at the end of their lives."

"And parsons as well," said Miss Lemaître; which further light upon the insufficiency shown, Miss Adam gave no sign of accepting.

"But I suppose there is something in the argument, that women must be what the development of ages has made them," she resumed.

"I think very little," said Miss Butler. "You

see, women are not descended only from women. Their heritage is from their fathers as much as their mothers. The development of one sex does not bear only upon that sex."

"A very good point," said Miss Cliff from the door; "and one that is not made enough of."

"Yes, there is truth in that," said Miss Adam. "But does not the life of one sex, carried on through generations, influence that sex? Do not some qualities go down in the female line and others in the male? In the evolution of any creature, is not that so?"

"The historian looks across the ages, as the heir of all of them," said Miss Butler, taking refuge in jest where she found it hard to keep cool. "Now I think of it, the lioness does not carry a mane in spite of her shaggy forefathers."

"She may owe much to her forefathers, nevertheless," said Miss Cliff. "We must not confuse the physical attributes of one sex, with the mental and moral part which is transmitted from both to both, and which the others hardly bear upon. We have known women like their fathers, though they did not carry beards. But to leave the sphere of science—to our brothers, if Miss Adam wills,—and take a practical view; the women of civilised countries outnumber the men; and as a proportion cannot marry, there must be a class of self-supporting women."

"Unless polygamy becomes an institution," said Miss Greenlow, the union of her manner and matter producing general hilarity.

"And even if they do marry," said Miss Butler, "why should learning unfit them for domestic duties? I suppose people think, if we heard a child screaming, we should wait to rub up Aristotle on the training of the young, before going to see what was troubling it. I have never seen evidence that learning has that effect. I am sure my cousin, Professor Butler, is the most erudite person, in mind and appearance, I have known; but to see his antics before his baby daughter, when she is at the point of decision between crying and not crying, is to lose faith for ever in the theory, that learning is prejudicial to domestic ability."

There was a general moving amid the laughter; and the little band dispersed down the corridor.

In her first treading of the same corridor, unpitiedly silent in a chattering stream, Dolores met the old, youthful experience of the earnest academic novice. On the brink of the student world, where the schooling was no longer a childhood's need, she felt the sense of her child's achievements fade into an older humbleness before better of her kind—saw it of a sudden a world of rushing generations, and quailed under youth's clear knowledge of the transience

of things. The principal's greeting—the welcome
accorded as part of another's duty, strengthened
in its formal well-wishing the sense of being a
one where the many only was significant. The
next hours passed as a dream—the setting in
order of the narrow student chambers, the wandering in the corridors barren of the messages
of memory. It was only the awakening that
lingered. Returning from the evening meal, in
the common hall, which seemed a sea of voices,
she came upon a student standing in the corridor
alone—turning from right to left with an air
which marked her a novice.

"Are you perplexed about anything?" said
Dolores, pausing. "You are a newcomer, as I
am, I suppose?"

"Yes, that is what I am," said the other;
"and an unfortunate thing it seems to be. I
am sure I wish I had arranged to be something
else."

Dolores looked at the short, plump figure; and
met an expression on the face, which brought a
smile to her own.

"Is there anything you want to find?" she
said.

"Nothing to matter. Only the rooms where I
live. I do not know why you should trouble. I
had come to the conclusion, that I was not a thing
to be taken into account."

"I had come to the same conclusion," smiled

Dolores. "Perhaps we could find your rooms between us."

"Thank you very much," said the other, following with a rollicking gait, which seemed to fit her. "It must seem presumptuous in me to feel a need. But it is embarrassing to odds and ends to be left about."

"Were they on this corridor?" said Dolores, as the short, quick sentences ceased. "I suppose your name will be on the doors."

"Why, yes, now I think of it, there are names on all the doors. But I am sure it was natural, if I expected to be known simply by a number. My name is Murray—Felicia Murray; if I am worthy of such an appendage."

"Felicia?" said Dolores, smiling. "Your meaning is the opposite of mine. And it fits you, does it not?"

"I have not thought. I am ashamed that I have ever felt interest in myself. Oh, here is the name on a door. This is where I am kept, then. Will you tell me your name before you go? Do you know, I believe all the people here have names? Is it not thoughtless, when there are a hundred? May I look out for you in the morning?"

Dolores found that the word with a fellow had somehow cleared her path. Her own rooms, with their narrow bareness, already had a certain welcome. The sense of living and working

amongst many with her life and work was
gathering a charm. The academic spirit was
weaving its toils.

It was not till the morning that she took a
real survey of the hundred student - maidens.
The nicety of the novice drew her with the
earliest in the direction of the chapel bell; and
as she stood with those, who followed her in
promptness in coming and eagerness of glance,
the faces that were appearing around her drew
her eyes. Young faces she saw them, not carrying less of youth that they carried things hardly
youthful. Here and there, in signs of waning
girlhood, she read of the teacher whose early way
had been vexed.

When the hundred in the order of their standing had filed from the chapel, the hall laid out
for the morning meal was the stage of an intricate
drama. Silent, except for response to courtesy
or question, but watching the easy actions of all,
as they passed in and out at will, she felt the
pervading spirit of effective freedom. When the
hall was deserted, and she followed in the general
wake, she found herself standing in a corner of
the corridor, where written notices covered the
walls ; and a voice struck strangely on her ear as
familiar.

"Oh, here you are! I had lost you. Not
that that is a thing to call attention to. I have
lost myself three times this morning. I see by

the lists that you are to read classics. You are short-sighted? How proud you must be! I read it was a mark of high civilisation. We are to interview Miss Butler at twelve. Advantages are already to be ours. You know she has edited a Greek play. It is easy to see in her face that she has. She looks at you as if she could read your soul. I hope she will not read my soul; and know that I better my mind simply because I must earn my bread, or go to the workhouse. I have an old nurse there. She told me she felt in her heart we should meet again. Do you suppose Miss Butler will ask us what classics we have read? I will go and decide what I have read. Have you such a book as 'Ideal synopsis of works to form a basis for classical scholarship'?"

Dolores knew, as she watched the little round figure rollick away, that the ground was laid for a student friendship. Three hours later she learned the meaning of Felicia's judgment of Miss Butler. The eyes under which the new-coming students dispersed to desks, had certainly no lack of insight. The little waste of manners and minutes seemed in keeping with their survey. The words to be said were said with precision and clearness, and said but once. The nature and hours of lectures were given; and a word of general advice was offered, in whose hinted severity of tone Dolores detected a tempering of nervousness. A student stammering a doubt

was gently answered ; another disposed to quibble
on a point that was passed, quelled with a
touch of sharpness as marked as courtesy permitted.

" I always thought souls were private," said
Felicia with a sigh, as they mingled in the stream
that poured to the hall for the midday meal.
" It was all a waste of time, preparing that ideal
synopsis. There is no good in precautions with
people who can read souls."

The meal in the common hall was what was
already familiar. The students entered and left
at will ; easiness of action was the feature of the
whole. But to Dolores, no longer silent and
alone amongst many, the sameness was less than
the difference. Felicia found a place at her side,
and poured out prattle ; and Miss Butler passed
to her seat with a smile already accepted as a
thing of price. The remaining hours of the day
were hours as those before them. But the comprehension of their spirit of striving self-govern-
ment was not all that they carried. They were
filling with the human interest, which to Dolores
was the greatest thing the hours could give. As
other days followed, bringing other such hours,
she found herself with a place and purposes in a
passionless, ardent little world — a world of
women's friendships ; where there lived in a
strange harmony the spirits of the mediæval
convent and modern growth.

Walking one day in the cloisters of the college, she came upon a figure standing in the shadow of a pillar, which arrested her scrutiny. It was the figure of a man—a visiting professor, as she knew from his gown, and the trencher lying at his feet,—in seeming buried in pondering; for he stood unmoving, with his eyes gazing before him, and his hands folded in his garments. His aspect was grotesque at a glance; for his massive body and arms were at variance with stunted lower limbs, and his shoulders were twisted. His face was dark and rugged of feature; his eyes piercing, but unevenly set, and so small and buried in rising flesh beneath them as hardly to be seen; his clothes and hair unkempt. An uncomely figure Dolores confessed him, as she left him to his musings. On reaching the doorway, and turning for a further glance, she was startled by the sight. He was standing with his feet set apart, his body swaying and his head and limbs working to contortion. She stood and watched him; and was startled anew when he ceased his gestures, picked up his cap with a lightning-like movement, and went his way. That evening, seated at table next to Miss Cliff, she spoke of the experience.

"Oh," said Miss Cliff, "that was Mr Claverhouse. Have you been startled? You will soon get used to seeing him about."

"Claverhouse?" said Dolores, with a sudden

awakening of thoughts. " Any relation of Claver-house, the dramatist ? "

" The dramatist himself," said Miss Cliff. " It is pleasant to hear his name so ready. He comes here to lecture."

" Comes here to lecture ? " said Dolores. " Why, what does he lecture on ? His own plays ? "

" Oh, no," said Miss Cliff. " He lectures in classics—usually on the Greek drama. He is a classical scholar apart from his writing. You will be numbered in his pupils yourself in your last year. His plays would hardly be suited to academic purposes."

" Would they not ? " said Dolores, smiling. " I should have thought they would bear elucidation."

" You have read them ? " said Miss Cliff, with surprise. " Yes ; they are obscure, as you say."

" And very profound, are they not ? " said Dolores.

" Yes, yes, very profound. Read as they should be read, they take one very deep."

" I wonder if they will ever be produced," said Dolores.

" They would hardly bear production, would they ? " said Miss Cliff. " There is so much that would not carry across the footlights. It is his ambition that they shall be read."

" He talks about them then ? " said Dolores, with an instinctive feeling of surprise.

" No, no," said Miss Cliff, half smiling ; "indeed he does not. He never comes out of himself. His only friend is a cousin of mine ; or he would be a mystery to me as much as to you. He lives in Oxford with his mother ; and supports her by private coaching, and by giving lectures here. His story is the old one of struggle with poverty and publishers, made bearable by the sense that he is giving his art his best."

" I suppose what I saw was the visible part of the process," said Dolores, covering with lightness a sense of being more deeply moved than was natural. " I must have seen him in the clutch of the creative spirit."

" No doubt of it," said Miss Cliff. " His habits would become a genius."

" I suppose a few would say, they do become one," said Dolores.

" Yes," said Miss Cliff; "and there will be many more."

" He must be a very fine man," said a student who was sitting next to Dolores.

" I hardly think the words ' fine man ' give him," said Miss Cliff. " His personality is too strange, to be fitted by such a current description. He wants something that goes deeper, and is not so wholly complimentary."

H

" But the eccentricities of the great do not take from them, do they ? I have known a good many remarkable people, and I have always loved their quaintnesses," said the student with smile-begetting naïveté.

" No, no, I daresay not," said Miss Cliff. " I only meant, they should be suggested in a full description."

" I really think that genius is enhanced by superficial eccentricities," went on the student, with a short, quick utterance which seemed intended to suggest, that her words covered more than appeared. " Would Socrates' personality mean so much to us, if he had not been like a Silenus ? "

" What do you think, Miss Hutton ? " said Miss Cliff.

" I should think it would," said Dolores, with a strange sensation in the remembrance, that she had heard the last words before from the same lips. " We should just associate the other attributes with him, instead of those of a Silenus. There is not much in external attributes themselves, is there ? "

" Is there not ? I don't know," said the other, slightly shaking her head.

" Well, I will leave you to convince Miss Hutton, Miss Kingsford," said Miss Cliff, turning with a smile at Dolores to her neighbour on the other side. " I feel quite inspirited by having met some one, who reads Mr Claverhouse's plays so young."

"Why, his plays must be read by any one at any age, might they not? I should think so myself from what I know of them," said the student, addressing Dolores, but failing to disguise that her words were spoken for Miss Cliff.

Dolores looked at the speaker—a student of her own standing with whom she was barely familiar; and felt her sense of being jarred yielding to a spirit of pardon. She knew that Perdita Kingsford knew nothing of the plays; but as she met the liquid eyes in the face that changed with the moments, the knowledge lost its estranging power. There was that in Dolores which yielded to womanhood's spells. She hardly judged of women as a woman amongst them; but as something sterner and stronger, that owed them gentleness in judgment. From the first hour to the last of their years of friendship, she read Perdita as an open page; and loved her with a love that grew, though its nurture was not in what she read.

"It is very inspiring to be brought into contact with a great, neglected life," said Perdita, as they left the hall. "So many great lives have been unrecognised; and in a way they grow greater from the very neglect. One feels one would give or do anything for a chance of smoothing

one of them ; and that if one were brought into
touch with it, one's own interests would not
count."

These words were heard and forgotten, as
other words, as they fell. But a time was to
come when Dolores recalled them. This day
which brought Perdita and Claverhouse into
her life, was to gather significance in its twofold
bringing of change. The change grew daily,
widening and deepening along its threads. But
at the first it widened and deepened slowly ; and
at the close of the term, we may watch her with
the two who had come through her into friendship, without meeting any token that her life
was not as theirs.

" Well, I am glad the term has an end," said
Felicia. " Things might have become monotonous if it had not had one. It will be cheering
to join one's family, and find oneself a recognised
item of something."

" I never understand you when you talk like
that," said Perdita. " I felt myself recognised
from the first. Did not you, Dolores ? "

" Perhaps at the first," said Dolores. " For
a few hours I clung to interest in myself, and
thought it natural that others should share it ;
but soon I hardly included myself in my own
survey of life. I agree with Felicia that the
change is painful."

"Happily it is quick," said Felicia. "In my case its climax was reached on the first morning; when the lecturers' enclosed pew struck me as a convenient hiding-place in chapel; and I was ushered into general view—hard treatment when the floor is recognised as the only congenial passage of the embarrassed."

"Well, they say that suffering is the truest education," said Dolores. "A foundation like this is right to accord its advantages early. Were any of them in the pew? If so, they would understand you to take them for your own kind."

"I did not think of that," said Felicia. "To think that I wasted gratification that the pew was empty! But Miss Butler came in, as I slunk out; and looked at me with a twinkle in her eyes. You know my view of Miss Butler's eyes. I am growing accustomed to violating truth beneath their scrutiny."

"Violating truth?" said Dolores. "I find they have the opposite influence."

"It is the questions she asks, while she uses them," said Felicia. "She asked me this morning, whether I did not find that classics had a growing fascination."

"And what did you say?" said Perdita.

"I said 'yes,'" said Felicia, turning a grave face to the laughter of the others.

"But, seriously, I don't think one can study a subject without feeling its fascination," said Perdita. "My way of looking at my work is quite different from what it was. I can't help feeling and knowing it."

"And I can't help feeling and knowing that mine is the same," said Felicia;—"the view natural in the daughter of a parson with eleven children; brought up on the principle, that life is a time for becoming qualified to teach, and then teaching; resolving itself into week-days devoted to secular studies, and Sundays to scriptural."

"Are not scriptural studies postponed till the day of scriptural instruction?" said Dolores. "To remember them longer than is needful seems sheer prodigality of brains—extravagance in a scarce luxury, that is unbecoming in daughters of parsons with families."

"But when Saturday's studies are postponed to the Sunday, there is little difference," said Felicia. "Things just move on."

"As the daughter of a parson myself, I should regard Saturday's studies as contraband on Sunday," said Dolores.

"Yes," said Felicia, smiling. "A memory lives with me of a Sunday of my youth, when my father brought a clerical brother 'to see me doing my scripture;' and it wasn't scripture."

"What did they say?" said Perdita.

"Little at the time," said Felicia. "But my father said things afterwards. But I must be about my business. I have some books of Miss Butler's, that she lent me a month ago; and I feel the cutting of their leaves a seemly step to returning them."

CHAPTER V.

THE spires of the university pierced the greyness of dusk. Among the many figures that trod the streets, which every age has trodden in its chosen sons, one figure passed lonely, bareheaded, marked of glances.

In the gateway of one of the colleges it made a halt; and remained stooping and still. Other figures passed it; nudging, muttering, or stepping aside with silenced tread. Two youths in cap and gown put their heads together, whispered, and broke into laughter. The ponderer started, glanced at the breakers of his musing, and stepped from the gateway. As he went his way, he cast another look at the youths. The look was long; and spoke of something that was neither resentment nor denial of heed.

On reaching the door of a dwelling in a street, that was little accounted and echoed of the past, he paused, and moved his hands in search. His hand lingered in his garments; his head bent; and the minutes past unheeded. All

at once he drew himself up with one of his
sudden movements, clasped his hands, searched
again with wandering fingers; and at last struck
the knocker with violence on the door. A moment brought the response. It opened to disclose a little old woman, tiny to the point of
dwarfishness, but strongly and squarely built;
with a skin as dark, and eyes as piercing and
deeply set as her son's. She bent her gaze for
a moment on the stooping form; and then stood
aside in silence, as it brushed past her, and
hastened up the staircase. A door sounded on
an upper floor; and she returned to the room
whence the knocking had summoned her. A
remarkable - looking old creature she was, as
she sat in the lamp - lit chamber, with eyes
rivetted to a printed page, and fingers empty
of trifling of needle. She was clearly of a great
age. Her tiny hands were dark-coloured and
deep - veined; the whiteness of her hair was
the streakless whiteness of the time when grey
and raven tresses share the past. But age,
though it showed its presence, had wrought no
further. There was no faltering of limb, no
trembling of the lower jaw, no wandering of the
piercing eyes that passed down the page. They
scanned it eagerly, neither missing nor recurring
to a word. When an hour had passed, she laid
the marker in the book; and taking the lamp
in her hands, went up the staircase. Her gait

was curious—a mingling of a slight lameness
with the combined ungainliness and energy,
which marked her son's. At the door of an
upper room she came to a pause, and stood
with her ear to the keyhole. She stood for
long, the bentness of her form and her childlike
stature giving the posture easiness. The sounds
from within — an irregular tread on the floor,
betraying it bare of cover, and from time to
time a deep voice breaking forth, brought no
change to her still features; save that once,
when the voice grew almost to a shout, a spasm
of emotion gave them a fleeting softening. At
length the steps and the voice grew silent; there
was a sound of the drawing of a chair across the
boards and the rustling of handled papers. She
bore the lamp to the lower chamber; and began
to limp about it with purposeful movements.
The service of eyes and limbs was readily rendered, though the rendering would have carried
to an eye that watched, no lessening of that which
marked her very far in years. She spread the
cloth for the evening meal, and brought vessels
and platters from a closet and ordered them for
three. There seemed to be a servant helping
from a kitchen; for she went once or twice to
the door, to receive some article of food or
crockery; but she gave no sign of communion
in glance or word. Her tiny, aged hands wrought
without faltering: the doing from time to time

of the duty of one by both, or a grasp for an easy holding, was all that betrayed that the days of their service were numbered. When the task was ended, she returned to her seat at the table, trimmed the lamp, and resumed her book. It was a little book of worn and sombre binding, containing a drama. She read as before, absorbedly; holding the volume closely to her eyes, and turned to catch the light of the lamp. The travelling of the eyes was rapid; and at certain passages they gathered fire, as though the inspiration were known. When she came to the end, she turned the pages read, with a touch that lingered and almost caressed. The caressing movement gained deepened meaning from the hard experience in the face above it. With the turning of the blank opening leaf, her hand and eyes were stayed. It bore a written inscription. The tracing of the pencilled words was too faint for her aged sight; but she read them with eyes that knew them. "To Janet Claverhouse, from her son, and the author of —— " beneath there followed the printed title of the play. The sunken features quivered. Motherhood had come late, and widowhood early to Janet; and through the fifty years from the day which brought them both, life had held them for her simply.

A step on the staircase brought an end to the yielding to emotion. She closed her book, and pushed the lamp to the middle of the table. There was a sound as though of groping at the door; and the playwright entered, wearing his working garb—a ragged coat of some fabric that looked like canvas,—and bearing a pile of papers in his hands.

"Is Soulsby coming to-night?" he said, as he set the manuscript down.

"To supper at eight o'clock. It is the hour now," said his mother, in guttural aged tones, which a German accent made curious.

Claverhouse took the seat that was nearest, and rested his elbows on the table, pushing his hands through his hair, and glancing at the clock.

"It is finished," he said. "I can read it to him to-night. He is long, is he not? I am in the vein for reading. He is very long."

"He is coming to supper," said Janet, resting her eyes on the disordering of the table, but taking no further heed. "We must have supper first, Sigismund. You have eaten nothing since midday."

"I want nothing," said Claverhouse, rising and moving excitedly. "I need nothing. Is he not coming? The last scene—it has lived so long with me. He is very late."

"Well, but what of your old mother, Sigismund? There are not so many suppers before a woman of ninety, that she should waste the chance of one," said Janet, with a laugh that was deep but pleasant-toned.

"Ah! we will have supper, my little mother," said the son, with a smile that brought a sudden difference to his face. "But Soulsby is long. He prevents our beginning."

Mrs Claverhouse laid her hand on the worn little volume at her side.

"I have been reading again the play, which I call my own play," she said. "I wept again over it, my son. You have given the father you never saw, to me again, if not to the world. It needs something to bring tears at ninety— at the fiftieth reading."

"Ah! it is a good play," said Claverhouse. "But I was a boy when I wrote it. It is different now. There is the knocker!"

He hastened from the room and went to the outer door; but on reaching it paused and fumbled.

"The door will not open," he called. "It is fastened."

"Turn the key," said the guttural tones from within. "It is locked on the inside. It does not keep together else; it needs to be mended. You have only to turn the key."

"The key?" said Claverhouse, stooping and fumbling, and finally clutching it, as though his hands had found it, and not his eyes. "Ah, Soulsby! you are late. Come in, come in."

A rapid, nervous utterance responded, as a tall figure stepped into the passage.

"I am sorry—I am sorry; I had no idea—no idea at all that I was late. I hope—I hope it is of no matter."

"No matter, no matter," said Claverhouse, standing aside, and not heeding that his friend was at trouble in the discarding of his outer garment. "You are good to come. The play is written to the end. I wrote the last scene to-night. It is different from all the rest. You shall hear it in a moment. Come in."

As the guest entered the lamp-lit sitting-room, he was a contrast to the figure he followed. Tall and well-moulded, with large, sensitive features, tended waves of glossy grey hair, and a manner marked by the nervousness of over-culture, he looked what he was, a type of the university don. He was the tutor of one of the colleges — a large-hearted pedant, to his finger-tips gently academic; with the tastes and talents rather of the scholar than the man of letters; but an instinctive knowledge of the genius that lived unsought, amid the many grey walls that stood in the sanctity of genius dead. The bonds that bound him alone of men to the dramatist, were too subtle for disentwining. They were not less strong that they were subtle.

"I am afraid—I am afraid I have kept you waiting," he said in his quick, hesitating manner, as he greeted Janet. "Pray—pray do not rise —pray do not. I had no idea—no idea I was behind the time."

"You are very little behind the time," said Janet, as she lifted the manuscript from the spread table, and placed it elsewhere. "And for Sigismund to take any one to task on exactness in time, is a case of the pot calling the kettle black. Sit down, Sigismund; and let William have his meal in peace."

It was a habit of Janet's to address Soulsby, though she had not known him till his youth was past, by his baptismal name. It was one of her few evincements of greatness of age; and Soulsby accepted it with the unnoticing courtesy, with which he accepted all that was unwonted in the genius' home.

The three now seated themselves at the table. A dish was brought in by a bent old servant, and set before Janet; who dispensed it with perfect precision of movement; paying covert heed to the fancies of her son, and attending to Soulsby with pretty courtliness. The servant knew her duties well. She was ready to the moment with a supporting touch, if Janet's hands showed signs of faltering; the extras of the meal were set with unobtrusive closeness under her master's dim-sighted eyes, some wonted attentions, with which Janet and her son dispensed, were paid to the guest; and all was done with

a silent evenness of movement, which covered the
actions.   It was clear to which member of the
household her devotion was given.   She watched
her master through every unoccupied moment;
lingered over the supplying of his needs; and
observed the extent of his justice to her culinary
skill, with eyes that were almost jealous.   He
had spoken truth when he disclaimed desire for
food; but when he was brought to settle to a
meal, other things, as Julia knew with rejoicing,
had their turn of being forgotten.

When he had finished, he threw himself back
in his seat, pushed his hands through his hair,
and looked at her with a smile.

"That was good, Julia," he said.

Julia's face illumined, and relapsed at once into
its usual neutral alertness.

"Ah, Julia," went on Claverhouse, who always
had a word with his old dependent once in the
day; "you are a clever housewoman.   You will
make a good wife some time."

Julia's face assumed the conscious smile of
sixty-three years of unwooed maidenhood.   The
jest was an old friend; and as such she loved
and welcomed it.

"Ah, Julia!" continued Claverhouse, "you are
coy, I am afraid; you are coy.   Where did you
learn those naughty proud airs?   It is time you
grew out of them.   Is it not, Soulsby?"

Soulsby looked up in some uneasiness.   Supper

in the playwright's household was an old experience; but it was a case where custom had
wrought little. He had sat, as was his wont,
in apparent discomfiture—though no eyes saw it
but Julia's,—fidgeting with his nervous hands;
and glancing from his hostess to her son, as if
reluctant to thrust his voice on the silence. He
was grateful that the talkative spirit had come
on his friend; but this appeal to himself was not
of a kind he would have chosen.

"Ah—yes—yes, yes," he replied; "yes, very
possibly."

"You talk too much nonsense, Sigismund,"
said Janet, in her deep tones. "Let us move
from the table, so that Julia may clear it."

"Ah, my little mother? Yes, you are right;
you are right. You are always right to me,"
said Claverhouse, perceiving that Janet's jealousy
was touched.

"How about the reading of the play, my
son?" said the mother. "It is growing late;
and William will be leaving us."

"Ah!" said Claverhouse, with a world of
remembrance and emotion. "Late, is it? It
is of no matter. Take some seat, Soulsby—no,
no; not there, not there. There—where I can
see your face. Sit here, little mother—here; so
that the ear that is not deaf is turned to me.
Quiet, Julia; or go, go. Now, Soulsby, find
what you think."

I

He sat in a low chair, with the manuscript set on his knees, and his eyes nearly touching its pages. The friend sat opposite, his fine frame in repose, the grey waves of his hair glossy in the firelight, his large, shapely hands twining and untwining at his breast.

Claverhouse plunged at once into the play. The harshness of his voice and his eruptive utterance at first gave colour to what he read : but as the drama unfolded, Soulsby leant forward in his seat, ceasing his nervous movements, and rivetting his eyes on his face ; and Janet almost crouched in her chair, her strange eyes gazing before her, and gathering tears or fire as the deep tones fell. The reader's voice, under the veil of its own qualities, became the voice of each character. At one time he sprang to his feet, and read for minutes standing. His tones swelled, sank, and carried trembling or tears. At the end he neither raised his eyes nor moved his limbs. He sat unseeing and silent, living yet in his self-created world. Neither Soulsby nor Janet broke the silence. The hours had passed ; but neither had heeded them. The silence lingered, and seemed to be deepening, when suddenly Claverhouse turned, and looked at Janet.

The aged woman was exhausted. She was lying back in her chair, with features and limbs relaxed. Crouching thus, with her eyes closed, and energy and motion gone, she looked what

she was — a fragile, aged creature. The playwright rose; and stooping over her, raised her
to her feet with an easiness which showed the
service familiar; his face betraying some depth
of feeling, but his voice abrupt and harshly
toned.

"Let me have that lamp, Soulsby. Push that
chair aside, and open the door. My mother is
worn out. I will be down in a moment."

The strange-looking couple passed from the
room, and mounted the staircase; the son walking
close to the mother, slackening his pace to hers,
and keeping the hand not hampered with the
lamp on her arm, in readiness to tighten its
grasp. The scene was a daily one on the steep
little staircase. He was as mindful of Janet's
years in the matter of bodily danger, as forgetful
of them in the dealings of their daily life. He
feared to trust her on the stairs of the narrow
old dwelling; and never forgot to help her to her
door at night, or to wait in the morning to support or carry her down. He knew nothing of her
many unattended journeys to the door of his
working-chamber; for Janet loved the tender
service, and shrank from robbing of their value
the many times of its fulfilment. She had
spoken no word on the matter to Julia; but
the faithful old servant watched and was wise,
rejoicing in the trust she had earned; and when
her master's eyes were safe, paid no heed to

the disobedience, but otherwise guarded the forbidden ground from unaided steps.

This evening Julia's doings told much of herself and her place in the household. Through
the reading of the play she knelt with her ear
at the keyhole; though her face betrayed that
her pleasure was rather in her master's voice
than in what he read. When the silence came,
she rose to her feet, but remained in a posture
of listening; and when Claverhouse and Janet
appeared, neither started nor stepped aside, but
stood in quiet waiting. When the former returned, she watched him out of sight with
venerating eyes, and then made haste to the
tending of her mistress.

Claverhouse made his appeal to his friend
almost before the door was open.

"Well?" he said; "well?"

Soulsby was sitting in the firelight, his hands
passing up and down before each other, and his
eyes fixed on the glowing coals. He had been
moved to strong emotion, and his nervousness
had left him.

"It is wonderful," he said in grave, musical
tones, turning his large grey eyes to Claverhouse.
"It is wonderful. It is great—there is no doubt
it is great."

"It is true, is it not?" said Claverhouse. "It
is that, that I strove for. Have I got it, Soulsby?
Ah, but I have."

"The play is wonderful," repeated Soulsby. "It is marvellously deep."

"Deep?" said Claverhouse. "Yes, it is deep. There is no great play that is not deep. But there are great plays that are not true. Mine is true, if you could but know it."

"If I could but know it?" said the other with a return of his nervous manner. "Yes, yes—you are right. I hardly follow you."

"You do not follow me?" said Claverhouse, leaning forwards, and speaking low. "Listen! When Althea hears that her father is dead, she utters no sound, no word — that is true. The madman in his lucid days thinks more of the life he shares for the time with his kind, than of the certain madness before him—that is true. When the teacher is enfeebled beyond the toil of his years, his thoughts are of the pupils whom he taught in his prime, rather than of those he is yielding up with their present gratitude. When old Jannetta is failing, she is cold to the friends who tend her age, and yearns towards her kin of blood."

"Yes, yes, I follow," said Soulsby. "I see that it is true—that all—that all your plays are true."

"No, no, that is not what I said," said Claverhouse, rising to his feet. "In all of them there is truth; but the two last are all true; this one, and the one that lies unread in the closet." Then with a change of tone, "Ah, well! Well,

Soulsby, what is there in this, that offends your scholar's judgment?"

"There—there was—there seemed to me — amongst other things," said Soulsby, "a slight— a slight discrepancy between the opening speech, and the reference to it later in the play. I—I think, if you consider it, you will agree with me."

"Soulsby, you are a pedant — a quibbling schoolman," said Claverhouse, moving his limbs impatiently. "You love the letter; and the spirit escapes you."

"No, no, believe me, it does — it does not," said Soulsby. "I was only—only answering the question you put. And I think you will see— will see I am right. A superficial inelegance remains—remains an inelegance."

"Inelegance!" said Claverhouse, fuming in contempt for the expression, and then changing his tone. "Soulsby, you are a friend and helper I value greatly. You understand it, is it not so? I knew it; and too well to be showing it so overmuch. So there are other 'inelegances'? Well, let us see to them. Tell me them. I will be grateful."

The friends talked earnestly over the manu- script; Soulsby showing his points with nervous insistence; and Claverhouse alternately fuming and complying. He chafed less as the talk proceeded, and he felt the spirit of the drama tighten its hold. He read on rapidly, often losing sight of the task of revision; and at last became utterly lost in it. He rose to his feet, holding it closely to his eyes, and read on aloud, in forgetfulness of Soulsby's presence. It was one o'clock in the morning. Soulsby noiselessly rose to his feet, crept to the door, stood for a moment watching the stooping form, and then slipped from the house. Julia came from the kitchen, fastened the outer door, and went up to bed. An hour later her master followed her, walking wearily, and carrying the manuscript under his arm.

Day began late in the playwright's strange little household. The many clocks of the university were striking the hour of nine, when Julia entered the living-room to clear the day's disorder; and the sun was strong, when Claverhouse and Janet sat at their silent morning meal. Janet had recovered from the previous night's exhaustion. She was one of those aged people who sleep readily and long; and thus put on their waning energy the minimum daily drain. The daylight had neither injustice nor mercy for the seamed, dark-coloured skin, the strong, sunken jaw, and the hair's dead whiteness. When the meal was over she rose; and seating herself on a covered stool by an ottoman that was wont to serve her as a table, spoke her first words of the day to her son.

"Sigismund, I will read the play to myself."

Claverhouse nodded, as though half-gratified; and going from the room, returned with the manuscript. He set it by his mother, after holding it closely to his eyes, to ensure his placing it the right way up before her; and left her without a word. In the narrow little hall he came to a pause, and pushed his fingers through his hair, as though he were schooling himself for a task that was distasteful. After a moment he made his way to his attic study, to await the pupils whose teaching was the trial of his days, and the means of his sustenance through them. The room seemed to fit its owner. It was bare of board, and of sparse furnishing; disorderly and paper - scattered. The table was hacked and scored; a pile of used quill pens flanked a broken inkstand; a smaller table, clearly profaned by any touch but his own, was littered with crumpled papers and grey with dust. He seated himself at the larger table, and drew towards him a pile of papers, scored and overwritten in his own hand. Till late in the afternoon, with the respite of an hour for food, he laboured at his irksome toil. His pupils came and went — strong - limbed striplings, rejoicing in their youth, ignorant or heedless of their contact with genius, ready to hail any carelessness of duty as a pedagogic favour. He laboured with a simple conscientiousness; recognising the prostitution of his powers, and giving of them fully. When the last had left him, he rose and stretched his limbs ; and then went at once to a wooden cabinet, and drew out a pile of manuscript. He held it for a long moment, almost dandling it in his arms ; and then replaced it with a lingering touch. " Ah ! " he muttered. " There is another now."

He broke off, seated himself on the table, and drew towards him paper and pens. Half an hour later a limping step came softly to the door, and was silent.

CHAPTER VI.

IN the living again of the early time of after years, Dolores was to see in her student days the things of the student's life as strangely least amongst many. There seemed from the first to be strange, bright promise in this being to face and in touch with the one, whom her young reverence had placed apart from the world, in the sphere which youth creates for those it sees the world's great. Hence, underlying her visible lot, was a hidden thing to which other things grew to be nothing. In secret she watched the self - absorbed being, that seemed to think and move in regard of none, and when perplexity's edge was blunt, of none regarded. In secret her hours were given to the dramas, which had fed her early eagerness for knowledge of her kind; and, grasped by her mind as given by his own, they seemed to bring her soul and his into subtle mutual knowledge. She spoke no word of this current of her life which was deeper than that which carried her fellows; sensitive to shame upon feelings she could only connect with her earlier self by yielding that self to their force; and in light discussion of the playwright, yielded her part to the lightness, drawing over what she sanctified the closest veil.

With the opening of the last and lived-in year of this life which to others was passionless, the student - experience of reaching the fulness of student days, and facing their wane, was robbed of its heed by the knowledge of near communion with the creature first to her judging. The strait routine continued to give of what seemed so foreign to itself. It was at the first hearing of a lecture from his lips, that there came the first awakening to the hidden truth.

She took long to forget what her pale calmness hid, as its minutes passed and its words fell. It was not that the words were as those she had looked for: there was little that strained the feelings or powers of those who listened. There was nothing but an academic dealing with the drama prescribed, with holding to the hearers' needs, and checking of instinct to rise or probe beyond their following. But poor Dolores! There was little need of what her fancy had painted, for the begetting of tumult within her. As surely as this would have brought it, it was born of what was afforded. This simple doing of a common thing by the man of genius, this expending of the greatly-achieving energy on the unhonoured service, given for sustenance—it was an awakening of deeper heart-throbs. That month was a dream, bound up with the real by the struggle with the lassitude of mind, which came of the long emotional strain; and at its end, no word had passed between the teacher and the pupil who would have given this worth to a word.

But there was difference in the months that followed. The classic drama was held a subject calling for some individual teaching; and there came a moment when she stood, with limbs that trembled, at the door behind which he awaited her alone. The essay whose judgment was to fill his hour of duty to her, passed from her hand to his, with a faltering of the one and a casual grasp of the other, which showed her herself as she was in his sight — one in an insignificant many. His dealing with it struck no note—as she had had a formless fear that it might—discordant with her conception of him. He propped his face in his hands with his eyes almost touching its pages; read them from the first to the last without diversion of glance; and then accomplished his task with as great a despatch as permitted its doing; limiting critical words to the parts that needed them, and showing what offended by drawing his pen through the passage. When he gathered up the papers at the end, he stayed his hand, and turned them as if he had found them not as their kind. Then putting them into her hands, without encountering her eyes, he pushed back his chair from the desk, and seemed to sink into musing. The lessons passed thus for weeks, even to the doubt at the end. At last, urged by the thought of their lessening number, she embodied in her essay a passage that showed a knowledge of his dramas. It was not an actual quotation or eulogy ; for her instinct guarded her from stumbling—simply some words which implied a reading of his latest play. She saw his eyes arrested by the passage ; and felt rather than saw, his glance at herself ; but he spoke no word. Her sense of repulsion revealed in its pain how much the action had held of purpose ; and she summoned her strength, and faced the following meeting with no emotion free. As she entered the room, his eyes went to her face.

" You read my plays ? " he said.

" Yes," said Dolores, feeling no power of further utterance.

" Ah ! that is well," he said, looking into her face with a peering gaze, that seemed to be straining to grasp what it held. Then, turning to her papers, he added in his harsher tones, " Well, for your own sake ; " and gave himself to his task.

No further word, apart from their formal dealings, was said till the close of the term. As he gave her her papers for the last time, he fixed his eyes on hers in a manner to hold her in waiting for speech. When they had stood for some moments, he spoke in quick, deep tones.

" How about some lessons with me on my own plays ? "

Dolores never recalled her answer. The memory she summoned was of his turning away with the words, " Ah, well, well ; we shall see to it."

Coming upon him in the cloisters early in the following term, and passing him, believing she was not perceived, she was startled at a distance by his voice.

"Five o'clock will do," he called, as though some discussion of the hour had passed. " Five o'clock on Fridays. We begin this evening."

From that day Dolores knew the great man as a teacher, and was dealt with by him as a pupil. He laid aside the conventional mask he wore with women ; and showed her himself, sparing her nothing of the brunt of his moods. At times he was full of forbearance and kindliness, in control of his nervous temper, and delighted to gratitude by the insight into his aims, which her early study and the affinity of their minds had given ; at others, intolerant of the faintest faltering of grasp ; and at others, in a mood of cynical bitterness to the world that ignored his service, which held her in heavy constraint, in its grudging of sign that exception was made of herself. He

accepted no gratitude for the service he rendered;
and presumed in no way upon it unless in assumption of a right to guide. It was not in chief his
own plays that he taught, but, as he told her in
a moment of emotion, " the greatest thing that
life offered to men "— the study of men, as shown
in nature, and, as grasped from nature, in the
plays of the greater dramatists of different time
and race; in whom, with a natural dignity which
thrilled her to passion, he numbered himself : and
at times he demanded not only understanding of
these, but studies of character from her own pen.

As the months grew few and priceless, and the
days heavy with the knowledge, that this sufficing
lot was but a passage of her life, about to be
resolved into a burden of memories, for the rendering her other than she seemed in a barren
sphere, Dolores found that her daily service to
duty was a daily wrestling. The approaching
change seemed the tearing of her being from the
only nurture that was sustenance. And comfort
was not a thing to be sought. There was denied
to her grief the bitter softening of waking and
moving in thraldom to itself. The public tests
of student-proficience, which were in name the
end of these passionate, prosaic years, lay before
her, as they lay before those whose unchastened
youthfulness had welcome for their young emula-
tion. It was due from her to strive for much
that had grown to be of childish things ; and the

hours and effort given to the dramatist's demands, were owed in duty to the feebler ends.

Dolores' living of this time showed her the same as we have known her. Her bearing marked her light of heart, when the hidden burden lay heavily; the daylight hours of helpless wrestling were atoned by labour in the silence; and her voice was as calm, as her lips were white, when she showed the playwright that his counsels must be second to her academic toiling.

"Ah!" he said, and was silent; but Dolores heard his confession of error in thinking her not as her fellows.

"It is not," she said, not trying longer to smother what came to her voice, "that I do not value your teaching far above other things. It is only—you see I have given time to what I have done for you—that I have no choice but to work for credentials. I shall be obliged to support myself by teaching."

"Ah!" he said again; and Dolores again read the meaning of the word, and went away comforted.

But this twofold struggling was not to meet the mockery of missing its purpose. There came other days with another struggling—days with the generous honour which is the portion only of the student in a student world; where the winner of success has no fellows but those

who strive for the same, as worthy of striving.
These days carried more of bitterness. The
need for hourly effort was gone; and the
reaction brought a time, to which nothing
remained but the suffering knowledge of its
passing.

For a moment of this time we may watch
her; as she sits at Miss Butler's side in the
common hall; and suffers in the sense, that to
the other she is one of a generation going
forth, and her lightness the natural lightness
of youth rejoicing in its laurels.

"You must be thankful that your degree
belongs to the past," Miss Butler said. "When
a thing like that is looming, it is so much
better behind than before."

"That is not the first time I have been
admonished of thankfulness," said Dolores, with
humour in her tones. "I had a letter from a
neighbour at home, observing that as success
was the result of gifts and perseverance, so
the way to avoid its snares was to be thankful
for both. There is something new in the view
that we should be thankful for perseverance.
It is usual to be thankful for more pleasant
things."

"The neighbour was your clergyman, I suppose?" said Miss Butler, laughing.

"No," said Dolores, with a rising smile as
Dr Cassell's image took shape in her mind;

K

"in that case he would be my father. He is a doctor; but he does do religious work. I believe he is—or used to be—a Plymouth Brother."

"I once had a governess who was a Plymouth Brother," said Miss Butler; "and I remember she used to tell me to be thankful for things. It was a perplexity to me that she was not a Plymouth Sister; but she was not. I have it on her own authority that she was a Plymouth Brother."

"The child is the father of the man," said Dolores. "You were naturally sensitive early to genders. I remember how nervous I was under your grammatical probing, when it was new to me."

"Nervous?" said Miss Butler, with a twinkle in her eyes. "Why, what was there to be nervous of?"

"*What* was there?" said Dolores. "It is a pity that confusion should begin at this stage. You would have little mercy for another in a similar position."

"I am afraid I am given to impatience," said Miss Butler, as the laugh ceased. "You must take a lesson for your own experience."

"I hope I shall take many lessons from you," said Dolores, colouring in the effort against the real reserve of the outwardly genial bread-winning woman.

Miss Butler answered the effort with a smile
which said enough to Dolores; and broke in a
little nervously, colouring herself.

"You will be thinking about your plans for the
future soon, I suppose? I was going to speak
to you of a plan—I mean I had a suggestion to
make. Would you care to stay up here and
work under me? The students are getting too
many to be managed without help. The salary
for some time would be nominal; but the
principal thinks it would be increased as the
duties grew heavier, and the post became recognised. It would be good for your prospects;
and you are more than equal to the work."

The self-command which, with its hard exercise, had grown with Dolores' growth, stood
her in faithful stead; though afterwards she
feared she had betrayed the bonds, which bound
her to this straitened lot.

The next days were graven to the end on
her soul. She looked back on them many
years after, and saw then her youth's days of
possibility. She saw them the last days of her
youth. They were days of hope. It seemed
that her nature expanded in their promise.
Her power of friendship grew. For Perdita,
the friend she loved, that love seemed hourly
to deepen. It happened that she was another,
who was not to pass from the college in the
passing from its children. She was to remain

to give aid in minor duties to the principal, for whom, as for so many others, she exercised a charm. Dolores, in foreliving the time which she saw a time of her own approach to joy, rejoiced also in seeing it a time of a comrade's watchfulness. There was relief, in the fulness of her own experience, in the loving and guiding this weaker moral creature.

It was with faith in her father's pleasure, that she wrote to her family the news of this bending of her future. His awaited letter lingered in coming; and there was an expectant smile on her lips when at length she broke its seal.

"MY DAUGHTER,—I have considered the plan for your future which you laid before me, and see there is much to be said for it. I have, however, another to suggest, with which it is my desire that you shall comply, and that your compliance will be willing, and for your happiness. Your sisters and youngest brother are at an age when education must begin in earnest. There is no school for girls within daily distance, and none for boys but that where Bertram is teaching, and which offers little in its lower forms. I cannot send them away to school. The decrease in my income puts it out of the question. My proposal is, that you shall settle at home, and undertake their teaching. A governess able to do this as you would do it, would require a salary larger than you could supply, if you should accept the post you describe, and offer to provide it; and would occasion trouble in the household. I need not tell you that your mother would not consent. Bertram will welcome your help in his studies; we shall all be glad of your companionship; and a life at home will in many ways be better for yourself.

"God bless you, my daughter.—Your affectionate father, CLEVELAND HUTTON."

Dolores went with the letter in her hands to be alone. The first hour of blind belief, that this was a thing which clashed with her own claims on herself, was by the others an hour of ease. But soon the hours were dark. Soon she saw what her father asked through her father's sight—simply the accepting of a service to her kin for one to strangers. She neither rebelled then, nor set her face to sacrifice. It was her way to see her life, as in the background rather than the fore, of the lives of others. It was to duty she owed her service—the choice that held the best for the lives on which it bore; and a service untouched by generous effort — given simply as owed. She knew that her father's letter had truth in its every word. But that which bound her, was the something deeper

than its words. Beneath them she read the
outcry for her companionship ; of declining years
in a home that held its weariness ; of yearning
for the presence, which shadowed the prime knit
with a nobler soul. Dolores' survey of a crisis
in her own experience was primitive and stern.
For others might be honest doubt, and blameless
wavering at a parting of the ways : for herself
there was a road to be taken, and another to be
left. On the one side lay effort for strangers,
to whom others' effort sufficed ; on the other
the claims of kindred, of her father and her
father's children.

She grew older in the days that followed. It
was not that she struggled : the struggle had
been but of an hour. It was simply that she
suffered, and that the suffering went deep.
Through the much that was hard to say and
do, she still saw grief a lesser evil than justice
a good. And when the hardest came, it was as
one who lived the unreal that she saw and heard.

"Ah, you are going ? Ah, well. Do not forget
what has passed between us. I shall not forget.
I have spent much time in teaching here ; but I
have taught none. They have all been strangers.
You have been my pupil."

CHAPTER VII.

The village lay in its silent, unprogressing peacefulness—meeting Dolores as it had met her four years earlier, on the threshold of her womanhood. Now that womanhood seemed old. Those four bright, troubled years, which had left this early world the same! As she spoke and moved beneath the pressure of her pain, she found herself simply dwelling through a dream on their difference, had nothing been sought but the sameness. But the living beneath her pain was not that which was before her. It was the living above it: and she found she had hardly faced what she had freely chosen — the suffering living of this visible, unmeaning, demanding round. For there were other things that were the same.

"Oh, Dolores, I cannot be thankful enough, that you have come home for good," said Bertram. "In a life that grows more hopeless with every day, it seems the last straw to have nobody to make a companion of."

"Why, Bertram, what is the trouble?" said Dolores.

"Nothing, beyond what you know. But it is enough to feel one's youth slipping away; and have no chance of doing what must be done then or never; and which will spoil one's life if it is not done."

"Oh, Bertram, is it so impossible that you should go to college?" said Dolores. "Cannot you or father see any way, in which it could be managed?"

"*I* can see a way very well," said Bertram. "Simply by the mater's making a little effort against expense for a few years. But father cannot—is not allowed to see it; and I can drudge on in a schoolroom of bumpkins, when a course at Oxford would open a career. It is not a light matter to me, Dolores. I am nearly two-and-twenty; and the years for it will be gone. One cannot begin one's life too late. But not a farthing further is to be wasted on me. Father takes credit to himself for having kept me sheltered and fed, while I should have starved or died of exposure, if he had not."

"I suppose his income is really very much less," said Dolores, in nervous uncertainty how to respond. "This fall in the tithes has made such a difference. He cannot do things for the younger ones, as he once intended."

"But they are not living the best years of their youth," said Bertram. "It does seem that some sort of effort might be made, to save the whole of my life. Father and the mater think that so long as I can just support myself, so as to be off their hands, I am not to be troubled about."

Dolores moved in silence. She felt a bewilderment in this forcing upon her of bitterness other than that of her own, which had filled her world. She looked about her, as one troubled in a dream. The familiar road seemed laden with suggestions of the old, monotonous round; the gabled parsonage was in sight. It was with an effort that added paleness to the set lines of her lips, that she crushed her despair in the denial of a lonely hour, for her sympathy's release; and set her face to the unknowing, family greetings.

" Why, Dolores, you are looking very pale and thin," said Mrs Hutton. " You do not look so after you have been at home for a few weeks."

" She needs a rest," said Mr Hutton, who could not repress an unwonted buoyancy, in welcoming the return with academic honours of the child of his hidden tenderness. " The news of your place on the lists gave me great pleasure, my daughter."

" Will you be glad to be settled at home, Dolores, or would you rather be at college ? " said Mrs Blackwood, who was calling with her husband and children, and whose presence had determined her sister's words. " Which life do you prefer ? "

"I have had many happy days at both," said Dolores. "I should not compare them."

"Do you think you will like teaching your sisters and brother?" pursued Mrs Blackwood, who had had a difference with Mrs Hutton earlier in the day. "With the home duties that are sure to crop up, you will get very little time to yourself."

"I am fond of teaching," said Dolores; "and I have no especial pursuits to make me anxious for much spare time."

"You are a very good sister, and a very good daughter," said Mrs Blackwood; "and I think we may say a very good stepdaughter too."

"My dear Carrie, you need not talk as if teaching three intelligent children were a condition of slavery," said Mrs Hutton. "We did not heap advantages on Dolores, for her to make no use of them. She really ought to be teaching away from home."

"My dear, that would be a foolish arrangement from your point of view," said Mrs Blackwood.

"Well, Bertram, what does your sister think of your new prospects?" said the Rev. Cleveland, interposing with a note of weariness.

Bertram, who had been talking in lowered tones to Elsa, looked up as if reminded of something jarring.

"Oh, I have not mentioned them to her, sir," he said.

Mr Hutton was silent; and Bertram continued in a casually bitter tone, in answer to Dolores' question.

"Oh, I have been offered a higher post at the grammar-school—the mastership of a house that takes boarders; so that I can settle down to give up my life to farmers' sons, and their welfare—mental and bodily."

"It is not a question of giving up your life," said the Rev. Cleveland. "Promotion is not tabooed any more to you than to other men."

"It is tabooed to me, as much as to other men with no qualifications, sir," said Bertram.

"My dear Bertram, learning is not only to be had at Oxford and Cambridge," said Mrs Hutton. "I am getting tired of this harping on that subject. You talk as if learning were a thing to be bought with pounds, shillings, and pence. Books are the same all the world over, surely. You have plenty of spare time; and you are not a baby. There is no reason why you should not give yourself as good an education, as any one need have."

"I have given myself as good a one already, as most people have," said Bertram. "I should have thought I need not tell you, that it is not only that, that Oxford and Cambridge give—are supposed to give, if you like,—it comes to the same thing. No good post is open to a man, who is not turned out of one or the other. Any man understands that."

" Yes ; to hear Uncle Cleveland talk, one would think his years at Oxford were the only time in his life he found worth living," said Elsa.

" But, really, though I suppose the atmosphere and ancient associations of Oxford and Cambridge must influence all that one reads and thinks in them, the learning in itself must always be the same, must it not ? " said Lettice.

" Letty, your habit of talking as one possessed by an imbecile spirit, has been wearying to me from your cradle," said Elsa. " I am sorry to see it growing upon you."

" Ah, there is a great deal of truth in anything that Letty says, I have no doubt," said Mr Black-wood, preferring passive conviction, as less exact-ing than active judgment. " I have no doubt of that."

Elsa resumed her talk with Bertram without yielding her father a glance ; and neither gave heed to the general company, until Mrs Black-wood's awakening to the need for leaving ; which occurred at a discomfiting point in argument with her sister, and was proof against pressure of hospitality.

Bertram escorted the guests to the door ; and on his return, Dolores was struck by a difference in him. He was buoyant, as she had known him only in unwitnessed moments of the younger time. His spirits lasted till the parting for the night; and apart from their giving of perplexity, in their bearing on the mood they followed, they seemed to sit on him strangely. To-day she had power to follow what she saw, only through sorrow's dazing sense of living the unreal; but the memory was to grow into meaning.

Poor Dolores! She wrestled along in the silent hours that night—holding to her own nature in the wrestling; neither weeping nor rising to pace the ground; but lying with dry eyes and worn face, and hands clutching the coverings tensely. When the morning grew light, she rose schooled for her lot.

The day was the Sabbath, which brought more of friction than peace in the parsonage household. She walked with her father in the garden after the constraining morning meal, at which Bertram's moodiness returned, to diffuse a general oppressiveness; and strove to give the daughterly comradeship, for which she gauged his unworded yearning. But it was not long hidden, that this which she felt the chief of her hard service, it might be a greater service to leave undone. Mrs Hutton's voice fell cold and repelling on her ear, as they passed down the churchyard to the church.

"I shall expect you to take your share of what has to be done, now that you are at home,

Dolores. I shall not expect you to enjoy yourself with the men of the household, and leave
me *all* the brunt of the general management.
The mere teaching of the children is not a work
which exempts you from everything else. There
were a good many things you might have done
to save me between breakfast and church; which
would have left me free for your father, at a time
when he always likes to have me with him."

Dolores was silent. Thrusts of this kind could
not strike without leaving a wound; but the pain
was lost in that which pressed without ceasing.
And it pressed heavily. The little familiar church,
failing by the side of the childhood's conception
which she carried; the loved, familiar face, whose
aging struck again the painful note of discord
with memory; the familiar, ponderous utterance,
whose words were alone in harmony with what
had foregone—being exactly those, which a few
years earlier had celebrated the corresponding
Sabbath;—all went to bring home the straitness
of the lot, she had taken for that which she held
as fullest.

At the midday meal her brother's vivacity
returned; and the casual manner of the notice
which met it, revealed that his changes of mood
were wonted. At its end, he suggested that his
sister and he should take a walk to the meeting-
house; where an afternoon service was to be held
by Mr Blackwood.

"You seem to have a fondness for that meeting-house, Bertram," said Mrs Hutton. "Do you approve of his going to dissenting-places so often, Cleveland?"

"I do not understand his preference," said Mr Hutton; "but it is not a matter upon which I should interfere with a son of mine."

Bertram looked a little embarrassed.

"I think the Blackwoods like some of us to go now and then, sir. They come to your church sometimes, to hear you preach."

"It is hardly a province where reciprocation should be regarded as an exchange of civility," said the Rev. Cleveland, following his son and daughter with rather ungenial eyes, as they left the room; "and I think 'sometimes,' and 'now and then' might be reversed in their connections."

The meeting-house showed a scene that was typical of Millfield experience. The seats were covered—or sprinkled—by such of the district's labouring and trading folk, as combined dissent with admiring confidence in Mr Blackwood, as oratorical evangelist. Mr Blackwood himself was standing near the platform, with bent head; twirling his moustache in frank evolution of the coming discourse. Dr Cassell was seated in the front, with an air half-critical, half-approvingly expectant; allowing his eyes to dwell at intervals on the toilette of his wife, whose gloved hand lay on his arm. Mrs Blackwood sat with her son and

daughters, with her eyes fixed on her husband,
and a rather tense demeanour. An elderly labouring man, whose face expressed that order of goodwill, which may be described as evangelistic, was
conducting strangers to places, with a deportment
fitted to the reversed proportion of visitors to
empty seats. Dolores and Bertram had hardly
been ushered with warmth of welcome to the
front, when Mr Blackwood stepped upon the
platform; opened a hymn-book in which his finger
had been keeping a place, and gave out a hymn.
A woman took her seat at a piano; which bore a
small brass plate, with the inscription: "Presented by Dr Cassell"—to which Dr Cassell's
eyes showed a tendency to turn;—and the as-
sembly sought the place, with a bearing in keeping with apprehension of results, should the first
line pass, unsung by any one of them. The rustic
official showed an almost painful anxiety, lest lack
of books should conduce to this pass; and did not
consider it too late to hasten to supply the need
—his own lips not ceasing to move the while—in
a case which had escaped his notice, during the last
verse. This attitude was common to most of the
audience, especially the men; two of whom resigned their own books, not failing to point to
the line being sung; and stood empty-handed; in
one case singing, with an air of struggling with
complacence in knowing the words, and in the
other remaining silent, as if deprivation was

nothing to a sense of it in another. At the end
of the hymn, Mr Blackwood broke upon the
general standing in wait for the "amen," with
the suggestion that the last verse, as carrying
peculiar benedictiveness, should be sung a second
time. This done, and a prayer pronounced in
a declamatory tone, he delivered his discourse;
which imposed no particular strain upon either
himself or his hearers. It was dogmatic in tone,
and tending to the antagonistic, as though with
unexpressed reference to holders of other faiths;
and was unhampered by line of argument, or
ruling aim. It provoked consentient murmurs
and rustles, which he clearly found congenial;
not failing to be inspired by them with greater
power of emphasis. The sentences tended to
rise and swell with ease, but to fail towards
the end, or even to meet some trouble in attain-
ing an end; in which cases he made compensation
for balance of language in impressiveness of utterance. Mrs Blackwood did not take her eyes from
his face while he spoke; and wore the air which
is observable in parents at the public perform-
ance of their children. Many of the older people
were provided with Bibles; and when a scriptural
allusion was made, bestowed some tedious precision on seeking the place; as if the neglecting
to regard what they had heard, in the text, were
an omission more serious than losing the words
that ensued. Dr Cassell lived the hour with the

L

bare endurance of a bad listener; and once sat
suddenly upright, and looked with flushed eagerness towards the speaker, as though the duties
of an auditor and the corrective power of his
normal character were at sharp conflict; and then
gave a glance at his wife, and settled down with
an air of restless resignation. At the end of the
final hymn and prayer, he at once made his move
to leave the chapel; and his face fell as his friend
made public a hope, that no one who desired a
word with himself would have hesitation in remaining : and two old people availing themselves
of this thoughtfulness, incurred from him a glance
of a hardly brotherly nature. Outside he stood
in silence, giving his wife no word of his pause,
as though feeling that the demands of speech
might tend to disarrangement of the matter in
his mind. When Mr Blackwood appeared, he at
once began to speak, making his habitual gesture
with his hand.

"You made a statement, Blackwood—I should
say, perhaps, quoted *the* statement, that, 'In
my Father's house are many mansions.' The
word, 'mansion,' does not signify in this context,
as you implied — the accepted meaning of — a
sumptuous dwelling; but merely its derivative
meaning, 'resting-place.' It is the Latin word,
'mansio,' used by the translators of the Bible in
its native significance."

"Ah, is that so, doctor?" said Mr Blackwood,

not very gratefully—the transition from emotional exaltation to acceptance of correction not coming very easily to pass. "Well, but now, *I* don't believe, you know, in this finding some new interpretation for every *text* in the Bible. *I* believe in the old gospel meanings, that have been *dear* to us from our *cradles*—that is what I believe in. I like the *old* meanings of the *old* texts—that is what *I* like. Why, there are some people who would go on giving us their new meanings, till in the end we shouldn't have any of the old meaning left."

"But—er—it is not a question in this case of giving a *different* meaning; it is a question of getting back to the original meaning," said Dr Cassell, feeling the peculiar injustice of these implications in reference to himself. "It is surely better, to take every method of getting nearer to the truth."

"Ah, well, the Truth itself is what I care about. I don't care about the different methods of getting near to it," said Mr Blackwood loudly; producing in poor Dr Cassell a hardly bearable sense of seeing the fallacious point in his reasoning, but being unable in a moment to locate it. "Now, I have just been having a talk with a poor old body, who was so *anxious* to get a word with me, that she hardly *knew* what she was doing; and it was wonderful the *faith* and the *joy* she showed she had in the *gospel*. 'Ah,

sir,' she said, 'you little know what you do
for us, your poorer brethren, in preaching the
gospel to us; and looking after our needs in the
matters where we have the *greatest* need—you
little know it,' she said.　That is the sort
of thing it does one good to hear—that is the
sort of thing, that makes one feel that the *Gospel*
is the thing that is wanted, and not *interpretations*, and *criticisms*, and things of that sort."

Dolores, standing with her brother in hearing
of this dialogue, found that the old, half-tender
sense of the humour of its kind was dead within
her.　She was living in two worlds; darkly groping in the one for a spot of solitude, that she
might in the spirit live wholly in the other.
A glance down the road brought the pain of self-
reproach.　A heavy figure was moving slowly
into sight.　So not for an hour could her father
still his yearning for her fellowship.

It was as she thought.　He shook hands in
silence with his friends; and motioning her to
his side, turned at once towards the parsonage.
Bertram and Elsa followed; and behind came a
group of Cassells and Blackwoods; of whom the
doctor had secured the reins of the talk, and was
enlightening a now receptive audience, an excellent example of attentiveness being set by Mrs
Cassell.

Dolores gave her power of effort to yielding
her father what he needed; but on reaching her

home, and meeting his wife on its threshold, she was again brought face to face with the knowledge, that seemed to render as vanity her hard faithfulness to that which she had seen as just.

"Dolores, I hope you understand that I meant what I said to you this morning. It is not my habit to say one thing, and expect people to do another. I wish work to start in earnest to-morrow. Have you looked out the children's books, and got everything into order?"

Dolores answered, with heavy feelings hidden by her courteous tone, that all should be in order by the morning; and the following day was a pattern of many that succeeded. They were days whose trials would have been embittering, had not daily trials become as childish things. Mrs Hutton did not leave the teaching wholly to her judgment, but in theory gave the direction herself; and her unfitness for the task, and the irritable jealousy which sprang with each day into easier life, made a round of hourly friction. Bertram continued his changes of mood; and was at one time depressed and silent, at another in the spirit that carried no less of painfulness. Her father at the outset spent much of his time in her company, at first in carelessness, and then in defiance of the results in his home; but by degrees, in weariness of discord, and the poisoning of his wife's companionship, fell back into formal recognition of his fatherhood; making his wife his apparent associate, and burying the deeper loneliness; though with a suggested wistfulness which made each glimpse of the bent grey head the begetter of a pang.

One day she received a letter from Perdita; which she read with a deeper paleness than its fellows brought, in their hope of a word of the creature who filled her heart and life, and on whom her lips were sealed. It held a request to be bidden to stay in Dolores' home; as the writer was an orphan, poor in kindred, and this was their only chance of renewing their friendship. Dolores wondered at her little suffering in asking the favour of her stepmother. Her natural, easier feelings seemed all but dead; and the one thing of moment was the chance of staying her yearning with some scanty food. But the result of her effort seemed a rebuke. Mrs Hutton was not a stranger to remorse, for the much that clouded her stepdaughter's days, and was often given in spite of an effort of will; and welcomed a means of making amends, and showing her sister her manner of fulfilling her stepmother's duty.

Perdita found great favour at the parsonage, where she showed herself full of understanding. She paid Mrs Hutton a pretty deference, petted and praised the children, implied a view of her host as an eminent scholar and divine, and avoided betraying too open a preference for being with Dolores, or encroaching on the hours of her duties. Her visit showed her Bertram at his best. His spirits ceased to fluctuate, and were natural and pleasing. He seemed to have become resigned to his future, and talked of the offered post at the school with evident purpose to accept it, and even with jests of the airs he should assume, when the head of a household. In a moment of being alone with Dolores, he observed that the boys in a country school were not without lives to live, and need to be fitted for living them; and she knew she was to hear the burial words of the university dream.

She noticed that her brother earned Perdita's prettiest dealings. With his high-bred comeliness, and the early growth to maturity in which he followed herself, he unknowing wielded spells over the woman coming with her young needs from a world of women; and Dolores looked into the future, and saw herself bound by further bonds to the friend she loved. When he left the village for a holiday, some days before Perdita's visit ended, her quickening instinct was alive to the change in her friend, and the purpose in the guardedly sparing words she spoke of him. It was not in her nature to know content, that the love of either should be wholly her own; and she grew to think of the two with tender looking forward.

But this was too frail a tenderness for this

troubled time. For herself the presence of
Perdita had made darkness and hidden strife.
The sacrifice of her choice, lived day by day and
silently, was hard to the brink of bending her
will. The parting, faced with the knowledge
of the sphere of the other's life, all but ended in
failing of heart; in its conflict with the passions,
from which it was a further conflict to withhold
the shame of jealousy. With Dolores it was
going sadly, when she forgot her brother's life
and her friend's, and bowed beneath the living
of her own.

But her experience was, as always, bent by the
lighter experience of others. As she stood on
the station, with her courage faltering, and her
face old for her years, she was accosted by
Elsa Blackwood; whose return from a visit had
been timed for the reception of her luggage by
the parsonage trap; and who joined her in such
bright youth, that it would have been strange
hearing to a watcher, that the days which had
seen the lives of the two were the same. Elsa
was in the lightest of her moods. She yielded
her possessions, without the soberness of injunc-
tion, to the lad who was gardener and groom at
the parsonage; and tripped by Dolores with a
flow of prattling, which spared her the effort
of words. As they neared the place of their
parting, her chatter suddenly ceased.

"Why, there is my mother coming to meet

us!" she said, in a voice with a studied lightness.

"Elsa, what is this?" said Mrs Blackwood, as she came into hearing. "This letter came for you from your friends this morning. I noticed the postmark, and knowing you were supposed still to be with them, opened it. It was written yesterday; and they were under the impression that you were on your journey home."

"You have no right to open my letters, mother," said Elsa. "Surely I am old enough to have a private correspondence."

"You are clearly not old enough to have any liberty at all," said her mother. "Where have you been to-day and yesterday? Your father insists on a full account."

"Oh, mother, am I never to have any friends of my own choice? Am I to be a child under you and father, till all my youth is past?" said Elsa, with tears in her voice. "What shall I have to look back on, when I am as old as you are? You have had your own youth. Why should you grudge me mine?"

"Elsa, do not be foolish," said Mrs Blackwood. "If you have been with those friends your father does not approve, say so, and we will forgive you this once, and help you to do better in future. It would be a dreadful thing to have such a burden on your conscience. There is a guidance we cannot understand in these things."

"Oh, well, mother, if you have guessed it, it is no good to say any more," said Elsa. "Here is the gate to the churchyard, where Dolores leaves us. Let us say good-bye at once, and spare her a family confession and pardon."

Dolores was used to Elsa's wildness; and gave her thoughts, as she bent her steps to the parsonage, to preparing an account of the scene for her father, who was always indulgent and amused over the mischief of his wife's comely niece.

But as she entered her father's study, whence a hum of voices sounded, thoughts of Elsa were banished. Mrs Hutton stood by the fireplace, looking flushed and nervous, her dress betraying some elaboration of its daily simple fitness; and by the window two portly, sable figures seemed to block out the light with their ample sombreness. They were the figures of the Rev. Cleveland Hutton and the Very Rev. James Hutton. The latter's greeting came deliberate and deep.

"Well, Dolores, it is a great pleasure to meet you. It must be two years since I visited your father, and found you at home. What a likeness——! She looks more the student than ever, Cleveland."

"She has done very well at college," said Mr Hutton. "I am told I ought to be proud of her."

"And you are not, I suppose?" said the Dean,

with rather laboured pleasantry. "Well, you must leave the being proud to me. I am sure I am very ready to be proud of my niece."

The Very Rev. James showed little change for the years. He was yet in the prime of his pomposity and portliness, his fondness for kindly patronage, and his contentment with himself and his ecclesiastical condition. Experience had dealt with him gently. His hair was less grey than the Rev. Cleveland's, and his figure straighter for all its greater cumbrousness. His personality was simple and inclined to transparence. Many had said that a minute of his company sufficed for the knowledge that he was married and childless.

It was only of late that this state had struck the Very Rev. James, in its aspect of difference from that of his brother. It was not that he had given no reflection to the comparison of himself and the Rev. Cleveland. It was a matter which had had some attraction for his thought; but it had seemed to him fairly summed up in their professional relation, or, more vaguely, in the position that he was himself the greater man. The new line of his fraternal considering had a climax which afforded him surprise and a degree of amiable excitement.

"You do not owe my visit to chance, or even merely to brotherly feeling for your father," he said to Dolores, repeating a speech he had made to Mrs Hutton; and improving the effect of its ending by subjecting one of his eyes to a wink in the direction of his brother. "My coming has a purpose. Your father will perhaps explain it."

"Your uncle has made a most generous suggestion," said the Rev. Cleveland, turning to his daughter with an air of elation at once nervous and laborious. "He has offered to bear the expense of a college course for Bertram. As I have told him, we know it to be the wish of your brother's life. I am most glad and grateful."

"Oh, so am I," said Dolores. "It is the thing of all others that Bertram would have chosen; and I have so wished it for him."

"Ah, James, you see what your offer means," said the Rev. Cleveland, adjusting his tone between the morose and pathetic. "My children are good children to me. My daughter knew that I could not afford what she wished so deeply for her brother; and I have heard no word of it. My lot has been hard in many ways, but in my children I am blessed." Mr Hutton felt an attitude of mingled pity and complacence to himself suitable to intercourse with his brother.

The Very Rev. James looked uncertain whether to be gratified by the happy direction of his bounty, or ruffled at the presence of pleasures in his brother's portion, which were lacking to his own; and Mrs Hutton's suggestion was opportune, that they should "walk round the garden and find the children;" who had been given hasty, covert directions to make change for the better in their apparel, and place themselves there at general avail.

The presence of the dean was oppressive in the parsonage, by the time that his nephew returned to learn his altered relation to him.

Bertram had not made known the hour of his coming; and he entered his father's study, where voices summoned him, without word with parents or sisters. Dolores saw that his mood was the temper of strained buoyancy, which had wearied her perplexity. The dean did not choose on this occasion to leave his liberality in his brother's treatment. He dealt with it himself, with an elaborate precision befitting its greatness, and an air of indulgence towards any impropriety, which should result in his nephew's deportment from the shock of grasping his fortune.

Bertram's wordless quest of beseeming response met such smiles and exchange of looks as it merited ; but his answer, when it came, brought his hearers to dumb bewilderment.

"Oh, I do not know, sir. I had quite given up thoughts of going to college. I am old for it now. I—I am very grateful to you, sir; but I cannot — must not think of accepting your generosity."

"Why, you are upset by the news, Bertram,"

said Mrs Hutton, earning a grateful glance from her husband. "He has wished it so long, James, that he is quite startled by its being made possible."

"Ah, ah, I expected as much," said the dean, as Bertram hastened from the room.

Dolores followed her brother; but he repulsed her advance, and turned to her words an unheeding ear. For the next hours he wandered alone in the garden and lanes, avoiding speech, and turning on his heel at the sight of his uncle or his father. Dolores was deeply bewildered, but he gave her no chance of words; and the next day greater perplexity came. It was known in a troubled and almost guilt-stricken household, that he had met his uncle's offer with becomingly grateful, but absolute refusal, on the ground of scruples of conscience, which it was not in his power to reveal.

The next days dragged by heavily. A burden of constraint seemed to lie on the parsonage. Mr Hutton showed an uncommitting moroseness; not referring to the conduct of his son, and avoiding all but conventional dealings with his brother. The Very Rev. James was an embarrassing union of courteous guestship and lofty forbearance with unthankful folly. Mrs Hutton was nervous and constrained; and Bertram forgot his spirits, and sank into unbroken depression, repulsing effort to learn his position

almost with anger. The person to break the
oppressiveness was the Very Rev. James. He
suddenly laid aside his discomfiting bearing, and
began to show Mrs Hutton courtly attentiveness,
and to display great interest in her children. She
responded in accordance with maternal diplomacy,
treating him as an indubitable source of superior
counselling; and it was known that he held to
his desire to benefit his brother's family, and was
to undertake the education of his youngest boy
and girls. On his leaving the parsonage, his
partings carried a new geniality, which was
accorded to Bertram with the rest; and the Rev.
Cleveland was supplanted as escort to the station
by Evelyn and Sophia.

Dolores looked into the future, questioned her
duty, and saw it clear. Much in her home
showed it clearer. Her father, as though he
regarded the late perplexities as giving him a
right to mould his habits afresh, fell back into
open seeking of her fellowship; and, although
while his wife was engrossed in arranging for her
children, the course was safe, she felt its covered
danger. Mrs Hutton's dealings with herself put
an end to anything that remained of choice.
She excused her children from study for their
time at home, and did all to be done for them
wholly herself; neither seeking Dolores' aid nor
accepting it when offered; so that Dolores' time
was her own from dawn to dusk. Her purpose

was not of the things to which Dolores was easily
blind.   She knew she was being shown her presence in her father's home as no more needed.
She saw her case, simply and without rebellion,
as it was; spent one dark hour, looking at the
little good to her kin that had cost all to herself;
and set her face forward with her old faith in the
just.   Full happiness in her father's lot was not a
thing that must be sought.   She must seek for
him peace in his loneliness, the content which—
albeit in blindness — he had chosen, made untroubled.   She would not act without his sanction
and counsel; and she told him her purpose, in
words that were few but bore their meaning.   As
she ended, he spoke in a new tone.

"My daughter," he said, "you are a good
woman.   Your mother lives on in you.   I will say
nothing.   You know better than I.   Your way
will be opened for you."

The father said words of truth.   Dolores' way
was opened for her, and for a space her days were
light.   She needed the accustomed tribute to her
fitness to teach ; and her appeal brought an answer
with hidden meaning.   The place she might have
held in the days that were behind, had met support, and was open to her need.   Then thoughts
of her own life came; but they were second to
those of her brother's, till the others grew to
purpose.

As she waited one evening in the churchyard,

knowing that Bertram chose this path to the parsonage, she met Dr Cassell, on his way to her sisters in some childish ailment; and asked if he knew of her brother's whereabouts.

"Ah, history repeats itself, does it not, Miss Dolores? There comes a time when the best sister is not enough," said the doctor, with a wink and a gesture towards the road.

Dolores saw that comprehension was accepted, and asked no question; but waited with a sense of seeing a dawning on what had been dark.

When Bertram came up the churchyard, the dusk was gathering; and she started at the sight of the sombre figure breaking the shadows. The start was a help, and she spoke the words she had been schooling herself to utter.

"Bertram, I am going to ask you a question, and I want your answer to be true and full. So it is no longer your wish to go to Oxford, if the way should open?"

Bertram started and whitened.

"Yes," he said in a shaky tone. "It is a small thing to wish so much, and feel so hopeless; but I do still wish it, Dolores—more than I can say in words."

"But the reason you had for refusing to go— the reason you will not disclose—does not that remain? What meaning had your absolute refusal of my uncle's offer? I would rather you should give up all, than do what is against your conscience."

"What do you mean?" said Bertram. "It is not possible for me to go."

"Yes, I think it is possible," said Dolores, gently. "I am taking a post at my old college —I am going away from home; it will be better so, Bertram,—where the salary would enable me to give you some help; and father could do something now, with the children's education settled. But if in some way it cannot be, we will not speak of it."

"Dolores, I will tell you it all," said Bertram. "I will tell you it all, and then you will know what you are doing; or I could not accept your sacrifice, much as I *can* accept from you. But do not speak to me while I am speaking. It began with my being so hopeless over being denied the chance to make a name as a scholar. My life seemed so narrow, and I saw no hope of its widening; and I was in despair, and made a grasp at all that was within my reach. I—I will not speak of my feeling for—for Elsa. You either know it, or you do not know it,—in either case we will not speak of it. The thing I have to tell you is—is that we are married. No; do not speak, Dolores. We met in that time when we were both away from home, by her leaving her friends before her people thought. We knew that our families would oppose, as my prospects

were so poor ; but we meant to disclose our marriage, and settle down at the grammar school-
house, where I was to be master. Well, you
understand my feelings when I returned, and
was met by my uncle's offer. My manner of
meeting it is no longer a mystery. Of course, I
saw my accepting it as impossible. But with
the suggestion the old longing returned. It had
lived so long with me ; and Elsa was sorry for
both our sakes, that I had given up the chance of
fulfilling it. She saw the difference it would
make to the lives of us both ; and thought
we might have kept our secret, and lived
apart in our homes, as betrothed to each other,
till my college years should be over. I was
troubled and bewildered by her thinking I should
have done differently ; and I simply revealed
nothing, and did nothing : and—well, that is all,
Dolores. It is not less than enough, I daresay
you will think."

Bertram pressed his hands to his head, and
leant against a tree, dropping his eyes to the
ground.

"Then that is why you have been sometimes
so excitable, and sometimes so depressed, ever
since I came home ? " said Dolores, too startled
to think of anything but following her brother's
course.

"Yes," said Bertram, in the tone of one simply
giving a desired explanation. "I alternately

worried over the passing of my youth without the chance I longed for, and yielded myself to thinking of Elsa, and our secret betrothal."

For some moments Dolores was silent, the image of Perdita vivid in her mind.

"Well, and what now?" she said at last, in the same voice.

Bertram hesitated.

"If I could go to Oxford—you are generous, Dolores—it is the dream of my boyhood—I— I do not see why it would not be right."

"You are married—" said Dolores.

"We have been through the marriage service," said Bertram. "Not that that is not enough. We are married for life, of course; and I am grateful that it is so; but I cannot see that the living apart for a few years, especially as be-trothed, is such a wrong thing that our prospects for life must be sacrificed. Anyhow, *I* do not think so, Dolores. It is my honest opinion that it is not so; and I think I have a right to decide. I am a man of three-and-twenty, and not young for my years. I have a right to act according to my honest opinions."

Dolores was silent. The last argument was a strong one to her, and Bertram had known it in choosing it.

"I think the decision of the matter rests with me," he repeated. "I do not see that you have a right to question my conscience. If you would offer me help if things were otherwise, I think you should offer it now."

"Well—then be it so," said Dolores slowly. "You are a grown man, as you say, Bertram. I may have no right to value your opinions more lightly than my own. So we will leave it so."

"Dolores, I must ask one more thing of you," said Bertram. "I have asked so much that I cannot hesitate. It will not count. We shall never speak of this—to others, or between ourselves. Not a word of it will pass my lips, and must not pass yours. I must have your promise. The matter concerns me solely. I have told it to you of my own will. It is a promise I have a right to exact."

"Ah, you know me well, Bertram," said Dolores, with a half-sad smile.

Bertram waited in silence.

"Well, up to a point, I think it may be a promise you have a right to exact," she said. "I promise never to disclose what you have told me to-night, as long as my silence does not involve — seem to me to involve — an injury, or anything that I consider an injury, to any human being."

CHAPTER VIII.

" No, no ; read more slowly, Sigismund. I cannot
follow what it means. You used not to read to
me so quickly."

There was a querulous, quavering note in the
aged tones. The last days of the many which
Janet Claverhouse had seen, had carried a change.
That which sorrow had failed, and the ills of the
flesh had spared to bring, was wrought by the
surer force of days. The grasshopper had
become a burden, and filial tendance was an
added weariness.

With the sound of the feeble voice, the son
slackened and lowered his tones ; but before he
had turned the page, it broke in again.

" No, no ; I do not hear, Sigismund. You read
in a whisper. You can shut the book ; I will not
listen any more. You do not try to make it easy
for me. I am old ; and you do not care to help
me any longer."

Claverhouse laid down the book he had
been holding closely to his eyes, and placed

his hand on the shrunken fingers on the coverlet.

"My dear old mother!" he said.

Janet's eyes filled with the easy tears of bodily weakness.

"I am old, and complaining, and you do not care for me," she said with faint sobs. "But I shall not be with you much longer. You will soon be rid of the burden of me. But when you were helpless, I never thought you were a burden."

Claverhouse moved his hand and was silent; and the aged creature saw that the wounding power of the words of her feebleness could not be deadened by their helpless utterance.

"Ah! I am an ungrateful old woman," she said, as if half-speaking her own thoughts, half-quoting those she judged to be her son's. "I expect too much of every one. I expect them to bear with me, and suffer with me from morning till night, and give them nothing in return but more to bear with. It will be a good thing when I am gone, and my son can live his own life without the burden."

Claverhouse was still silent. This prostration of the vital creature, he had honoured through the years as her who had borne him, in the aged weakness of other women, was a grief with a subtle bitterness. He could almost find it in him to wish, that the end had come some seven years earlier, in a sickness which had stricken her first feebleness, and given in its passing a new hold on life.

"My dear little mother!" he said at last, taking the tiny hand. "Weakness and weariness are hard for a spirit such as yours. But endurance, as other things, grows great in you. You need not doubt me. I know when it is weakness speaking, and when it is yourself."

Janet shed a few more tears, but of a quieter kind which brought a calmer mood; and then lay back on her pillows, and presently passed into sleep. The son sat by her chair, with his face towards her, but his eyes looking into space. He was sitting thus, when the door of the chamber opened, and Julia entered with a covered cup in her hand. Her look of venerating tenderness at the face on the pillow was followed by another that spoke of deeper things, as her master yielded her his seat and stole from the room. It was not till the uneven, heavy tread on the stairs was succeeded by the sound of the upper door and silence, that the expression of listening eagerness died on her face, and she seated herself to await the end of the sleep, that checked her tendance. The light slumber of age was readily broken by the change in the ministering presence. Janet awoke, and rested her eyes on the watcher at her side. After a moment she suddenly staggered to her feet, and took some struggling steps, as though continuing in action the experience of her dreaming. A gesture of her hand towards the floor above, and the movements of her lips and limbs, showed that her purpose was the old pilgrimage to the door of her son. Julia checked her gently ; laid her back on the pillows, and soothed and fed her. She received the ministrations in a silence that told of inner weariness, broken by words in which complaining and gratitude were mingled. But she seemed to gain strength from the food as she swallowed it ; and when the cup was set aside, her talking gladdened the humble, waiting heart with its shadowing of the old self. A colour rose to her shrunken cheeks as she spoke. It was of her son that she talked, and her desires for his comfort when her mother's care should be lost to him. Her voice seemed to lose its high-pitched quaver, and regain its old deep tone. But she appeared to be agitated ; and more than once repeated herself unwittingly, or stumbled over her words. Julia perceived the signs of change, but could not interpret their certain message ; and when she sank into sleep, left her without uneasiness.

In the upper chamber the son, in the mood of emotional ardour, which was brought him by grief in greatness, but held from begetting wrestling of spirit by its birth in the workings of nature and days, was living in a world of his own ; with no knowledge of the moments, and his senses closed to the things that touched them.

A feeble, limping footfall, growing slower and feebler with its steps, fell on his ear to stir no response in his mind, save a slumbering power of remembrance. A sound of a fall, and a long, feeble, guttural cry, mingled with the other dim impression, and wrought no further ; till other sounds—another footstep, and another cry— awakened perception and memory, with the fear they brought. He rushed from his room; and on the staircase there met his sight the scene which his moment of dread had painted. He pushed the trembling Julia aside ; and taking up the weightless form, bore it to the lower room, and laid it on the bed. The eyes were closed, and the limbs drooping ; but something in the face showed that the mind was awake. It was the hour for the doctor's daily coming ; and the chance was well ; for the man's strong limbs were trembling. He turned to Julia with his breath quickened.

"How dared you leave her, without fetching me to watch her ?" he said.

"I was getting the supper. The work had to be done. We always do leave her when she sleeps. I never do disturb you—she will not have it. O, my dear, my dear !" sobbed the old servant, kneeling by the bed.

" How came she to go to the staircase ? " said Claverhouse, leaning against the wall for support. " It is years since she has been there alone. She must have been wandering; but, even so, how did it come to her mind ? "

The eyes of the aged woman opened, and turned to Julia's face; and one tiny, shrunken hand made a gesture pitifully imperious in its bare achievement. Julia had raised her head to speak ; but she bent it at once—the last office of her long obedience,—and wringing her hands, continued sobbing. The doctor's entrance brought silence, and the words that were awaited and dreaded.

" Yes, it was the end. The fall on the stairs was due to a kind of paralytic spasm. It was possible there had been some wandering of mind. The cause of all was age. There was nothing to be done save quiet watching and tendance as long as they were needed."

And they were not needed long. A spell of unconsciousness followed ; and in the early hours of the morning the final stillness came. For the farewell of the mother and the son there was no word spoken ; but Julia, in her daily dwelling on the last knowing moment, knew—though in the silence of the loyalty that did not die with death — that the years of selfless service had had no unfitting end.

Claverhouse stood for long, gazing on the

shrunken form stretched on the bed. His mood was one of exalted emotion that was almost congenial. The many years of the powerful life had closed—had joined the infinitude of unwritten history. It was still — the heart of many struggles; still in the unutterable dignity of having worn itself out. His was an exalted grief. He moved away, and seated himself at the fireside; sought about him for paper and pencil, and began to write. Julia crept from the room; and going to the upper chamber, gathered up the papers that lay half-written on the table, and carried them to the room of death. As she passed the bedside in leaving it, her look at the face on the pillow showed that it was not for one alone that she rendered the ministering action. Claverhouse wrote by the light of the fire, till dawn supplanted the service of its dying embers; and at last fell, pencil in hand, into sleep. When he awoke, the last ministrations had been given to the dead; the bed and the body were disposed as was fitting; and Julia was standing at the bedside, smoothing the coverings with her wrinkled hand, as though loth to acknowledge finished the last act of her life's service. Claverhouse rose to his feet, and came to her side. She gave a glance at his face; and then covered her own and burst into weeping. He walked from the room without giving her a word, and passed to the living-chamber. With the wrought-up feelings which came with the awakening from a short sleep after a long weariness, he could ill bear with the reminder that other eyes had wept, and other hands wrought, while slumber stayed his own. As he opened the door, a tall, grey-haired figure turned from the fireplace.

"Soulsby!" he said, peering forward as though he had felt, but not yet perceived, the presence. "When did you come? You have heard then? How long have you waited?"

"I—I came about an hour ago," said the nervous, musical tones. "I—I came really to inquire. I—I did not—did not know before. The old servant told me you were asleep; and I waited till you should wake. I——"

"You are a good friend, Soulsby," said Claverhouse. "I should be lonely indeed but for you. I shall always be lonely without you now. Yes; so it is over. Julia has told you; so I will not. Ah, well! it was to come; and it is a marvel that it did not come sooner; but it must be as it must be, now it has come. I am alone now."

He walked to the chimney-piece and leaned his head against it. His face was older.

"Yes — you would like me to go?" said Soulsby, making a movement towards the door.

"No, no; stay," said Claverhouse. "I am not broken down, and I shall not be. I shall go on

in the old way—living and working. It is what
is left to me."

He laid his hand on the bell; and Julia
brought the morning meal with a readiness that
showed it in waiting for the summons; and fulfilled her duties and those of her mistress in
her wonted unobtrusive silence; nothing but her
features' traces of tears and watching speaking
of the change in the household whose needs were
her life. But the change was great. It was not
till the burial was past, that it seemed to come;
but when it came it was great. Before the burial
Claverhouse was quietly himself. His friend
spent many hours of each day with him; and
they talked, as was their wont, of his work,
reading and discussing it together. He showed
interest and gratitude, and gave little sign of
sorrow; seeming to avoid imposing on his friend
too great a share of his burden : but there seemed
a restlessness about him, as if he was in waiting
for something that was to come and bring a
change. The something came surely, and as
surely brought its change. It was the knowledge of his altered lot; and on the day of the
burial it came.

They were heavy days which followed. It
was not that they were marked by wrestling
or passionate grief. The watcher of men knew
the natural and timely as they were, and as such
he met them. But they brought loneliness—the

loneliness which his life-purpose of human study
made tragedy for him; and which, while believing himself the loneliest of men, he had never
known ; and they brought the understanding,
that the hard endurance of the neglect of his
race had been softened by the human sympathy
of his close lot into easiness. He wandered in
house and streets, unable to concentrate his
powers, in a restlessness that at once wore him
with its scanty respite, and held him in dread
of the relieving spells of the old losing himself
in his labour, as bringing each another waking
to the change.

And there was sadder than this. He fell to
dwelling on the years of his sonhood, and those
of his mother's life which had been of his ordering ; and his mind, with its habit of analysis of
feeling, and giving of significance to human
experience, was a soil where there sprang into
early life, and throve on a bare nurture, the
dire growth of remorse. His mother's aged
years, with the bounding of their joys in himself, and what seemed to his instinct of bereavement their scant repayment in filial duty, were
ever before him—a never-exhausted source of
pain. His hours with Soulsby were less a
relief for himself, than an unacknowledged
burden for his friend ; and were worthy of their
afterward honouring in his memory, as a
tribute to the faithfulness that had no power

of faltering. At one time he was sad and silent, and impatient of break on his troubled pondering; at another eager to dwell by the hour upon his mother's fading years, thirsty for reminders of all that spoke for her content. For weeks it was in this way with him; and then there came the beginning of a change. It was not the wonted change of the end of a struggle through a sorrow — the passing from the old self crushed by grief, to a different self in which the grief is woven. It seemed to be rather a passing from the grief itself to the surveying of it. His talk with Soulsby showed it. He had hitherto shrunk from probing in words the deepest of his own feelings. Now he began to speak of them; and as though less with a desire to assuage their pain, than to gain understanding of them. At times he seemed to be striving to recall them in their early bitterness, not so much through love's recoiling from the acknowledgment of their deadening, as from a yearning to grasp them in their essence. The dramatist-spirit was grappling with itself, that it might gauge its fellows.

One evening Soulsby waited long in the darkening room for the coming of his friend— at one time an almost daily experience; now, as he thought, but a chance happening, pregnant with sobering reminder. But it was not as he thought. When the playwright appeared, he came quickly towards him, and began to speak without heeding the need for greeting—another thing once habitual, but coming now as another echo of the fuller past. He was wearing his ragged working garb, which met Soulsby's sight for the first time since Janet's death.

" Ah, Soulsby," he said, " it is a strong thing—sorrow !—that in which remorse feeds on nothing, and solitude grows to loneliness. I have shown it as it is to-night. I have not suffered what was strange to me, and gone no further. I have shown its ways as I have known them."

Soulsby went from the humble dwelling under a great thankfulness for his friend. The creative spirit no longer lay crushed beneath its burden. It had risen above it ; and was even lifting it to carry it forward, as an addition to the richness that was its own.

N

CHAPTER IX.

"I WONDER if it would be any good to ask Mr Claverhouse to join us again," said Miss Butler. "I think he must have been designed for the proving exception to the rule that man is a social creature. I suppose advances are of no avail, if it has really been arranged like that."

"In that case, I wonder he was allowed to join us at all," said Miss Lemaître. "A pure piece of carelessness in the higher sphere, I suppose."

"Miss Kingsford, you will have to set your spells to work again," said Miss Dorrington, her eyes going from Miss Butler to Miss Lemaître, with twinkling appreciation of the words of both.

"Why, has he ever joined you in here?" said Dolores. "I thought he had nothing to do with you beyond what he could help."

"Oh, yes; for a time he quite unbent," said Miss Butler. "He came to the common-room four times, and we only invited him seven; and every time but twice he spoke. It was Miss Kingsford who seemed the softening influence. Once he said five things to her in one week. We were all quite proud of her."

"Your gift of numerical exactitude would be very useful to me in my duties, Miss Butler," said Miss Greenlow.

"It is his mother's death that has altered him," said Miss Cliff. "His relapse into aloofness is not the only change. I daresay time will be a help."

"Yes, we must hope so," said Perdita. "It is hardly time to expect him to rouse himself yet."

"Well, I am sure one cannot help hoping so," said Miss Lemaître. "I caught one glimpse of him last week, and have felt oppressed ever since."

"Well, this week you must try and let him work upon you homœopathically," said Miss Greenlow.

"And hope in general charity that I may work upon him in the same way," said Miss Lemaître.

"A very good line of idea for curing one another of trying moods," said Miss Dorrington.

"We can do very little for each other at times like these," said Miss Adam. "There is only the one kind of help."

"You knew him better than most of his students, did you not, Miss Hutton?" said Miss Cliff. "Do you think him much altered?"

"I have not spoken to him yet," said Dolores. "Outwardly he is altered. He looks worn and much older."

"You passed him in the corridor just now," said Miss Adam. "I suppose he did not see you? I think he is more short-sighted than ever."

"No; he did not see me," said Dolores, rather faintly.

"He seems to see very little now," said Perdita. "He spoke to me the other day, looking straight above my head, as though he thought he was looking into my face; and he said that he could not see that it was I, but that he *felt* I was there."

"Yes, yes; it is a sorry business," said Miss Butler.

"It is your spirits that are in sympathy, then," said Miss Lemaître. "We may acquit you of calling coquettish influence to your aid in taming him."

"Yes, you may acquit me of that," said Perdita, smiling; "as much as you may himself."

"Is he trying to tame you, then?" said Miss Lemaître.

"I am not aware that I require taming. If

what people give me to understand is true, he is certainly different to me from to them," said Perdita.

Miss Adam looked a little uneasily from one speaker to the other.

"I am afraid his sight is really worse," she said, in an unnoticing tone. "Just lately he has never opened a door, without fumbling for the handle; and he seems not even to try to look for it, as though he felt his eyes were no good. One does not like to think what the end may be."

"It would certainly be irony on the part of fate for him to lose his sight, when he could clearly be deaf and dumb without any deprivation," said Miss Lemaître.

Dolores, as she left the room by Perdita's side, felt no power of hiding that which was within her with lip-spoken words. She could no longer sully the creature she loved, with the idle speech which was the alternative of silence; and silence held her. The following days of effort and renewal of friendship took from her more than they gave. Calmness and conscious courage went; and a life opened whose every day was a struggle—a life to which she clung with the grasp whose slackening speaks destruction.

More than once she came upon Claverhouse in corridor or cloister, and passed him unper-

ceived; but she was driven at last by her sense
of his knowledge of her presence to watch for
him, and give him greeting.

He started at her voice — a different voice
from her own,—and met her eyes with a straining, troubled look, verifying all too plainly the
words that were said.

She spoke again; this time in tones that
were natural, and did their service. His face
lit up; and, as he took her hand, he uttered
words of friendship and pleasure in the meeting. The words were few; but he did not
relax his grasp as he spoke them, and they
only ceased, when it was said that the hour
of counselling should be resumed. He left her
with the old blunt suddenness; which thrilled
her as strongly as anything the meeting held,
in its showing that the days of sorrow had
wrought no difference.

But it was not wholly thus; and as the
weeks passed, she found it. Something had
gone from him — the old eager singleness of
purpose; the rejoicing in a service that was
thankless, if at the same time it was great;
the power of leaving the world where he moved
and breathed, and moving in another. The
hand of sorrow was heavy yet. He yet could
not see the lives of his fellows, for the stretch
of emptiness that made his own. In the hours
they passed together, it was the service of the

teacher to the pupil he rendered. It was not as it once had been. It was she to whom his thought was given, and not himself.

But as the days passed, they carried with them that which was of them. She was gladdened by the change which was lifting the burden from another watcher's heart. The old self returned — the old living for the chosen labour. Once more was demanded less the deepening of her own conceptions, than the true knowledge of his own. One day he laid before her some manuscript pages of a play. The writing was large and straggling, as if the hand that traced it owed little to a guiding eye.

"It is my last," he said. "I am yet writing it. It is as yet for no one's eyes but mine. But you may read it."

Dolores read it; and knew that he had lived his grief to the end. His own deepest experience, which had lain covered from sympathy's touch, was bared to the probing of the world, which had shown itself unloving. She gave it back into his hands in silence, and raised her face with the message she could not speak.

But it had to be spoken. His eyes sought hers with the groping, helpless look she was learning to shrink from meeting; and his gesture showed his need of words. The words were easily given. The forces which bound them

were broken in the shock of a sleeping dread
awakened.

There was a different dread to come.

The self restored as it had been before sorrow
touched it, was not the self she had known.
The days which had been denied to her sight,
when the shadow of bereavement was looming,
were not as those when it was yet unseen, and
after it fell. But she learned to know them, as
if she had watched them; for she watched the
days that were lived now, and knew them of
their image.

Of the manner and swiftness of the change
she could learn nothing, save what she read
into purposeless words. But now it was revealed from its hiding, it was a change which
she witnessed with what she was forced to
acknowledge pain. For the days of genius
proud in its isolation, of neglect accepted and
given, lived in the past. That which was
before her now — genius indeed; but genius in
the half - conventional surrounding of mingled
adulation for itself, and humouring of its eccen-
tricity seemed less great a thing. The student
of men in the little crowd of these daughters
of his age, was not the student standing aloof,
that the ages might lie the same before him.
But the change was not as it first seemed; and
as she watched it, she came to see its essence—
greater and less than she had thought. In the

little company that paid him court, he was simply as he had ever been—blunt, austere, or responsive, as it pleased him; seeming to take the tolerance that met his moods as his due. The change was of straitened surface, but going deep. She knew its presence and its further daily growth; but demanded blindness of herself. But a moment came, which brought the knowledge, that from its earliest signs she had watched it.

She was standing with Perdita in the common library, searching through a shelf of books, when Claverhouse stepped from an alcove in the wall, and joined them. It was to herself he spoke — some trivial words on a change in their hour of meeting; and he turned away when they were spoken. But she read his groping glance aside from herself. The shadow she had seen on the floor, which had shrunk away with his figure's passing from the alcove, she knew had lain there long.

She turned her face from her friend, and sought alone among the books.

CHAPTER X.

"No, you may not be wrong, Bertram; but I cannot help feeling certain that you are. Nothing but my being certain could justify my speaking."

"Then I am quite sure you are certain," said Bertram. "I do not ask for a surer proof, than that otherwise you would not feel justified. You see, I do know something of you, Dolores."

"Bertram, you are old to look at the matter lightly. Another person's life should be to you in your dealings as much as your own. My poor little helpless friend! I wish I had opposed her coming again to see us. I blame myself greatly."

"Well, I cannot help it," said Bertram. "Miss Kingsford knows that—that I am betrothed to Elsa. If it is as you think, I do not know that I am the object for your moral urging."

"Bertram, I must say it for Perdita's sake,"

said Dolores. " What is there in your behaviour
to Elsa, or Elsa's to you, that speaks for your
betrothal? If Perdita thinks it a mere weak-
ening compact of your youth, that may at any
time be broken, is it to be wondered at? But
I am asking you to do nothing more than
remember, that you owe to her what we all
owe to every one."

Bertram whitened, and turned his face from
his sister; and she was spared his reply by the
entrance of Perdita.

" I am despatched as embassy to summon you
both to the drawing-room. Some one has come
to see your father, and Mrs Hutton is out. I
only just caught a glimpse of him. He is tall,
and has grey hair. Your father seemed very
pleased to see him."

" Uncle James," said Bertram. " The pater
is an excellent actor when he chooses; and for
these conditions he has had some practice."

But the figure that rose as Dolores and Perdita
entered, bore merely the generic resemblance to
the form of the Very Rev. James; and Mr
Hutton's tones were not of a kind to be designed for the ear of his brother.

" My daughter, it is a great pleasure to introduce Mr Soulsby. He has a double claim
on our friendship. He was a contemporary of
mine in my undergraduate days; and he is now
the tutor of Bertram's college. He recognised

Bertram's name, and learned from him of my whereabouts ; and being in the neighbourhood for the fishing, has done me the kindness of looking me up."

" No, no, the—the kindness is on your side. It is a great pleasure to me to renew our—our very early acquaintance," said the guest, glancing round to see that the ladies had taken seats, before he resumed his own.

The stranger's manner was felt as constraining by those for whom its youthful form was not discernible through it ; and Mr Hutton found that his precautions for support had left him self-dependent.

" Well, Soulsby, though I have not followed you myself in your academic experience, I have a child who is on the way to doing so. My daughter here is a lecturer at one of the ladies' colleges. I daresay you are surprised to hear it. She is certainly more like a child of yours than mine."

" At—at which college ? " said Soulsby to Dolores, with a slight bow, and a note of deprecating the suggested affinity.

Dolores answered ; and the guest suddenly spoke with musical fluency.

" Then you know Claverhouse, the dramatist ? "

" Yes," said Dolores after a minute's pause, striving to hold her face from changing.

"You were perhaps a pupil of his?" said Soulsby, with a touch of earnestness and apology for it.

"Yes, and I am still in a manner. I have had great kindness from him," said Dolores.

For some moments the guest appeared to be eagerly on the point of speaking; and before he was successful, Mrs Hutton returned, to the relief of Dolores, who felt herself flushing and paling.

The next weeks were a passage by themselves to the master of the parsonage. He found the society of his early friend the greatest happiness. He had been the latter's senior at Oxford, where the closing year of his own deferred and forgotten course was the first of the other's brilliant, early experience; and Soulsby was not the person to whom afterward difference was a ground for unmindfulness of honour owed once to an academic superior. The memories common to both —and both were men in whom academic memories were strong—tended much to his advance in self-esteem; a process which could hardly have been more congenial and natural to him, and which the stationary condition of his own lot, which he had yet to look upon easily, had condemned to a painful tardiness.

But there was another reason underlying the welcome, which drew the diffident scholar daily to the parsonage. The Rev. Cleveland saw

something that other eyes did not see. The
grey-haired pedant, who had passed his prime
without seeking the love of women, saw the
child of his hidden yearning as his own eyes
saw her. He lived this passage of his fatherhood as his nature guided. He built no definite
hopes, and cast no glances over a self-created
future; but standing aside, reconciled to the
one issue or the other, he of purpose seconded
the common view, that the familiar dealings of
his daughter and his friend were an outcome
of their characters too natural to call for
question.

But the bond between Soulsby and Dolores
had its binding from the hidden source. The
life-interest of both was sacred to each, and
was the same. The chambers of each heart,
that were covered from human sight, could be
opened to each other—in the one with freedom,
in the other in slight but grateful part. From
the moment when the common thread of their
lives was known to them, it formed a growing
bond. And for Soulsby it was true that the
bond was more than this. The friendship of
this woman, who gave of friendship as a comrade; whose venerating knowledge of what was
great to himself, was free in its imparting from
the womanly spells which would have held him
wordless and troubled, was growing into a place

of its own in the precision of his life. The
father's eyes were not deceived in what they
saw.

But Dolores? As far as her life was touched
they were wholly deceived. To her the presence
of Soulsby was but the shadow of another. Her
days grew heavy and sadly perplexed. Three
lives lay ever stretched before her—her own,
Perdita's, and that to which she told herself
her own was as nothing. She told herself this.
Could she show herself, in deed, it was truth
that she told? She was saved from darkness
only by the suffering need of living the surface
life, as one amongst many who were living no
other. She bowed to need, as always, calmly;
moved and spoke as one whose life was easy;
kept her passion clothed in the guise of the
feelings of a pupil for a teacher beloved; even
faced the mockery of wrestling to make it thus
in itself—faithful through all to her old religion
of the duty she owed her kind. And now the
duty went deep. It held her from forcing from
herself her knowledge of Claverhouse's love for
Perdita, from grasping the persuasion that his
feeling for herself was love.

When she bade farewell to Soulsby she bade
it blindly; unable to do else than blindly think
the thought, that what he had given was a
deepening of her love in her deeper knowledge

of what had given it birth. She gave him her
hand, knowing nothing of what might be read
into her pale silence.

That day was the day preceding their own
return to the duties of the session. The farewells were made at night, by reason of early
leaving on the morrow. As Dolores passed the
chamber where Perdita slept, she caught a
glimpse of a figure leaning against the wall,
just within the half-shut door, with the hands
on the heart, and the face as a face in death.

CHAPTER XI.

DOLORES returned to the little emotionless world where she had her lot, sustained—since sustaining was her need—by the hope that what she had seen had its being only in her eyes. She knew it was not as she hoped; but had not strength to carry the knowledge.

And it was not as she hoped. Other sight than her own saw the change. Perdita was the mark of the glances of many eyes, and the words of many lips. Poor Perdita! She could not but know a feverish joy, in this feeling herself seen the one of these many bright souls, which had earned homage where any heed was of price; and she did not shrink from the giving of her ear to words, or her eyes to the meeting of glances. To her nature bending was easy, and she bowed to present force. But beneath, no less than Dolores, she lived a hidden life. It was not that the hidden life was as Dolores'. It had no place for struggle or searching of self. But it held a passion—a passion which for all its differ-ence, was enough to bend her yielding soul. She

o

bowed before it ; and the visible life bore signs of
what was within.   It was said that she could not
yield what was sought to the man of genius, and
that her sufferings were sore in her helpless giving
of pain.   Words of sympathy and pity were spoken.

Dolores heard them ; and saw that as far as
they were knowing, they were true.   But she
could give her thought to her friend only at
times and hardly.   Her own experience was
growing vexed to the utter clouding of her soul.
She lived in wavering between two states—
demanding and different, — the state of being
borne, conscious and struggling, on her passion's
flood ; and that which followed as reaction, and
seemed a sort of exhaustion of her nature, in
which she questioned the two lives other than
her own, which were threatened by the same
undoing.

Her hours with Claverhouse laid bare the
change in him before her.   The old self was
again dead — the old dramatist spirit.   Again
he was as teacher to pupil.   Again he was
living his own human life.   One day, as she
rose to leave him, he suddenly laid his hand on
her arm.   His eyes, with a piercing expression
pitiful with their straining to fulfil their purpose,
seemed groping for her own.

"You know what is my aim ?" he said, speaking low and deep.

Dolores felt herself trembling.

" Yes," she said, barely finding utterance.

" And you know her ? You are her friend, as you are mine ? "

" Yes," said Dolores.

" If you can, you will help me ? " he said. " I feel helpless—I am helpless. And yet I am a man who has done and seen much. If you are able, you will help me ? "

Dolores was alive to nothing beyond the look and tone.

" Oh, I will, I will," she said, her voice the voice of one taking a vow.

" Ah ! I knew you as a friend," he said. " You have been my friend. If it were not to be——"

Dolores left him with blind steps ; the surging of her feelings aroused by the last words, making her see the promise she had uttered doomed to be falsely spoken.

That day she sat alone through the evening hours, with books and papers untouched before her, and her face pressed into her hands ; living, since no power she had could help her, in the future which the words, " If it were not to be——" forced before her sight. She was living in it, alive to nothing beside, save that which alone lay deeper—the knowledge that she could live in her actual life in no other. She did not hear an agitated footfall in the corridor. Her door was flung open ; and before her thoughts were clear,

Perdita was on her knees at her side, hiding her face in her garments, and sobbing almost with struggles.

Dolores spoke no word; her voice seemed dead; and her question needed no utterance.

"Oh, Dolores, my friend! It is to you I must come. I cannot carry it myself. I am so utterly alone. But you will bear with me? Tell me that you will."

Dolores answered by a movement of tenderness. She knew that the movement came without the bidding of her will. She was stunned by this sudden awakening to actual things. A jarring, formless feeling was creeping over her, that Perdita's words and actions were less helpless than they seemed.

"He has said it—as I knew — as every one knew—he must say it soon. He spoke to me—when we were alone. Oh, it was so dreadful, Dolores."

Dolores flung her arms round the crouching form that clung to her. It seemed to herself that the action had love and hatred in it. What she suffered was something stronger than suspense.

"Oh, it is so dreadful," sobbed Perdita. "He is so great; and it would be such a privilege to give up to him a life like mine; but I cannot, Dolores, I cannot; it is not through my own will. It is not in my power."

Dolores was silent and still.

"I cannot," said Perdita, raising her face. "I have prayed that I might be able; but I am not able. Speak to me, Dolores."

Dolores uttered no sound. As never before in the years she remembered, her own life was all in all. Perdita's choice for her future was a clearing of her own. Claverhouse's sorrow was a thing for herself to heal. For the moment it had this meaning and no other.

"Speak to me, Dolores," said Perdita, in a voice that was almost a cry.

But Dolores spoke no word.

"I cannot stay here," went on Perdita, again hiding her face; and again giving Dolores the dim, jarring sense, that her words came as they were purposed. "I cannot stay where I must see him, and watch him day by day. I must go away. I shall go far away, where I can never meet him. I shall go and live somewhere where I can see you, Dolores; somewhere near your dear home, where you were all brothers and sisters to me; where I shall not be a creature utterly alone. I shall find there some way of earning my bread; and when you are at home, I shall see you all, and be comforted."

Dolores heard the words, and knew their hidden meaning. She felt that the hidden meaning was as nothing.

"I must go away," said Perdita again, the

words seeming to come more easily now once
uttered. "I must go and earn my bread near
your peaceful home; and when you are there,
you will let me see you? You will always love
me, Dolores?"

"I shall always love you," said Dolores suddenly; her words with their terrible inner
significance causing her a feeling that seemed
to be shame struggling through a deeper
passion.

Perdita rose to her feet. She was lost in herself, and could give no heed to Dolores' pallor
and silence.

"I will leave you, my sister-friend," she said,
caressing Dolores' hair; while her voice seemed
to lose its emotional tremor. "I have troubled
and bewildered you. Come to me when you are
willing to be wearied; and I will tell you my
plans for the future."

Again Dolores spoke suddenly.

"You have plans already?" she said.

"Yes," said Perdita, with a swiftly checked
touch of uneasiness, as though words had escaped
which had better been unsaid. "I have thought
of them before to-night. I have seen this coming
for some time, as you must have seen it too. But
its coming unnerved me."

She hastily left the room; and Dolores rose and
walked with aimless, rapid movements. She yet
lived in her own future, in a spirit of feverish

grasping at it, which belonged to a creeping sense, that its supplanting was at hand. She lived in it till the conception seemed exhausted, and the reaction came without effort. Perdita's words! They returned to her one by one, with their weight of meaning. Perdita's soul was laid uncovered to her sight. The unquestioning repulse of what held so much in the sphere where she had her lot; the use of her helpless emotions for her voluntary ends; the grasping at a life that afforded her that which she believed she was honest in clutching! Dolores saw it as it was, fraught with covered purpose.

And it was not only Perdita's soul that seemed to lie quivering before her eyes. There was the other, which she would fain have forced aside, that she might be spared the torture of her own. And she surveyed it almost with passiveness. She saw these two lives, that had crossed her own, with a simple, just survey, as it was her nature to see them. She saw her own life, with its power of ordering the others, with a simple, just survey, as it was her nature to see it. But the survey, she told herself, was taken thus, merely because it was her nature. It was to beget no purpose. This which had come to her soul from the other soul—upon which the lips which had the disclosing power, were silent— where was the binding force on her, to see it as laid forth, for the imposing as a duty of the

devotion of herself? But a moment, and this
hour would end.

But it was many moments that she stood
with her hands clenched, and her face still and
strained. The minutes were hours, and midnight
had passed, before her limbs relaxed, and she
pushed the hair from the brow that was lined
beyond her youth. She left her room, and passed
down the corridor to Perdita's sleeping chamber.
It was as she had thought. The room was
lighted, and Perdita was standing in the day's
garments; her looks, as she turned to the opening
door, telling of a startled pause in agitated pacing. Dolores went toward her, and stood with
one of her hands on her shoulder.

"My dear," she said, her voice having a
strange impressiveness, as though it were the
voice of an older creature that had outlived
passions; "before I leave this thing to your
own heart, I must say a word—a word which
by one as much older than yourself, in all things
but years, as I am, should not be unsaid. Do
nothing that may bring repentance on your later
years. Do nothing in haste. I think of my
brother's early mistake, and fear for you."

Perdita turned her face so suddenly, that
her shoulder was jerked from under Dolores'
hand. She set it back as though the movement
were unthinking; and Dolores continued in the
same tone, as if it had escaped her heed.

"My dear, I may trust to your silence, and tell you my brother's story? It will show you how an act of young rashness may alter a life. He married on a youthful impulse; and by that impulse must abide. Be on your guard lest you fall into the same error on the other side. The pity of it would be deeper."

"Married?" uttered Perdita. "He is not married?"

"Yes, he is married," said Dolores, looking away from Perdita's face; and leaving her hand on her shoulder, as if she did not feel its trembling. "He is married to Elsa Blackwood. After his years at Oxford are over, they will make it known, and live together. His chance of an Oxford course came after their marriage, and led to its concealment. It was one of those actions on youthful impulse which order a lifetime. I want it to help you to realise, that your judgment now is for your life."

"But—but if there is no love between them—and it is quite clear there is not—they will not—they need not live together, and spoil each other's lives?" said Perdita, in a dry voice whose easiness startled Dolores, with her knowledge of what it covered. "Surely a mere ceremony need not carry that. It—it surely could be managed otherwise?"

"They neither of them wish it to be otherwise," said Dolores, in a natural, firm voice. "They have neither given their love to another, and neither has thought of it. Besides, now that Bertram's career is so full of promise, Elsa has no regrets; and I think that Bertram is not conscious of them. I trust they will be happy in their union. That is why I have told you, Perdita; to show you that a decision of this kind is made to the end; that regrets must find no place. But you are worn out with your feelings. Good-night, my dear one. May you come to the judgment that is best for you."

Dolores laid an arm round the shaking form, and kissed the cold brow; and then passed from the room.

The hours of this night, which were so often re-lived in the souls of the women who knew them the hours that bent their experience, were lived to their end by them, as by themselves. Perdita, when Dolores left her, stood for some minutes trembling and white; and then walked with feverish movements till exhaustion came to her help, and brought with the breaking dawn a sleep that was the stupor of energy spent.

Dolores reached her room; and, with her stronger will, at once lay down; not thinking of sleep, but forcing calmness and clearness of thought, that her actions for these two, whose destinies had come to her hands, might be well for them. She looked into the future calmly; for it did not seem that the future was to be lived

by herself. It was a stretch of years, whose
meaning was the course of two lives through it.
And she saw it clearly. Perdita's soul was, as
always, open to her scrutiny; and she knew that
the pliant nature would bow to the altered lot;
that the fostered instinct to live for the sight
of men, would clutch at the portion which carried
the bending of eyes.

Even sooner than she had thought, the change
was clear. It was a very few days after that
Perdita came to her, and spoke some faltering
words.

"Dolores, I am so grateful. I see how much
my folly might have led me to throw away."

Dolores waited and paled, before she gave her
embrace, and her words of earnest wishing of
good. She seemed to be stunned by a sudden
rush of perception. In a moment she read many
things. She read that Perdita knew the purpose
of the words she had spoken on the night that
lived with them both. She read that her instinct
impelled her to act as if she did not know it; and
to protect her dignity in her counsellor's sight, by
showing her valuing of that which was given unsought, greater than of that denied to her seeking. Moreover, for an instant the knowledge
came, that before herself also there were years
that must be lived.

But the moment she dreaded as her final trial
was not to come. Claverhouse gave her no word

of her friend's acceptance of his hand. She had
from him as little heed as in the earliest days
of their mutual dealings; and the others he had
known in the college were suddenly as strangers.
As the pain grew numb, and went, she found
that perplexity followed in its wake. The soul
to which her soul was knit, was primitive in its
workings. The object of communion was gone:
and hence it was ended.

But Perdita was far from showing eagerness
to cease her mingling with her kind. Dolores,
as she watched her, learned that this surface
living of her life was also its inner meaning.
The feeling awakened by her bringing of this
glimpse of romance into this world of women's
friendships; the unconscious deference accorded
her as the holder of the homage of genius, were
things that meant much. It seemed to Dolores,
that the days when she lived the old routine
with this sweetening, made more for her content
than those when her lover's presence demanded
her staying at his side, and unwitnessed hearing
of his words took the place of their naïve repeating, as proofs of his love and confidence. On the
whole she told little of him, though she spoke
of him much. Her manner seemed meant to
mark understanding a thing reserved too fully
for herself, for words to be other than vain.
On being asked if his work was much to her,
she answered, "Everything, as it is to him";

and in response to sympathy on the trouble of his failing sight, she said with sensitive repelling of the subject, that his sight was not really failing; that, though it had long been weak, it was growing no worse; and that he saw much more than it seemed.

But it was not through any of this, that Dolores' heart misgave her. It was at a moment when her thoughts were not of Perdita, when her will was passive, exhausted by its long struggling. One day, when she was going up a staircase at the side of Miss Butler, talking of daily duties with the yielding of surface thought to surface things, which was gaining from custom a strange easiness, she saw the two figures coming down the corridor.

It was a sight that no longer demanded question or meaning glance. Miss Butler passed with a smile for Perdita, and a look, half kindly, half curious, from the one to the other. But Dolores, as she followed, had a memory of something beside. Perdita had met them with the look of studied unconsciousness, with which it was her wont to encounter eyes, when seen with her lover; and continued her talk with an easy flow of words, as though to mark their familiar communion. But as they came to the staircase, the dramatist's tread grew uncertain; and he gave a groping gesture as if he sought guidance. Perdita made a slight, but certain sidelong

movement, and passed on as though unperceiv-
ing; continuing her talk, and throwing a glance
behind, as if perplexed by his slower following.

Dolores felt a throb that had a fiercer than
the bitterness of jealousy. So service could only
be accepted, never rendered. That was deemed
a shame, which she had renounced as a privilege
sacred beyond her lot. What of that great,
suffering nature and its burden? Into what
keeping had she given it?

But there was no place in Dolores' soul, for
remorse for that which was wrought with pain
for the sake of conscience. Misgiving, in bringing anguish to her spirit, could bring it no cloud.
The great life flung by an ignorance on the brink
of bereavement—the young life rushing in darkness to its undoing!—the yielding the light she
had to yield, was owed without question. She
could not have done other than she had done.

But she went and stood alone for many hours.

CHAPTER XII.

THE marriage of Claverhouse and Perdita consisted in visible deed of little beyond the ceremony. They were people poor in friends, and poorer in kin. The weeks that preceded it Perdita spent in the parsonage at Millfield.

Poor Perdita! The reality of joy she had sought, had shadows behind it to be grasped. She clutched at the stimulant of living before Bertram's eyes, as the woman chosen of the man of genius. She looked at herself through the days as it were through his sight; and found her words, and even her thoughts of the life that was at hand, moulded for the consciousness in which she saw herself mirrored. Dolores knew how it was; and forced the knowledge from her.

Perdita was married by the Rev. Cleveland in the Millfield church. Claverhouse stayed in the village for a time before; spending the nights at the inn, and the days in wandering in the lanes and fields, alone or with his betrothed. To

Dolores these weeks were such, that years were to pass, before she could follow their memory without finding her thoughts repulsed by unfaceable pain. She had thought the struggle behind her, fixed and graven on the hours of that night, which seemed as large a part of her life as all the years before. But through the minutes and hours it lived with her, in the darker form of conflict with the unworthiness of remorse that it had been sustained. For the stimulus of selfless effort gone, its moral exaltation dead, it was bitter to live and look for hard, empty days, with no human knowledge or pity of the accepted bitterness.

On the eve of the marriage she sought her farewell with her friend; and the words had for neither less of weight, for the coming witnessed parting of the morrow.

"You will always be in my thoughts, Perdita," she said, with the unconscious impressiveness·which came to her voice with strength of feeling. "You will let me hear from you through your husband?" The last words came calmly. Dolores in her actual dealings was strong.

"Oh, you will not have trouble in getting Sigismund to talk about me," said Perdita. "It would be different if you wanted him to talk about something else. I tell him I shall keep my friends away from him, when I value their goodwill. Other people may have the power of getting tired of me, even if he is without that gift himself."

Dolores was silent. The further purpose of these words seemed to set a barrier between her soul, and the weaker soul it yearned over. The face of the bride of the morrow was pale and sharpened in the waning light.

A great flood of emotion came over her—her dominating love of her kind gathered into a single channel; misgiving for this bending creature on the brink of an untried, unchosen lot; questioning of what it held for her young need- fulness—a flood in which her own life was carried as a straw on waters; and she opened her arms, and gathered Perdita into a strong embrace.

"My dear one, may all go well with you. May you find yourself fitted for what is before you, and able to need only what is given."

For a moment Perdita's arms returned the clasp with all their feebler strength; as if the pressure of the throbbing hearts were the dis- burdening of the one upon the other of all to which outpouring was denied. Then she drew herself away, with the constraint of the returning to her surface life.

"Well, we have had our good-bye," she said. "To-morrow it will be our duty to spare our friends the trial of wedding-day emotions. There is really no need for a real good-bye. We are not to spend our lives a thousand miles from

P

each other. You must often come and stay with
us. Good-night, dear Dolores."

She left the room without meeting Dolores'
eyes; and Dolores stood, confronting the future,
as a stretch of years in which she herself had
nothing to seek.

The next day Claverhouse and Perdita were
married. The marriage, for all its strangeness,
hardly seemed to call for questioning or wondering words. Its unwontedness seemed in fitness
with all that pertained to it. The service was
conducted with unmoved demeanour by the Rev.
Cleveland. It was witnessed by the Hutton
family, and such dwellers in the district as were
drawn by curiosity or the heaviness of time. The
farewells, by Claverhouse's wish, were said at the
church; and they were hardly spoken, when the
bridal pair set out on their homeward journey.

"Well, that was a queer thing!" said Mr Blackwood, as he overtook Dr Cassell in the road; the
outdoor calls of gentlemen betraying them at
times into the curiosity which is really a feminine
attribute. "An out-and-out queer thing that
was; there's no doubt of that. How a young
and pretty woman can tie herself up for life to
an old, blind bookworm like that, is quite beyond
me; I must say that it is."

Dr Cassell came to a pause.

"I think that as a rule—in these cases—there
is something on the woman's part, that—explains

the attraction of the man for her—a reverence
for learning, or something of that kind; so that
the feeling between them is more that of teacher
and pupil, than of husband and wife. I should
think that is so in this case, very ,possibly."

" Ah, yes, doctor, very likely, very likely,"
said Mr Blackwood, twirling his moustache ;
" but I can't understand it myself, and that's
the truth. I shouldn't like one of *my* girls to be
up to that sort of thing. *I* should have something to say ; I should indeed." Mr Blackwood
shook his head, and parted with the doctor with
a sense of paternal qualifications.

Perdita and her husband entered on their
journey with few words. Perdita's feelings were
strange for those of the wife of an hour. Through
the day she had borne herself for Bertram's sight,
and watched herself through it. Even now, as
she travelled to her home, she was picturing his
thoughts of her—the woman entering her life
with the man endowed beyond other men, who
had chosen her of other women. A sudden
knowledge of the tenor of her thoughts seemed
to lay the future bare—the future chosen for the
eyes of men, and hidden from those eyes. What
must her days hold ? Unwitnessed service to
him who had chosen her, in passion that was not
the passion of his life ; who sat at her side, in the
first silence of the marriage-bells, with his eyes
turned from herself, and his being in a world

that did not hold her. And to the creature who filled her life, she was as dead. Tears burned in her eyes, and her fragile hands were clenched. Believing herself unheeded, she hardly strove to smother sobs.

" Why, my little one ! " said the deep voice at her side ; " you have no sorrow you are hiding ? "

" Oh, no, no," said Perdita, trembling. " Only —weddings—any great change in anything— always unnerves me. I am so easily moved. I am not like you—strong like men are. I have no trouble hidden. I am not unhappy."

" No ? I thought not, my little one," said Claverhouse, bending to look into her eyes. " You must have no troubles. They are not for lives like yours."

He laid his hand for a moment on her quivering frail one ; and then looked away, and seemed to sink into thought. His vain searching of her eyes had been less a look of anxious question, than of eagerness to meet them dimmed by tears. His love had brought him no knowledge of her. She had yet to give him a glimpse of the self, that was a needing, suffering self like other selves. She was almost a shadowy creature to him—a creature of surface life and elusive being, to be left to her own light lot without watching or question. From toil for her bread, unfitted for her tenderness, he had taken her to comfort unbought of weariness. For himself, in his empty hours, there would be the filling of newly-felt, natural needs. It was well for them both.

As they drove to the dwelling in the narrow street, which had not the power to strike him as it was, for its sufficing through the years to his mother and himself—he grasped her hand.

" We are home—at the home we are to share together," he said. " Welcome, my little one."

Poor Perdita ! Her pliant nature had been bending in the last hour to the lot that was at hand. She had been picturing with dawning of hope the untried experience of ordering a household, and knowing herself the mark of glances as the mate of the genius. Her eyes, gazing through the dusk as the wheels slackened, took on a half-frightened look ; and remained fastened on the scene before them. Her husband's touch and tones recalled her to the moment's needs.

As one in a dream, she felt her feet on the narrow pavement. As one in a dream, she saw a bent figure hasten down the steps, with eyes that seemed to miss herself for their rivetted gaze on the figure in the carriage. As one in a dream, she stood, and looked, and was silent. Claverhouse stooped from the carriage gropingly, with his hands on the sides of its doorway ; but missed the step, and violently stumbled as he gained a footing on the pavement. Perdita felt herself pushed aside ; and saw the old servant spring to support his staggering form ; while, still as through a dream, she heard a startled utterance.

" Ah !—See !—move, madam.   He is not safe without watching."

It was only the happening of a moment.   The next, her husband was standing at her side ; and Julia was speaking some words of respectful greeting, as if the disturbance had been unreal. But Perdita, as she walked up the jagged steps into the narrow dwelling, felt a sense of being jarred so deep and complex, that she could hardly sustain it ; and in the dim passage she stood with the eyes of a tortured dumb creature, speaking no word, and making no movement towards chamber or staircase.   Her husband, though his eyes were turned to her face, saw nothing in it that was not well.   But other eyes saw.

" You are tired, madam," said Julia.   " You will be glad of some rest."

" Yes, yes, she is weary," said Claverhouse. " Come upstairs with us, Julia, and show your mistress how things are done for her.   Come, little one.   We shall not have you weary long."

He mounted the staircase with the ungainly quickness which marked his movements on ground he knew, and which brought another change to Perdita's eyes, as they saw it for the first time.   She followed slowly, and without words.   As she entered the room prepared for

them, she found him standing just within the
door, turning his head with eager groping.

"Ah! this room!" he was saying. "It has
seen much, Julia! Where my mother was lying
a year ago! A year ago."

Julia made no reply, but her face said much;
and Perdita, in hearing these words of an unmeaning past, felt the pang of a sufferer awaking
from darkened days with memory dead. She
was jarred by an intuitive knowledge, that the
silence of the old servant was considerate feeling
for herself.

"Perhaps you will show me what is needful,
Julia; and then we will not trouble you further,"
she said; speaking with courteous, cold authority,
but with a knowledge that the sentence was to
be numbered in her store of memories, as the
first she had uttered under her own roof.

Julia gave one glance at the wan young face;
and then spoke with respectful brevity, put some
keys into Perdita's hand, and left the room. As
she moved about the kitchen, her face was as
neutral as if she felt herself watched. Her
thoughts would have borne any searching in
their worthiness of the years behind her. No
unloving feeling assailed her for this young
creature, who was to straiten her world in strait-
ening her place in her master's lot. In her faithfulness she closed her heart against it; and even
had pity not come to her with help, would have

held it closed. But the pity did not only help.
As she attended the husband and wife at their
evening meal, noted their words and their silence,
and watched the sharpened face of the bride of a
day, her heart misgave her for both. And there
came a different pity, with a different, deeper
pang. It was only her eyes that saw that the
face was sharpened. Her long dread was growing
surely into a swift and certain sorrow.

"Well, Julia," said Claverhouse, as the meal
went its way, "I see you are still a good house-
wife. I am bringing my little one into safe
keeping. I can trust you to care for her, when
I am earning the bread?"

Julia's mute signs of submission were ready
and full. No service for her master was hard.

"Well, my pretty one," said Claverhouse to
Perdita, "you are weary to-night. You are a
tender nursling for us to care for. Julia, it is
the second charge you will have fulfilled for
me."

Julia's face showed momentary lighting; but
she moved about in silence.

Perdita made an effort to lay aside her weary
unresponsiveness. She leaned from her place
at the table's head, and laid her hand in her
husband's.

"Ah, my little one," he said, returning the
caress. "There is only one whom I could see in
that place. I could say no more to you."

The tone was too much for Perdita's over-wrought feelings. Her lips trembled and her eyes filled; and she sat with her eyes bent on her plate. Her husband smiled into her face, but could not mark its change, and Julia seemed not to see it. Till the end of the meal the silence was unbroken — the silence that was an easy, daily thing to the one — so different to the other.

When Julia was clearing the table, there was a knock at the outer door.

Claverhouse sprang to his feet, and was about to answer the summons; but Julia was before him in the passage, with unconscious eagerness to be spared his groping for the fastenings. The tall, grey-headed figure hesitated to cross the threshold.

"I—I—Mr Claverhouse wrote and asked me to come to-night; but—but I know it is his first evening at home with—with Mrs Claverhouse. Perhaps——"

"Ah, Soulsby! I was thinking you had for-gotten," said the deep voice from the inner doorway. "Come in, come in. This is a different picture from what you are used to seeing here— and a prettier one, is it not so? I am glad for you to know my wife. I have told her much of you."

Soulsby gave Perdita a swift glance, and greeted her with a nervous uneasiness, which

somehow left him his full distinction of bearing;
his habit of silence on his own experience holding
him from giving any sign, beyond his look into
her face, that he did not meet her as a stranger.
Then, seating himself, as he was bidden, he looked
from one face to the other.

Claverhouse's words gave him a sense of
surprise.

"Well, Soulsby, I have done little since I saw
you last; but I am going to get to wasting the
paper to-morrow. A holiday is the thing for
courting days, even for a scribbling old fellow;
but I am beginning to long for the scribbling.
And I must be at my other business—the earning of the bread. I have a reason for doing
that in earnest." He laid his hand on
Perdita's.

Soulsby looked at Perdita.

"You — you take great interest in your husband's work, Mrs Claverhouse?"

"Oh, yes; it is everything to me," said Perdita,
with a soul-sinking feeling, that she had no choice
but to give this account of her seeking this life.

"You — you have had a long journey," said
Soulsby, with a gentle deference, in which a
note of perplexity was barely suppressed. "You
are weary, I fear. I should not have disturbed
you to-night."

"Oh, no; I should have been sorry for you
not to come. It has been my great wish to meet

you," said Perdita, speaking in her weariness simply for the ears of her husband.

"Ah, little one, you are certainly weary. Your voice is quite faint," said Claverhouse. "Go up to your rest. Do not stay for me. Julia will do what you need for you."

Perdita gave the guest her hand in silence, not daring to speak, and passed through the door, as he held it open ; her husband remaining in his place.

Soulsby walked back slowly to his seat.

"Your wife looks very frail," he said, in the easier tones which came to him with disturbed feeling.

"Yes, she is a fragile creature," said Claverhouse. "She has earned her living with her brains ; and it has been a lot unfit for her. I am thankful to feel her freed from the need to toil."

"She — I suppose — what will she do while you are working ? " said Soulsby, struggling with the instinct to be blunt. "She—she has interests of her own, of course. I—I meant—your life is hardly one which will bring her the usual pleasures of youth."

"No, no, indeed ; many young creatures would find it a dreary lot," said Claverhouse. "But she is different from others. She has no thought for what is called pleasure. If she could, she would not seek it. Her life has been monotony and effort; and it is enough for her to be free. She is a lover of books in her woman's way—an innocent lover as yet—prettily blind; but I shall teach her to understand. There is no one else I could see in my mother's place."

"She—you—she will enter into your work, as you do it?" said Soulsby.

"I shall teach her," said Claverhouse. "Little by little she will learn; and she will find it no burden to help me, when the years are heavy."

Soulsby was silent. He knew by the voice what was meant by the heaviness of the years. His misgiving for the helpless thing, he had seemed to see sacrificed in blindness, was lost in dread for the other—helpless no less—whose good he held of greatest worth. No word had passed between him and the playwright of the latter's failing sight; though the thoughts of each had long been read by the other. In this strange experience of meeting his friend on his marriage day, he felt an impulse to break the long reserve.

"Sigismund," he said—he had never used the baptismal name except in moments of significance —"should you not consult an oculist?"

Claverhouse gave a start, and was silent; his features contorting. "Have I not consulted one?" he muttered. "Have I not made my appeal to every one I have heard of? You think me a child or a madman. Which am

I, because I am blind? Should I let my life slip from me, without putting out one hand to save it?"

"What?" said Soulsby, in low, agitated tones.

"What?" said Claverhouse with bitter mimicry, —continuing after the word in a broken voice. "Do you want me to explain—to put it into words?"

Soulsby was silent, his over-sensitiveness holding him tongue-tied, his face telling of deep trouble.

Claverhouse was also silent; keeping his eyes averted from the face of his friend, as though with shrinking to show himself anew the vanity of seeking to read what it told. Minutes passed before the silence was broken.

"I am going to begin to write to-morrow," he said, with the constraint of passing to an easy subject from one which has moved unwilling emotion. "The conception I told you of has grown. I shall be able to work it out quickly."

Soulsby responded in a similar spirit; and the talk went on as of old, with the sad, deep difference beneath, till the minute for parting.

As Claverhouse rose to bid his friend farewell, he seemed to hesitate, as though on the point of some words.

"I—I have faced the future, as far as what we spoke of goes," he said, with a painful effort to save the next meeting from cloud. "It has

taken me years to do it; but it is done now.
I shall just go on, finding my happiness in the
work that yields it; and what help I shall grow
to need my wife will give. Do not let this
trouble you, Soulsby. Come to-morrow at the
same hour."

Soulsby dared not ask if the sad-faced wife
knew of what was before her. He wrung the
playwright's hand, as he had never wrung it
before; seeking to give in the grasp what his
lips could not speak, and his face spoke vainly;
and Claverhouse turned to the chimney-piece,
and covered his face with his hand.

In the upper chamber Perdita lay, with sleep-
less, suffering eyes. When she entered the room,
she had sunk on her knees by the bed; and in
the relief of solitude shed the tears of her weariness of body and soul. But as the shallower
griefs were wept away, the others that were not
to be met by tears, seemed to press more heavily.
It was before her—and it had never been faced
—the living the years out of sight of the creature, whose consciousness, mirrored in her own,
had hitherto sustained her in her struggling.
She rose to her feet, and stood rigid and dry-
eyed, while her being seemed going out in
unimaginable yearning; until the thought that
her husband might be with her, with question
of her tardiness in seeking rest, forced her to the
effort of ceasing from struggle before she was

exhausted, and the unconscious respite of bodily movement. She put off her garments and laid them aside ; and making signs about the room of what she would have done in quietude of spirit, lay down in the bed for further fellowship with grief. As her starving passion became exhausted by its own outcrying, she lay yielding her dulled powers to a survey of the life before her—the life in which the domestic ordering which had arrested her woman's eagerness, had grown to a sordid labour in a cramping sphere, to be shrunk from, and left to serving hands ; in which the content of knowing herself watched as the fellow of genius, had grown to shame in walking in sight, that had marked the conditions of this lot ; in which the sustaining effort of feigning grasp of her husband's aims, for maintenance in his eyes of the character she had sought, had grown to a stretch of wearying struggle, spreading over the weeks without respite or goal.

When her husband came to the room, she feigned sleep without effort; finding it the one thing yet in her power, to lie as if life was gone from her limbs. He came to the bedside, and caressed her hair, and kissed her lips. She felt the wandering touch of his hands, and his lips groping for her own ; but she made no response in body or mind, almost feeling that she had lost the power of stirring or feeling a pang. Through

the hours of the night she lay thus; fearing to
move or weep, lest she should rouse the sleeper
at her side, and dreading sleep for herself, that
it must bring a new awakening to all she now
had power to face.

At the morning meal she sat sick and silent,
unable to swallow food, or to care for Julia's eyes
and thoughts. It was not till it ended, that she
awoke to necessity, and forced herself to bend
before it.

"I am a perplexing bride, am I not, Sigismund?" she said, with a feeble grasping at a
natural manner. "I think I must be too weak
a creature to marry. I have a headache this
morning, as retribution for doing so yesterday.
You will not mind, if I rest for an hour?"

Her husband put his hands on her shoulders.

"Ah, you are a tender thing," he said. "That
is why it is well that you are married. Yes;
you go to your rest, while I go to my work.
That is the division of labour between us."

He pressed his hands on her shoulders, as
though seeking some passage to himself of her
young responsiveness; and she raised her head
with an effort at archness, which recalled the
Perdita of the past.

To him the Perdita of to-day was the same;
and she went to solitude, with a sense that his
blindness was pushing her from the only cherishing her lot afforded.

The days began to pass, carrying that lot with daily sameness. Claverhouse gave himself to his work; growing utterly absorbed as its old grip returned, and more than could be spared of his time was demanded by the toil for the bread. The breaks in the life were Soulsby's evening visits; and except for the hours for food, these were the only times of intercourse of the husband and wife. Beneath it all there was the hopelessness of truth. A want may absorb a life while it remains unfilled, and bear but little filling. Perdita lived joyless days, with privation of all that was good to her thought. Their only change was the growing of her suffering shame in her lot, to the indifference of feeling blunted by bitter use; and she marvelled, now with fierce resentment, now helpless wonder, that he could thus be blind to the claims of her youth.

For it was true that he went his way in blindness; the blindness of a consciousness so long absorbed in a purpose, that it has lost the power of fair survey of surrounding things. He had taken Perdita from the earning of her bread to freely yielded nurture. There was something repelling to his thought in a woman's working to live; and he had no doubt that this change in itself was enough for her content. For the definite things that her life gave—they were those which had sufficed to his mother with her stronger needs; and he gave them no

Q

thought.   He could not but learn that her
knowledge of his aims was a thing feigned for
his worthier judging of her ; but he judged of
her tenderly, as a creature calling for tenderness ; and as touched her faith and interest held
to his trust.

But it was sad that the trust should be held.
Poor Perdita ! It seemed to her the hardest
thing of her wifehood, that, when he joined her
at the end of his hours of toil, the lonely longing for human kindness, which had grown with
those hours, should be met by demands for expending herself on the labour whose own demands were bringing that self to starvation.
Day after day she raised her eyes from the
book or trifling of needle supposed to be holding them, with helpless appeal for some sign of
cherishing, or at least undemanding fellowship ;
and day after day she fought with anger and
despair, and forced from herself the weariness
of self-dissembling.   One evening, when a deeper
than her wonted depression was met by stronger
eagerness for the alien interest, her spirit faltered ; and she met the first appeal with silence,
and the question which followed with petulant
words.

Surprised, but hardly wrought upon deeply, he
made kindly question of her health or weariness.

She could not bring her courage to confession
of what was pent within her ; and, clutching at the

second plea, sought the loneliness which seemed to be draining her life.

The dramatist did not forget the occurrence; but the significance he gave it, though allied to the true one, had nothing of its depth. He made his demands on her interest and sympathy fewer; and formed a habit of trying to afford her what he sought for himself. He would ask her what books she was reading, and talk to her of them with gentle moulding of himself to her needs; or tell her stories of his youth, with his early struggles and ambitions. He even, in the thought of a moment, asked her what friends she had; and bade her seek them if she willed, or bid them to her home. These words she heard with leaping heart. Her soul cried out for Dolores. But her torturing shame on her daily experience, and the passion of pride which was fiercest touching the woman she most loved, wrung an answer from her lips which sealed the straitness of her lot.

CHAPTER XIII.

THE nine months of Perdita's wifehood had worn to their end. Perdita lay as still and sorrowless, as her child who had never breathed.

Soulsby, as he stood on the steps of the darkened dwelling, looked on the shrouded windows with feelings he could not name. The close of this passage in his friend's experience, which seemed already to have fallen back into a past whose life was in memory, was a bewildering, constraining thing. Would the old days return — with unwitnessed fellowship and unmarked words; as if the suffering eyes had never wearied of unheeded watching, and the sweet, faint tones had never struggled to be steady? He worked his hands nervously, as a step sounded in the passage.

"I—I did not know whether—whether the sad message was a request for my coming or not. I thought that—that I might just come to inquire, and either go or stay, as it was best. Can you — you will tell me what I should do?"

"Ah, sir! come in, if you please; come in," said the old servant; making a sign towards the living-room, as she spoke in a toneless voice. "He sits in there alone hour after hour. He has never uttered a word, except to ask me if the poor young creature seemed happy in the time she lived with us. And, indeed, she never opened her lips to say she wasn't; so proud to the end as she was, and such a spirit as there was in that weak body. Yes; go in, sir; go in. I fear he is taken, as after the mistress died, with looking back on things, and wishing they had all been different; and it will be a sad thing for him, if it is so, sir."

Soulsby entered the room, and paused just inside the doorway, as if to accept notice or repulsion, as either might meet him.

Claverhouse was standing by the chimney-piece. He did not turn, but moved as though he felt his presence; and beckoning him forward with a sidelong gesture, spoke without looking towards him.

"Soulsby, it was a wrong thing that I did— that taking a young creature's youth, and burying it. It is a thing for which I must live and die sorrowing. The memory of these months, as she lived them and suffered in them — for whether or no she knew it, she must have suffered — suffered starvation of her growing nature—must be always with me."

He talked on; and Soulsby listened in silence, except for needful response, and at times a restraining or remonstrant word. There was a feeling upon him, that he was living the experience for the second time. A similar hour after Janet's burial was present with him, in spite of an effort to repel it. Each word and look of his friend seemed in a strange manner familiar; and he found himself looking, without the bidding of his will, over the days that must be darkened, to the further inevitable time, when the cloud should surely have passed.

But there was different and sadder to come.

The following day he came as he was bidden, to fulfil this new demand on his unwearying friendship. With characteristic shrinking from breaking the silence of the dwelling of death, he entered the house without knock or ring.

The playwright was sitting with his arms stretched out on the table, and his head bowed over them. His friend was struck by a difference from the yesterday. His face was set in lines of hopeless misery, which on a face marked thus with the years and their burden, was tragic; and he gave no sign of knowing that his solitude was broken. On the table before him, almost covered by both his hands, was what seemed to be a small, black note-book.

After a minute's waiting, Soulsby moved to the door; and Claverhouse suddenly spoke, in a voice that was almost a cry.

"No, do not leave me—do not leave me. Do not leave me alone in my outer life, as I am in the other."

Soulsby returned to the hearth, and stood for some moments silent. When at last he spoke, he shrank at the sound of his own voice.

"Are you not—I think—are you not dwelling too much on the trouble? It—it is, I think, your nature to do so. It—it is—is it not a time for the exercise of will?"

Claverhouse made a sound and movement of the intense irritation, which comes from the breaking of thought that leads to a climax at once intensely shrunk from and sought; but Soulsby, at cost to himself, held to his purpose.

"What of the play—the play you have just finished? I have not heard it read as — as a whole. If — if you could lose yourself for a time in some other interest, you — you would be able to look more fairly at the trouble it-self."

The playwright started to his feet, as if a

thought had given him strength. He burst
from the room, with something of the old suddenness of action which was leaving him as the
failing of his sight demanded caution in movement; and Soulsby heard that his steps on the
stairs had their old uneven violence. In a
minute he returned, with a pile of manuscript;
and Soulsby fought with a feeling that approached to anger, for the helpless young creature, whose life was lost with trivial things as
one of them. The words he heard brought a
startled feeling, that grew to a sense almost of
guilt.

"Soulsby, this play is the master-work of my
life. It is to be put to the deepest use in my
life. You will never read it, or hear it read.
It will be buried with her. I can make one sign
of what I shall never put in words. I shall not
live, feeling that I have given nothing in return
for what I have taken."

He set the papers on the table, and fingered
them as though composing them to lie as he
said; and Soulsby looked on with eyes troubled
and incredulous, living the experience as a dream.

The blind man felt the unbelief, whose signs
were hidden from him. He suddenly swept up
the papers, sprang to the grate, and thrust them
on the dying fire. The embers leapt into life;
and as a flaring, crackling sound told its hopeless
tale, Soulsby darted forward with some agitated

words. But he held his ground with unyielding strength ; and by the time his friend had forced a passage, the moments had done their work. The flames were flickering to their death, and the sparks vanishing from their grey, trembling bed.

He watched them vanish with the strange gaze, at once straining and half - exultant, of growing blindness following something of a nature to be still discernible. When the last was gone, he knelt and gathered the ashes in his hands ; his eyes held closely to the grate, his fumbling fingers touching them as things of price. A softening came like a spasm over his face, as he rose with his hands helpless with their crumbling burden, and his dim eyes caught the white expanse of a cloth which Soulsby had snatched from the table, and held to receive them. He yielded them at once ; and glanced from his friend to the grate, with a groping wistfulness eloquent in its mute appeal. In a moment Soulsby was on his knees, gathering with his shapely hands the remaining cinders to their last vestige. He put them with the others ; and stood with a set face of sorrow, as the dramatist folded the cloth, and spoke his parting words.

" They will be buried with her, Soulsby. It is well that you drove me to burn it. How could I have known with my blindness that my words

were obeyed? And with it and her, will be
buried the happiness that might have remained
to me. So it is as it should and must be. I will
leave you for to-day. Through the hours of to-
night I must sit at her side."

He left the room, carrying the folded cloth in
both his blackened hands; and Soulsby took a
step backwards, and looked after him with his
fingers pressed to his forehead. As he moved
back, his eye was caught by the note-book on
the table. His hand mechanically sought it,
and his eyes went down its open page. He
started, and flung it from him as if it had
stung him.

It was Perdita's diary—the record of her hand
of the hidden history of her wifehood.

CHAPTER XIV.

"No," said Dolores; "I cannot think as you do. I cannot think that the way to honour the memory of one who was loved, is to make one's own life emptier. I am sure she would not feel it so. Surely the effort of rising above a life of passive remorse, and filling the days with striving, would be a better tribute."

"*Passive* remorse!" said Claverhouse, pressing his elbows on the desk.

"I mean that it achieves nothing," said Dolores. "Or, rather, as you were thinking, it has achieved harm. Why should you not set some object before you—some purpose to fulfil—as your token of your sorrow?"

"I will do it," said Claverhouse, rising and clenching his hands. "I will fling myself into the writing—the re-writing of the old play. In both of its forms—and in both of its fates, it will have been, as you say, my token of my sorrow for her—for her sufferings—of which I was the cause."

" I am glad," said Dolores, with her unconscious impressiveness; "more glad than I can
say in words."

"But I must tell you the truth," he broke out.
" I feel I must tell you all things. It is my wish
to write the play — my — my longing, the one
thing I desire. I feel that my remorse, the
remorse that made the year after her death a
hell to me, is lost in the old purpose. It has
fallen back into a part of my past life—a part
of the experience that has added to my knowledge of men. It has happened with it, as with
everything I have ever felt."

"Time must blunt the edge of feeling," said
Dolores. "Surely it is not right to clutch at a
grief. The grief that came in spite of yourself, is
as it is. You will not add to its meaning by
seeking it. Love and grief are different things.
It is only a tribute to the one, that it outlives the
other."

"But I do not know if it does outlive it," he
said, his tone almost querulous. " I do not know
if I ever felt love for her. What I felt was something different."

"It must have been something very near it,"
said Dolores, gently. " What you have suffered
must have had its root in love."

" Ah ! what I suffered ! That year ! I weary
you with my dwelling on it; but I must tell you
fully once. The memory of it, unless it is shared,

burdens me ; gives me a feeling almost of guilt ; and there is no one but you—and Soulsby, my good friend—to whom I can speak."

"It is my greatest joy—if I have helped you," said Dolores.

"It was a dark time," said the dramatist, in quick, low tones of shrinking, as though the subject still held unfaceable pain. "Day after day, and every hour of each day, I went through her feelings — the feelings I knew—I had learned—were hers, in the nine months she was with me, from our marriage till her death. I clutched at the knowledge of them. I felt myself straining after it ; that I might as it were endure them myself, and show myself their endurance was bearable. The moment of her seeing her home—of first knowing her lot —and all the others — I have spent days in grasping after each. And the deadness which came, when it seemed that my soul was exhausted — and the awaking from it!" He shuddered, and put his hand before his eyes.

Dolores was silent, waiting ; and he continued in an easier manner, as though narrating what was past the helping of emotions.

"But the times of exhaustion began to come oftener—more easily, as I now understand ; and the awaking had the numbness of having been lived many times. At first I barely felt the change ; but now I look back and see it. I have reached the feeling, I have had at the end of all my sorrows—though I thought this was not as the others, and would have no end —the feeling of almost rejoicing in my understanding of it, and of longing to — to create some creature with the same experience."

He ended as if he were making a confession; and when the words were uttered, was silent.

"You must follow the impulse," said Dolores gravely. "It is what your life holds. You are wrong in feeling that you are grasping at something which carries shame. Your having fallen short in a part of your life, if it is true that you have done so, does not justify your wasting what remains."

"No, I will do it," he said. "The play will be greater than it would have been. Ah, how I see what it needed!"

He made a movement as though to grasp a pencil; but suddenly a change seemed to drain the eagerness from his every limb.

"I am a broken old man," he said, in a voice with a startling change. "Blind; so that my powers are useless, for want of the one that is common to the things that breathe."

Dolores could find no words.

"I am blind; I cannot write. For I cannot see. I cannot read what I have written. There is no help for me."

There was appeal in his voice so simple and strong, that Dolores answered as though it were cast in words.

"You can do what you will, with some one to read what you write, through every minute of every day. Your deprivation is great; but in your greatest need it can be filled."

"I must tell you it all," he said, turning to her almost solemnly. "I must tell you what I have suffered, that you may know me; that no barrier may be between your soul and mine. When misgiving grew to dread, and dread to hopelessness, what I passed through! And I could not speak of it. I could not. I had not such great strength. How could I say, 'I cannot see. Tell me of what is before my eyes, for I am blind'—I, who could read a man's soul in his glance—who could see as no other man saw? No; I shut myself in myself; I did the one thing I could do. These coming days of passing into darkness will be happy compared to the learning they must come. But now I have told it to you, my soul will be free. In the other days I carried a burden; for — for she would not — could not know. Let us leave each other for to-day. When we meet, we will speak of the things that will be."

Dolores left him with a feeling she could only interpret as a great solemness. It seemed to her that the years she had lived, were the training-time for the work at hand; that this significance was the sole of her troubled experience; that had her struggles been a whit less hard, her suffering short of the fullest, she must have been too little tried and strong. A vision of the giving of her days to this great, sad-hearted creature, to whom for so long she had herself been given, brought a surging of passion that paled her lips. A straying of her thought to the future's passing from her, as she saw it, held her trembling and afraid. She went to her own rooms under a sense of being awestruck.

On her desk there was lying a letter—a letter left by some messenger's hand, as its cover bore a word of urgency. Sudden, inexplicable feeling gripped her, as it met her touch. As a flash, there came on her mind the day, when another of the letters with this look had turned for that time the course of her life. She had a sense of foreboding that approached to personal terror. She opened it, and read its words.

It was from the Reverend Cleveland Hutton; and it summoned her to Millfield parsonage, to the deathbed of her stepmother.

Closing her eyes to the future, and holding them closed, she spoke and wrought in strength in the next hours. She said what was needful to those who shared and ordered her life, and took the earliest journey to her home. A few

hours from her reading her father's words found
her entering its doors, marking it hushed and
darkened; and hastening with pitiful heart and
arms outstretched and strong, to the help of
those to whom all needed effort was owed,
whose claim was that of kindred.

She was thankful for herself in the days that
followed, that the yielding of her powers for those
who suffered of her flesh and blood, held her personal life an undercurrent in the stream of the
experience she saw, hidden and unheeded for all
its greater depth. The sad-faced young sisters
—Evelyn with her helpless sorrowing, and Sophia
with her self-repression betrayed by her thought
for the others who suffered; the boy, Cleveland,
in his sobbing grief; and the grey-haired father,
with his new loneliness, and gratitude wordless
in loyalty to the dead — they were creatures
whose need was a cry for her help — an unspoken claim that was clear and binding.

She looked through the future calmly. It
seemed to her that her power to struggle had
been worn to its death; that to suffer in secret
daily, and lie in the night hours helpless under
agony below the easiness of tears, was the lot
that was natural for her.

It was not till the evening before her return to
the college, that her father spoke of her settling
to the life of mistress of his home. As he spoke,
there came no change to her face. No paling

or quiver of a struggle was seen. It remained, simply, a face sad in its worn youthfulness.

"You will settle down at home now, and look after us all, my—— and look after us all, Dolores? That will be your duty now; and I trust you will not find it uncongenial?"

"Yes; that is what I thought, father. I see it is best," said Dolores, understanding the instinct that checked the words, 'my daughter.' "You must just do as well with me as you can; and I must just do as well as I can. I shall not try and fill any one's place."

"Dolores," said Sophia, "it was my dear mother's wish, that you should be at the head of things when she was gone. She said when—when she knew she was to be taken from us, that it was the one thing, that would let her die at ease about father and us all. She told us that her message to you was that she trusted us all to you. She said it would mean to you everything, she wished she could say to you herself."

As Sophia's voice broke, Dolores wept with her; with a feeling that she was weeping away the surface sorrows, whose melting would uncover those that held her soul as dead.

She felt that her soul was dead, when she made her lonely journey, for the winding up of the life she dared not look back upon. She felt it was dead; and had a strange, dull gladness in feeling it; for that it might awaken was a petrifying thing. But it awoke. When she saw the bent, still figure among the familiar desks, it awoke; and she knew that her hour was come.

Claverhouse did not turn as she entered. His aspect told of the old absorption; and from time to time his hands and head moved with the old suddenness. His roughly-hewn face wore a look of calm content; and the look laid a chill on Dolores' heart.

She closed the door with a sound; and he turned his head. His face lit up, with the swiftness of a happy knowledge that comes by a deeper power than sight. Dolores took the seat at his side, silent and cold.

He said no word; and his acceptance of a lot, in which closeness of comradeship gives countenance to speech or silence, brought a pang which seemed to shake her.

She began to speak—with a feeling that she must clutch the fiercest pain, her words and their work could cost, as the means of holding her emotions from following his.

"I am come to say—to tell you that this meeting is our last. My father has lost his wife; and he and his children have no one to look to, but me. I am needed in his home; and I must see that it is there I must feel my duty. There is one thing I ask you to do—to do for me, and for her — to give all your powers to the play."

As he turned his sightless eyes towards her, the manner of the change on his face blanched her own. After a long silence he seemed to be trying to speak; but it was minutes before the power of utterance came.

"What?" he said, in a toneless mutter.

She repeated her sentences, word for word, in a voice that had lost its life.

He sat looking before him; and his frame relaxed; as though he were sinking passively to utter hopelessness. Suddenly he turned to her, and sat leaning towards her, as though the whole of his being were straining in question towards the whole of hers. She knew the question as if he had spoken it. There was then in all her feeling towards him no love for him?

She rose and left the room; neither breaking through the doorway, nor throwing a farewell glance at the figure at the desk; but walking slowly and helplessly, as though the meaning of movement were gone.

She went to her own study and fastened the door.

CHAPTER XV.

FIVE years had gone, unmarked by word between Dolores and Claverhouse. From the recoil and quiver of the inner soul come the issues in the world that is seen. In their differing bondage of seeming to choose to forsake, and feeling lightly forsaken; with their differing helplessness before the barrier of his blindness; with their same night-searching of their fellowship's strange restraint, lest the one soul had read the other falsely as a mirror of itself; they lived in silence; while there grew into each heart, as a part of itself, its aching hourly questioning of the other.

At the end of five years, the utter sameness broke. At the end of five years, Soulsby—who at a word from Dolores before the years began, that marriage was against her heart, had gathered his shrinking being to himself; and gone from her sight to live for service to his friend; tongue-tied as always upon anything that could hint that he had a life of his own,—was again of good courage; and was seen in the neighbourhood of Millfield Parsonage.

Five years had gone unmarked. On the path
through Millfield churchyard, that led from the
road to the parsonage, there walked a man and
a woman. As the man spoke, his tones fell grave
and musical.

"Yes; it has been a sad life—a life full—full
of such troubles as must be borne alone, and
in which friendship seems of little help. It is
a great grief to me—the greatest grief I have
known, to watch him failing."

"You cannot say that *your* friendship has
been of little help," said Dolores, unable to withhold from her voice a deep, personal gratitude.

"Some years ago I should not have said it,"
said Soulsby, with his easier utterance of trouble.
"But of late it has been so. I am not enough
for him, as once I was. How it is I do not
know. He seems to be lonely. He shows a
longing for—for something or some one, of whom
he never speaks. And it is not for—for his wife.
At least—at least, I think I may say so. His
sorrow for her was different; and it was over
before this last change began. I do not understand. It is the one thing in which I have not
his confidence."

"He is really failing, is he?" said Dolores,
looking away from her companion to the ruddy
evening sky.

"Yes, he is failing," said Soulsby. "He never
leaves his house now; and he has given up

teaching. And it is more than that. There is disease—a disease of the heart, which must be fatal. It may be soon, or in years ; but it must be in the end. And he does not struggle to live. He feels his life holds nothing, now he is blind."

"He is quite blind?" said Dolores.

"He can distinguish light and darkness— nothing more. He cannot read ; and writing is no good to him—or so he says—as he cannot judge what is written. He has done very little since the issuing four years ago of his great play. It is a thing that will not bear words — that he has not power to give the time that is left him, to using his genius."

"But do not you read to him what he has written?" said Dolores, with a note that was almost a cry in her voice. "Cannot you make what changes he wishes? I cannot see that blindness is utterly preventive of his writing."

"No," said Soulsby, with simple sadness ; " I cannot—more than a little. He does not—does not allow me. I—I am—he does not feel me in sympathy with him—in my mind, I mean. He feels I do not follow him—and indeed often I do not ; and the feeling repels him. He seems to shrink from revealing to me his conceptions while they are growing. Even — even in the old days, I only heard what he chose to read to me. And—and even then, he was often im- patient of what I said and thought — even before—before feebleness and privation had made him hasty."

Dolores was silent; living in the sad picture which had grown to be a part of her consciousness. She lived in it with a heavy, simple grief. She had no wonder how the playwright in his blind and penniless age, came by daily bread and tendance; not needing to hear the words which she knew could not pass her companion's lips. As her eyes were drawn to the fine, spare figure, with the grey hair in scantier waves, and the saddened, older face, a rush of feeling came—a rush which she had been forcing back through many days. She yielded now. She let herself watch the other picture, which lay before her mind's vision—her own life bound with the life of this noble creature, who alone of those she knew of her kind, had given her more than she gave—her own life holding the tenderness and cherishing it had never held—carrying for the history of the first of its changed chapters, the deliverance of the greater life, that had waned too far to be knit except thus with her own. She could not but see the picture; and as she walked on, shrinking from breaking the silence whose significance she knew, her thoughts hovered round it, and drew it into the range of the possible and near.

For changes had grown in the parsonage household, in the five years in which Dolores

had been its mistress. The Reverend Cleveland
had buried his second bereavement more easily
and finally than his first; and was a happier and
less unresponsive man in his doubly widowed
days. Bertram was absorbed in the fair and
prosperous ordering of his own life; Cleveland,
with full, and quite unemotional paternal consent,
had been adopted by the Very Reverend James;
and of the young sisters, Evelyn was betrothed
and on the point of marriage to Herbert Blackwood, and Sophia had grown into a womanhood
beyond her years, and into much of the place in
her father's heart which in the earlier time had
been Dolores'.

For there was a further difference between the
Mr Hutton of to-day, and the husband and father
of the days of his second wife. The close of the
second passage of his wedded experience, by its
removal of the check upon remembrance of the
first, had seemed to rob the latter of its earlier
sanctity. Both were sunk in memory; and for a
man of his history and years, he lived little in
the past. Dolores' place in his life was hardly
larger than her sisters'; many of his old qualities,
in chief his moroseness and liking for thoughtful
companionship, were far less marked; and Sophia
was of an age and nature to sustain easily the
lightened burden, and fitly the greater dignity.
Dolores felt that her will was her own; that this
feebler and later promise of brightening in her

path was undimmed by looming shadows. When
Soulsby spoke, she felt it was her right to hear
him without struggle.

"Claverhouse has not—has not done and suffered what he has, without giving me a share of
his troubles. I miss his friendship — the real
friendship that once I had, deeply. I am thrown
much on myself. I have never been a man of—
a man of friends. I am—I am lonely. I have—
I hope I may have—a hope——"

He broke off. It was not his earliest effort.
The task was barely in his power.

They had reached the gate that opened from
the churchyard to the road. Dolores gave him
her hand. He pressed it with a deepening of
his usual deprecating deference, glanced into her
face as he lifted his hat, and while she passed
through the bushes from his sight, remained still
and bareheaded.

As she neared the parsonage garden, she saw
two figures pacing with arms entwined before
the porch. They were the figures of her father
and Sophia; and she paused in the blooming
rhododendrons, leaning on a firmly - growing
branch, and watched them.

No ; she was no longer essential to her father's
life. The years which carried the undoing of the
life that was supreme to her thought, and held
the supreme need, had seen the end of the duty
whose call had been her command. Five years,

and this change ! The cup was not to pass from her. It must seem—it seemed—that little was done, in the place of what might have been done. But her nature remained for her help ; and she was spared the wishing different what she had done hardly and sorrowing. The glimpse of the heavy figure and the youthful was pregnant with memories. Before these five years, she could not have judged otherwise than as she had judged.

And now her life was her own. As she stood leaning on the cold bough, with the damp earth under her feet, her hands clasped together, and her worn, woman's face towards her childhood's home, there were simple, pitiful feelings mingling with those which lay too deep for herself to name them. No ; it was not only the brightening of the darkened end of the life which was the meaning of her own--not only the living for the noble fellow-creature who sought her for herself ; —it was the other things of which her lot had been empty ;—daily cherishing, little hourly signs of a heart's homage, the glances of those who knew her early years, and deemed her unsought of men, and grateful that the shelter of her father's roof was ungrudging. It was such things as these, that left the others beneath, and struggled to the surface. For there are times when the heart is hungry, and cries out for the simplest sustenance as stay for its need.

CHAPTER XVI.

THE Blackwoods had bidden their friends to an
evening mildly convivial; and Mr Blackwood,
twirling his moustache in survey of his drawing-
room, had a sense that he was doing a pleasant
thing which he could ill afford, and which was
therefore generous as well as pleasant. In Mrs
Blackwood, who sat with a very upright bearing
and a studied air of ease, which seemed to clash
with each other, the sense of pleasantness was
rather painfully subordinate to that of the ill-
affording; and there were further misgivings to
give complication to qualms. The Huttons and
Cassells were to be supplemented, not merely by
Mrs Merton-Vane; whose acceptance of Blackwood good-fellowship was sufficiently rare—being
limited to cases when Mr Hutton was known to
be included in the company—to be held moment-
ous; but by Soulsby; upon whom Mr Blackwood
had pressed his invitation, without reference to
authority more domestic than his own impulse,
and with genial insistence unhampered by a

sense of acquaintance resting on a single meeting, or of the guest's probable experience of evening hospitality.

Mr Hutton had suffered some unperturbing amazement, that this chance of convivial experience had commended itself to his friend ; and Mrs Merton-Vane, to whom in confidence he admitted his view, easily entered into it. Mr and Mrs Blackwood, with the true instinct of hospitality —which is known to feel astonishment an unfitting attitude to the doings of guests,— had not yielded to surprise over any case of welcome extended to the pleasure they offered.

" Well, *Vicar!*" said Mr Blackwood; "I am glad to see you here with all your flock. And a fine flock it is, too—as fine as my own ; and I couldn't say more to please—to please any one you please. I couldn't indeed."

Mr Hutton's eyes sought the available chairs, rather than Mr Blackwood's face; and his reply seemed lost in a heavy taking of a seat, though his expression was well disposed.

" Well, you are a fine pair of girls!" said Mr Blackwood, taking the hands of Sophia and Evelyn. "I shall be proud of having one of you for my daughter-in-law. I shall indeed. I shouldn't mind if I was to have you both——"

" Herbert, come dear," said Mrs Blackwood, in her half-reproving, conjugal tones ; " here is Mrs Merton-Vane."

"I am *glad* to see you, Mrs Merton-Vane," said Mr Blackwood, very loudly, as though in amend for his involuntary disregard. "How are you?"

"I am pret-ty well, thank you, Mr Blackwood," said Mrs Merton-Vane, implying that her quali-fied words had allusion to her widow's weeds. "I felt I *could* not refuse your kindness, though I feel inclined to shut myself up, away from ev-er-y-one. But it does not do to give way to feelings like that *too* much, does it?"

"No, no, it doesn't do, Mrs Merton-Vane; it doesn't do," said Mr Blackwood.

"How do you do, Mrs Cassell?" said Mrs Blackwood. "We were all beginning to wonder if anything had prevented your coming."

"How do you know we were, mother? We have none of us said so," said Elsa.

"Oh, no, *thank* you, Mr Blackwood. It was John; he *would* be so long dressing," said Mrs Cassell, throwing an arch look at her hus-band, which he ignored with no failing in goodwill.

"Well, *doctor!*" said Mr Blackwood, ad-vancing. "Well, *doctor*, how are you?"

"I am—well, thank you," said Dr. Cassell.

"Why, Mr *Soulsby!*" said Mr Blackwood; "I am glad to see *you* here. I am glad to see you here at last; I am indeed. Come, find a seat. Do not treat us as strangers, I beg of you, after our having been neighbours at intervals for all these years."

"Come up to the fire, Mr Soulsby," said Mrs Blackwood.

"Why, Soulsby? Still at your old tricks of unpunctuality?" said Mr Hutton, knowing himself regarded as accosting the friend of his early days.

"I—I—you are most kind. No, no, no; this place is—is what I should choose, thank you," said Soulsby; managing to glance round the room, rest his eyes on Dolores, and push his fingers through his hair, in the second before he took his seat.

"Why, Mr Soulsby, I hear that you and Mr Hut-ton were boys to-geth-er," said Mrs Merton-Vane, leaning forward.

"Yes; yes, yes. At least—that is to say, we were at Oxford at the same time," said Soulsby.

"Now, Mr Soulsby, what do you think of this double wedding we are all going foolish over?" said Mr Blackwood; indicating the four young people concerned, with confidence in their hold upon any man's interest. "Brother and sister, to brother and sister. A pretty thing, won't it be?"

"Brother and sister, to brother and sister?" broke in Dr Cassell. "Brother and sister, to sister and brother, I believe?"

"Ah, yes, doctor; ah, yes, that's the coupling," said Mr Blackwood. "Well, what do you think of it, Mr Soulsby?"

"Oh—certainly—a very—a very pleasant arrangement," said Soulsby; throwing one swift glance at Elsa and Evelyn, as though feeling definite scrutiny a discourtesy, and clasping and unclasping his hands.

Dolores, who was watching Bertram, saw him make a gesture as though in response to a sign; and Elsa suddenly rose, and confronted her father.

"You can leave Bertram and me out of Mr Soulsby's 'pleasant arrangement,' father," she said, in a reckless voice with a quiver of laughter. "We have fulfilled our part early, to save so much complication."

Mr Blackwood looked easily uncomprehending; but Mrs Blackwood leaned forward.

"What do you mean, Elsa? Say what you mean plainly, and at once."

"Oh, Elsa, Elsa, you hussy, what now, what now?" said the Reverend Cleveland.

"Remember that you are speaking to Mrs Hutton, if you please, Uncle Cleveland," said Elsa.

"Oh, Elsa, how naughty of you!" said Mrs Blackwood, mingling the feminine attributes of swift comprehension and shrill tearfulness. "Now you have spoilt it all — the double wedding and everything. You never think of any one but yourself. You never have been anything but a disappointment to us from your babyhood. I shall be ashamed to tell any one. I shall never be able to speak of it. And my eldest daughter's marriage too! It is too bad. But I suppose it is all my fault, for allowing you and Bertram to be about so much alone. If you had had another mother. . . ."

"Oh, my darling, come, come. Young people will do foolish things sometimes. Why, you and I were on the point of doing something very much like it, about sixty years ago, if you remember. But it *will* be a bad thing, if *you* are going to fret about it. Come, come, now." Mr Blackwood crossed over to his wife, and awaited further revelations with his arm round her shoulders.

"Sixty years ago!" said Mrs Cassell, looking round with a smile. "Well, it isn't *quite* so long ago, that we were nearly culprits in the same way, is it, John?"

"Bertram, my son, should not the explanation come from you?" said Mr Hutton, as the doctor's voice gave no sign of breaking the silence.

"Yes, sir, certainly," said Bertram, going to Elsa and taking her hand. "It is just as—as my wife has said. We have no excuse to make; except that young people, as my father-in-law

s

has observed, will do foolish things sometimes. We must plead that we are not—are not considered to be—mature." Bertram spoke with a faint note of cynical bitterness.

"You are instead—considered to be"— said Dr Cassell, leaning forward and smiling, "a little *pre*-mature."

"Ah! So I am a father-in-law. So I am. I had not thought of that," said Mr Blackwood, as though taking some personal credit.

"Oh, de-ars!" said Mrs Merton-Vane. "How *could* you do such a naughty thing? De-ar, de-ar!"

"They may not be mature; but they are— universally agreed to be — a little *pre*-mature," said Dr Cassell, a little more urgently, arresting no eye but Mrs Cassell's.

"Cannot we have a coherent account of the thing?" said Herbert. "Evelyn and I would like some hints how these matters are managed."

"Oh, Herbert, do not joke about it," said Mrs Blackwood.

"My *darling*, you are upset," said Mr Blackwood, so loudly that Soulsby looked at him with uneasy question.

"There is no account to give. We simply did it, and there is an end of it. I am sure that is coherent. We will not thrust the whens and wherefores upon you, as my mother finds the subject so distasteful," said Elsa.

" Oh, my de-ar ! " said Mrs Merton-Vane.

" Shall we go in to supper, mother," said Lettice, implying that the subject was of a kind to be dropped as soon as possible.

" Yes, yes, Letty, my *darling*. You take the bottom of the table, and relieve your mother," said Mr Blackwood, ending in a resonant whisper, which he seemed to consider audible to his daughter, but not to the ear against his moustache.

The supper-table afforded bare accommodation for the party to be seated ; but Mr Blackwood was fortunate in not seeing this condition a ground for discomfiture. He pointed his guests to seats, with a loud geniality, and an easy consciousness of ushering them to the excellent, which in no degree failed him, even at the end of his efforts, when Soulsby was found to be standing in helpless survey of the spaceless rows, as a result of persistent passing on of the places pointed out to him.

" Oh, Mr Souls-by ! " said Mrs Merton-Vane. " How self-ish we all are ! Re-al-ly, I feel quite ashamed."

Soulsby took the seat that by some impenetrable process was put at his disposal, with some nervous words and gestures, which, as they came from himself, were perfectly dignified ; and found relief in aiding the passing of the plates; which Mr Blackwood was issuing from the head of the table, without exaggerated heed to their destination.

"Well," said that genial host in tones of some triumph, pausing with the carving knife and fork in his hands; "this is a nice thing! This is a nice thing, upon my word—upon my word it is! Ah, Elsa, you may well sit there, looking so innocent! You may, indeed, you monkey. As if we had not had enough trouble with you!"

"I—I suppose you were surprised to find that your sister was married?" said Soulsby to Lettice; finding this his best in the way of the urbane intercourse incumbent on a guest.

"Yes, I was very surprised," said Lettice, implying that surprise was one of the mildest of her sentiments.

"Lettice would never have done such a thing," said Mrs Blackwood. "She is very shocked; and I do not wonder."

"Neither do I, mother," said Elsa. "My power of wondering at Letty's being shocked at things, has been worn out with overwork long ago."

"How many days have you been married, my son?" said the Reverend Cleveland. "I do not like this living apart as husband and wife. You must take Elsa to the home you have ready for her."

"Yes, sir; I quite agree with you. We are thinking of dispensing with a honeymoon, and going to Manchester to settle next week," said Bertram, his manner seeming at peculiar variance with his supposedly recent freak.

"I only have one more Sunday to go to the Wesleyan chapel," said Elsa, with naughty complacence.

"Elsa, I hope you will make a point of attending the Wesleyan service, when you are in your own home," said Mrs Blackwood. "I cannot bear to think of your turning aside, to become anything but a Wesleyan."

"Oh, I have turned aside in my heart long ago, mother," said Elsa; "ever since I heard father's lecture on the 'Wesleyan Body, its origin and history,' in the meeting - house, when I was twelve. I am a churchwoman now; and you ought to be thankful, I am not a Roman Catholic, as I ought to be on any normal reactive principle. Are you not glad I am a churchwoman, Uncle Cleveland?"

"If I may say what I should feel, were I your father, I think I may admit that I am," said Mr Hutton.

"Dear Uncle Cleveland! What a nice father you would have made!" said Elsa, not subjecting Mr Blackwood to any parental pang.

"I have been thinking, Blackwood," said Dr Cassell, recalled by this talk of religion to his own particular pre-eminence; "of giving a series of—lectures—in the meeting-house, upon—Pro-

testantism, and the various causes which —
threaten it. I am thinking of arranging the
lectures in a course of six ; and giving them once
a fortnight for twelve weeks."

"Ah, doctôr, are you, are you?" said Mr
Blackwood, easily sinking such matters as his
children's marriages in this interest. "Well,
now—how would it be now, if I were to join
you *myself;* and give — say, alternate lectures
with you on some other subject—say *Temperance.*
That is the subject I am best up in. I believe I
could make the lectures interesting; I *believe*
that I could. I have had a good deal of experience in that line, as you know ; and I could bring
forward a good many practical examples, to give
the thing a *hold* upon the people. What do you
say to that, doctor ?"

Dr Cassell considered with some fall of countenance.

"Well, doctor, what do you say to it ?" said
Mr Blackwood.

"I hardly think," said Dr Cassell, in a rather
wounded manner, "that lectures on Temperance
would—alternate very well with my lectures. The
subjects are hardly—kindred ; and I had planned
that attendance should be required only once a
fortnight, with the purpose of—insuring a good
audience. I—I think, I do not think well of the
combination."

"Ah, well, doctor   Have it all to yourself

if you like," said Mr Blackwood, with satisfactory compliance, but, as it seemed to his friend, a rather crude frankness.

"I suppose you will not go—will not have time to go to the lectures, Mr Hut-ton?" said Mrs Merton-Vane, inclining her head.

"No, I shall not, I fear," said Mr Hutton, his non-committing tone leading in subtle manner to a silence; which Soulsby felt himself somehow impelled to break.

"So you have secured the post at Manchester university?" he said to Bertram. "I was glad to hear it."

"I have to thank you most gratefully for your influence in the matter, sir," said Bertram.

"To think that you have a son a pro-fes-sor, Mr Hutton!" said Mrs Merton-Vane. "I feel quite fright-ened, at sitting by the father of a pro-fes-sor. I suppose we must begin to call him, Pro-fes-sor Hut-ton?"

"I hope I shall not be Professor long," said Bertram. "I have only accepted a professorship at Manchester, as a stepping-stone to some smaller post in Oxford. I am obliged to take something that carries a house and a necessary income."

"I once knew a Professor *Long*," said Dr Cassell, brought into full form by the final relief of his dialogue with his host. "I think I may say that everything about him was *long*. His hair was long; his legs were long; his name was

'Long'; and the only anecdote he knew — was
long." Dr Cassell laughed; and finding himself
fairly followed, continued.

" He lived to be ninety-one; so I think we may
say his life was long. In fact, shall we call him
a second *Long-fellow?*"

Mrs Cassell looked round, with a smile significant of power of appreciative comment.

"Ah, Mr Soulsby," said Mr Blackwood loudly,
perceiving Soulsby's eyes resting on Dr Cassell;
"you don't know the *doctor*, do you? He's the
one for *anecdotes*, and clever *sayings*, and information of all kinds. He *is* that, I can tell you.
You will soon get to know that; I can tell you
that you will."

Dr Cassell glanced at Soulsby; and then looked
at nothing in particular with a smile wavering
on his lips; and Soulsby looked at his host, and
then at Dr Cassell, and opened his mouth; but
shut it again, clasping and unclasping his
hands.

"Well, Dolores, this will make a change for
you—this losing your brother and sister," said
Mr Blackwood. "You will have a much smaller
household to be mistress of. How shall you like
it?"

"I shall miss them very much," said Dolores,
in a quiet tone; but feeling a deeper than the
wonted wound, at this view of her duty to her
father as a privilege naturally grasped.

"Well, you must get married yourself," said Mr Blackwood, his tone betraying recognition of the impracticable nature of his advice.

"Oh, you would not leave your father, would you, de-ar?" said Mrs Merton-Vane, inclining her head. "She has been such a good daughter, has she not, Mr Hut-ton?"

"She has indeed," said Mr Hutton. "We all owe very much to her."

Dolores did not speak. She was held by feelings, whose bringing of joy and shame was no longer new. She found herself yearning for the time for taking her altered place, as a woman who held what a man gives once to one of her kind—for ending this view of herself, as a woman whose function was to give of herself in fair earning of her bread—for walking in the sight of those who knew her, honoured as one for whom honour was fitting. With the thought of the coming changes, came the vision of her father and Sophia, sufficing to each other in the parsonage life; and her eyes were drawn to her noble-looking sister.

Sophia's face was turned to Soulsby's; and Dolores saw, with a shock that held her stunned, that its beauty was of a worn and wistful kind for its youth. As she watched it, the large eyes met her own; and shrank and drooped, while the cheeks were stained. Dolores felt stricken, but not bewildered. Her old insight into things that

were suffered and hidden, which had seemed to
grow blunted in the years with the unstruggling
fellows of her flesh and blood, was again at her
command ; and Sophia's soul lay bare to her
sight — the pure soul, with its daily wrestling,
its daily vanquishing, its high resolve.

Rising as in a dream, when the move was
made, and crossing the passage blindly in the
idle throng, she found herself at Soulsby's side,
and spoke the words that rose.

" It will seem very strange at home, when my
sister and brother are gone, and I have only
Sophia to care for. I hope I shall not be called
on to give up Sophia, unless it is to some one
very worthy."

Soulsby's eyes went to Sophia's face.

" I hope not," he said, in easy, musical tones.
" There would not be many worthy."

Dolores' heart seemed to cease its beating.

" No, there would not," she said. " She is
so good ; how good I can hardly tell you. I
have always felt the living with her a privilege."

" Yes," he said, not taking his eyes from
Sophia's face. " I have thought it must be a
privilege, from the first time I saw her."

Dolores was silent ; accepting this new knowledge calmly. So—whether or not he knew it
—he had chosen herself for the smaller gulf
between them. Whether or not he knew it,
there was another filling of his life, that would

satisfy its need. And Sophia had given him
what she had not; though she knew what it
was to give it. She awaited the end of the
evening with eagerness and dread.

The evening had been, in a social sense, but
a bare success; though Mr Blackwood accepted
gratitude for what it had afforded, with much
good faith, and even some encouragement for
its fuller expression. Bertram and Elsa had
sat apart, taking no share in the talk, and
speaking little to each other; and Herbert and
Evelyn had followed their example. Mrs Merton-Vane had monopolised the Reverend Cleveland, who made no effort towards diffusion of
his social gifts; Mrs Blackwood had sunk her
character of hostess in that of disappointed
mother; and Mr Blackwood had given her the
chief of his attention, in no doubt that his
conjugal devotion was in itself a sufficiently
pretty thing for the pleasure of his friends.

Dolores felt the touch of Soulsby's hand, and
heard the words he spoke of meeting on the
morrow, with a feeling that seemed little more
than simple wonder, that she had believed this
thing for herself. On reaching the parsonage,
she was going at once to her room, perceiving
that Sophia winced before her eyes; but as she
reached the staircase, she heard her father's step
behind.

"My daughter," he said, placing his hand on

her shoulder; "so Evelyn is not the only one of you I am to lose?"

Dolores' face paled. It was a moment before she could meet the sacrifice of this oft-lived heart-throb. Her father waited with his hand still on her shoulder; and she forced herself to meet his eyes and speak.

"No, father. You are right that you are to lose two of us; but I am not to be one of them. You must ask no questions yet, and know nothing till it is told you. But I shall always be with you—for us to grow old together."

For a moment Mr Hutton was silent. Then he turned away with his usual ponderous neutrality.

"Well, well, my daughter; if it is in your hands, I suppose it is well. But remember that you owe a duty to yourself, as well as to others."

He went into his study and closed the door. No one was to know how much he saw of the happenings around him, or how far was moved by them in his hidden self. Dolores suffered anew, in the denial of a grateful word for what she had done and was to do for him.

She went to her chamber, and took the first seat that met her eyes. She sat with the darkness round her, with her head erect, and her lips set in stern and simple sadness. Her survey of her position was clear and calm. As far as Soulsby and her father were touched, Sophia and herself might either fill either place. It was Sophia's long, young life, and the waning days of the other life, whose fading, held from her sight, made her own life as it was hidden, that lay before her for her judgment. This was her choice.

A trembling came to her; for her conscience and her will clashed, and the clash seemed to shake her soul. As the hour of midnight struck, she rose and crossed the passage to Sophia's room. As a flash there came upon her memory that other midnight hour, which had seen her doing another thing, with another purpose, for another woman. She seemed to be living the minutes for the second time.

Sophia was standing, half-clad, at her open window; shivering as though in welcome of cold and weariness, for their relief in deadening the subtler pain. As Dolores came to her, she started, and stood for a moment trembling; and then yielded herself to the arms that were held.

"Oh, Dolores, Dolores! I meant that no one should know. But I cannot bear it. I cannot feel my happiness in yours. I am not like you. I am wicked; but I do not wish to be. I only wish that I need not live."

"My dear," said Dolores, folding her arms round the shaking form, "you have only to wish to live and be happy ; for it is that which is before you. It is coming to you—it will soon come—all that you seek. You are not wicked. These things are not of our own helping. Our feelings are often in spite of the strongest efforts of our will."

CHAPTER XVII.

DOLORES paced the path through the church-yard, looking at the things she saw with emotions that were new. They were after all the things that must be before her through the years. They stood, in their unheeded eloquence — the tombs with their two inscriptions ; so nearly the same, and carrying their difference—the tokens of the endings of two of her life's chapters. She paused before the stone with the fewer marks of time. " In memory of Sophia, beloved wife of Cleveland Hutton, vicar of this parish, who died in the fifty-fourth year of her age." With all her father had to look back upon, did he know the deeper things that were to be known ? She started at a step on the path at hand.

" I—I am going, at last, if I may, to speak to you plainly. You—you will listen to what I must say ; and tell me what I must know ? "

Dolores had turned and raised her eyes ; but as Soulsby's free words showed her the strength of what he felt, she shrank and turned them aside.

"I must ask you if there is any hope of your fulfilling the great wish of my life. I need not put it in language. It is the deepest personal desire I have known. If you can fulfil it, my happiness will not be met by words. If you cannot, I shall not wish I had kept it hidden. I shall be grateful to you, for permitting me to make it known to you; and I shall feel to the end, that I am the better for having felt it."

Dolores looked at him with mute beseeching.

"Ah! you cannot?" he said at once, with a great gentleness. "Then the words I have said are my last. I will not ask for your continued friendship. It would be to imply that I think there is need."

There was a long silence; and Dolores broke its pain with a sudden question.

"Will you do me a kindness?"

He did not utter the words that needed no utterance; but stood in waiting for her bidding.

"I am going away for a while to stay with my brother," she said, her eyes drooping to the ground; "and I should be very grateful, if you would spend the time—or a part of it—at the vicarage with my father. He will be lonely without me—with my brother gone, and my sister Evelyn preparing for her marriage; and I do not like to leave too much on Sophia. She is always too ready to sacrifice herself."

"The further I am allowed, the greater will

be the privilege," he said, with a courteous list-lessness which wrung her heart.

"I must go in," she said, with a feeling something like a shudder. "Do not think—pray do not think, that I am not grateful—deeply grateful—for all I have had from you this morning —and always. You are the only one who has ever given me so much without return. But the time will come, when you will be glad of my answer."

"No; you are wrong, if I may say so," he said, in gentle tones merely of rejoinder. "Unless—unless, of course, I see you united with some one, who—who——"

He broke off, and hastened away; shrinking from the freedom of seeming to ask if he owed his sorrow to a rival; and Dolores went into the parsonage, and sought her father.

"Father," she said, not trying to disguise in her voice, that her words had a deeper than their necessary meaning; "I am going away for a time, to stay with Bertram and Elsa. It is my wish, that you shall ask Mr Soulsby to stay with you till I return. I have spoken to him; and he has given his consent to come and be your companion. It will be well both for you and Sophia."

The Rev. Cleveland was silent, looking into her face. When he spoke, she was grateful that he did not feign to miss her meaning.

T

"You are sure you are right, my daughter?"

"Yes, I am sure," said Dolores, finding that she spoke calmly and steadily.

He looked at her again; and turned away with some words in the voice she had heard only once before.

"You are a good woman, Dolores. I see each day more clearly whose child you are. I am unworthy of either of you. It is companionship too high for me."

Dolores went to her room; but it was not at once that she began to prepare for her journey of the morrow.

When the morrow came, she left her home with a calm face and words of cheer. For one moment Sophia was clasped to her breast; and for the same moment, the father's eyes rested on the locked forms of the two dearest of his children. Then he turned and entered his study; and Dolores went on her way.

It came to pass as she had purposed, and taught herself to hope. On the day before her leaving her brother, after the doing of a needful work in smoothing the time of Elsa's settling to domestic duties, and Bertram's earliest efforts at forbearance, a letter was brought to her from her father.

"My daughter,—I believe that for you my tidings will hardly be tidings. Sophia is soon to be married to William Soulsby. We shall have after all the double wedding, the neighbourhood has set its heart upon. I will say no more —except to congratulate you upon the happiness of your sister and your friend, which I know is your own.—Your affectionate father,

"CLEVELAND HUTTON."

Dolores folded the letter, and told the news in natural manner to her brother and his wife.

"Sophia to be married to Uncle Cleveland's old crony!" Elsa exclaimed. "Why, he is treble her age. I thought he was courting you, Dolores; and that you were fully young for him. What a deep game he has played!"

"Dear Sophia!" said Bertram. "It is a surprise indeed. I hope she will be as happy as she deserves. There is often great happiness with great difference in age. So that has been Soulsby's business in father's part of the world. I suppose you had his confidence, Dolores? I confess I thought with Elsa, that he was courting you."

"I think I am not a very fit subject for courting," said Dolores, smiling.

"I suppose you are too clever to be fallen in love with," said Elsa. "I expect he thinks of you, as he thinks of Uncle Cleveland — a person to talk about colleges and classics with."

"There is certainly no better person than Dolores, to talk about things with," said Bertram, with something in his tone that made Elsa fidget and frown.

Dolores went in silence to prepare for leaving her brother on the morrow. She purposely had not written to Sophia the hour of her return; and she walked alone from the station to the parsonage. As she went up the path through the churchyard, she saw two figures coming towards her. She stopped short; and for a second her hand went to her heart. Then she hastened forward, to take her sister to her breast with tender wishing well.

The words she heard that night from each, remained with her, for her help through the years. Soulsby spoke to her little through the evening hours; but his manner was deferential beyond what it was to Sophia. As he was leaving the parsonage at dark, he met her in the garden; and, after a moment of nervous pause, spoke in tones that thrilled her with their grave music.

"May I speak once more to you of my feelings towards you? There is little to be said —simply that my wife and I shall always look up to you, as one who lives above a life that can be shared."

Dolores could not speak. She met his eyes in silence and gave him her hand. He raised

it to his lips, and walked hastily away with
his head bare. She watched him till the
hedges hid him from sight, and then turned
back to the parsonage. When she was alone
in her room that night, there was a knock at
the door, and Sophia came to her — a Sophia
with a younger beauty, a new dignity mingled
with the old.

"Dolores," she said, "tell me truthfully how
it is with you. You are so good, that I
cannot tell what you may have done. Did
you — do you — he says you do not — but do
you love him, as I do?"

Dolores laid her hands on her sister's
shoulders.

"No, dearest, no. I have strong feelings
towards him — deep respect and a great affection — the feelings I should wish to have for
the man to whom I must trust my Sophia—
nothing more. I have never felt to him as
you do—as it is your right alone to feel. You
need have no fear."

"Dolores," said Sophia simply, "I know I
do not know your troubles, as you have always
known mine. I am not like you — a woman
who lives for the troubles of others, and help-
ing· them through them. But if you have
them yourself, you would let me do anything
I could?"

"My dear, you have been perplexed about

me?" said Dolores, with gentle regret. "I have much to be forgiven, if I have added to the troubles of your early time. I will tell you, that you may be quite at rest. I have had a sorrow—a long sorrow which I brought on myself, and which is over now. You need have no fear for me; it is over."

CHAPTER XVIII.

THERE was much strong feeling in the rustic mind of Millfield, at the marriage of the two young daughters of its parsonage. It was felt that the occasion should be held as pathetic no less than great; and faces were clad in solemnity as well as bodies in holiday garb, for attendance at the double ceremony. This solemn aspect was enhanced by the presence of the Very Rev. James; who spent a week with his merely Reverend brother, with the purpose of giving this weight to the nuptials of the nieces, who owed him gratitude for their maidenly arts, as well as reverence for his honourable service to the Establishment; and Soulsby's grey head and unwandering glance could hardly be regarded as devoid of all moving bearing. In brief, the mother of the carpenter was felt to be fitly expressing the natural and general, if hitherto undefined feeling, when in the course of the service she said aloud with sobs, "Dear, dear! Poor, dear, motherless young things!"

Evelyn made a graceful, and Sophia a beautiful bride. Herbert did his part with a boyish
self - consciousness not unbecoming his youth;
and Soulsby bore himself with unfaltering dignity; betraying no embarrassment in sharing
his nuptials with those of an age to be his
children, but doing the things to be done with
simple compliance, as the steps to that which
he sought of his choice.

The afterward gathering at the parsonage consisted of familiar figures. Soulsby was frankly
friendless, and had been quite startled at the
notion of bidding his kin to his marriage feast;
and the sisters' and Herbert's circle of acquaintance was comprised in the dwellers in the district. The time to be spent in convivial well-
wishing happened to be unwontedly brief; and
Dolores was glad as its minutes passed; for
there seemed a general uneasiness which refused
to be dispelled. The Rev. Cleveland was ponderous and silent. The Very Rev. James was
pompous and officious, and exerted an influence
consistently constraining. Soulsby was passive
in the grip of a nervousness, which sealed his
lips on pain of discomfiture for himself and
others. Doctor Cassell held aloof, as if uncertain
of the etiquette, and Mrs Cassell felt forbidden
to leave his side; and Mr Blackwood's spasmodic
professions of appreciation of the occasion's qualities, produced more gratitude for his exertions

than relief in their results. It was not until the two young brides came down with their bridal garb put off, and the carriages which the Very Rev. James had hired from the local inn had driven to the door, that any one attained the feelings for which all had striven.

"Well, girls, well; so you are off," said Mr Blackwood, with equal emphasis and relief. "All health and happiness to you both. I am sure it is the wish of us all. I am sure that it is, Vicar."

"Yes; yes, I—second you, Blackwood," said Dr Cassell, his tone suggesting contentment with his choice of expression.

"Good-bye, my dears," said the Dean, in sonorous tones which drew to him general attention, and seemed to imply that the chief guardian of the brides had hitherto been himself. "God bless you; and may everything fall to your lot that is good for you."

"Good-bye, my daughters. You know what I wish for you without my saying it," said the Rev. Cleveland, embracing his children, and implying that this unexpanded farewell was irrevocably his final word.

"Oh, Herbert, my dear, dear boy!" said Mrs Blackwood, putting her arms round her son.

"Oh, come, my darling; come, come," said Mr Blackwood, finding his powers employed with less effort in a practised direction. "Young people must marry, you know. Why, there was a

time, when you and I were up to much the same
sort of thing. Good-bye, my son; good-bye.
May your wife be as much to you, as your mother
has been to me."

"Oh, de-ars, thank you both for the pret-ty
sight you have given us," said Mrs Merton-Vane.
"And take care of both your de-ar selves, *won't*
you? Prom-ise me that you will."

"While we are thinking of marriages," said
Dr Cassell, edging himself to a prominent place,
and speaking with twinkling eye and gesticulating hand; "there is a—story which has just come
to my mind, which I flatter myself may be—
appropriate. An old man asked another, why
he was marrying at his time of life; and received
the reply, 'Waal! I'd be fain to have some one
to close me eyes.' 'Well,' said the other, slowly
—in his turn—'I've had three wives; and they've
all of 'em opened mine.'"

"Ah, that's good, doctor!" said Mr Blackwood, with less involuntary mirth than laborious
effort to help things to go off well. "That's
good, and no mistake."

"Oh, Dr Cas-sell!" said Mrs Merton-Vane.
"And with these de-ar girls just starting off,
too!"

"Well, unless they make up their minds to
something of the kind, they will miss the train,"
said Elsa. "Oh, I am so glad I was not married
in a dull, ordinary way like this."

"It would in that case have been a *triple* wedding," said Dr Cassell.

"Good-bye, Hutton," said Soulsby quietly, giving his hand to the Rev. Cleveland. "I am grateful to you for all I have to be grateful for; and it is very much. We shall see you, and —we shall see you both at Oxford, as soon as we return from abroad." Soulsby had yet to bring himself to give Dolores a name.

"Good-bye, Mr Soulsby," said Mrs Merton-Vane. "You have a pre-cious charge to take care of. I am sure we all feel she is qui-te safe in your hands."

"Good-bye, mater," said Herbert, turning to take Evelyn to the carriage.

There was a little bustle and disturbance. The Very Rev. James pushed his way to the front of the porch, holding his handkerchief in readiness for its God-speeding office. Soulsby took Dolores' hand, and held it for several seconds; and then dropped it suddenly, and hastened down the steps. Mrs Blackwood began to cry, and Elsa to quote a poem on wedding emotions, which had become a domestic classic. Dolores went to the carriages, to leave a word and smile in the memories of the sisters leaving her care for their wider experience; and the Rev. Cleveland brushed his handkerchief across his eyes, and glanced towards the door of his study.

As the carriages drove away, Mrs Merton-Vane looked round the remaining company, and brought her eyes to rest on the Rev. Cleveland.

"It does remind me so of so ma-ny things," she said, looking down at her widow's garments. "The de-ar children! May their husbands be spared ve-ry long, to love and care for them."

CHAPTER XIX.

"Go on, go on," said Claverhouse, leaning with his ear towards the lips of his friend. "You hesitate and stumble, so that I find my conception constantly broken. Read more fluently. Begin the passage again."

Soulsby turned back the pages of manuscript, and read in a controlled expressive voice; but in a moment came to a pause, gave a troubled glance at the blind listener, and sat surveying the scored sheets with contracted brows.

"Go on, go on," said Claverhouse, moving impatiently, and still stooping forward, as though to drink in every whit of the meaning of what was read.

"I—I cannot—quite follow the—the manuscript here," said Soulsby, with a face of trouble. "The—it has been—I think there are some lines scored out; but—but the scoring marks are only partly through them, and the final version is written half across the other, so that—so that——"

"So that, so that!" said Claverhouse, with

bitter mimicry. "So that it is impossible to see what the old blind driveller meant by his scribbling. Put it aside then. Do not take any trouble to help me. Who am I, that I should exact so much from my friend?"

Soulsby sat silent, in grieved forbearance; until Claverhouse, in the nervous irritation of feebleness and premature age, made a movement of violent impatience, when he again took up the sheets.

"Shall—shall I—go on from the end of the—the doubtful passage?"

"No, do not go on at all," said Claverhouse, still in the painfully bitter tone. "Go back to your wife, and your life of happiness and love, and leave me alone; to get on, or to fail—or to die, as well as I may. What else do I deserve at your hands?"

"I think I have deserved a little better at yours," said Soulsby, laying down the papers.

"Ah, you have!" said Claverhouse, covering his face, and pushing the fingers of his other hand through his thin, grey hair. "But you do not know what it is to live in formless blackness, and see it swallowing the work of your days. May you never."

"I do not know it, indeed," said Soulsby, with gentle earnestness. "And I am wrong in saying you owe anything to me. The debt is mine."

"Ah! You pander to me, and soothe me with words with no thought in them, because I am an

old blind creature in my second childhood," said
Claverhouse. "Well, I shall be gone soon; and
you will have nothing to do for me, but look back
and congratulate yourself on your goodness."

There was a long silence; and at length
Soulsby spoke, with the constraint which resumes
after a break at embarrassing words.

"I—I have some relatives of my wife's—her
father and elder sister — coming to spend some
weeks with me. The—the sister is an old friend
of yours and—and of your wife's; and would feel
it a privilege—she tells me—to come and visit
you. She——"

"Oh!" said Claverhouse, heaving up his
shoulders, and speaking in a querulous manner
which gave him a strange resemblance to his
mother in her later feebleness. "I have earned
my bread amongst women. There are hundreds
who would be ' old friends of mine,' in speaking
to a believer in my powers — or rather in my
future fame. They don't care about me, or know
me, nor I them. Some relatives of your wife's!
You are heartless, Soulsby. I don't want crumbs
from your domestic happiness thrown to me."

"This—this has nothing to do with my domestic happiness," said Soulsby simply. "Dolores
Hutton was a friend and pupil of yours before she
knew my name." He gave a start; for his words
were no longer spurned.

Claverhouse made an agitated sound, half-lifted

his arms, and seemed to be shivering. Then he pressed his elbows on the table, and crouched forward, with his eyes seeming to strain for sight.

"What?" he said. "Who? What are you talking of?"

"Her name is Dolores Hutton. She is my wife's sister. Their father is a clergyman in Yorkshire. I have heard you speak of her to your wife," said Soulsby, watching him with changing expressions.

"When will she come? How soon will you bring her to me?" said Claverhouse, still stooping forward, and speaking in a hoarse tone that was almost a whisper. "Let there be no needless waiting. Have I not waited long enough?"

"She can come at some early hour to-morrow," said Soulsby, finding that his voice sounded strangely. "She reaches me to-night."

"Why at some hour to-morrow? What time does she reach you? Oh, you may wonder at me, Soulsby. What matters it what a man does on the brink of the grave? Tell her to come to me to-night. Five years! Nearly all there was left me!"

He sank back in his chair, and made a gesture for his friend to leave him.

"I will give her your message," said Soulsby, composing the papers with nervous fingers. "I —I see no reason why it should not be as you wish. I—I shall be deeply rejoiced, if—if——"

He saw his friend was giving him no heed, and

passed from the room. In the passage he came
upon Julia, standing with her hands folded in her
apron, and an expression on her wrinkled face he
could not interpret.

"You—you—I need not warn you—I am sure
you are the last person to need warning. But
I—I am bringing a—a friend—a lady, here with
me to-night. She is an old friend of—of Mrs
Claverhouse. You—you will know to take all
that happens as a matter of course?"

"I heard, sir," said the old servant, in a quietly
hopeless tone. "It doesn't seem as if much good
could come out of anything now. But I hope
there can't come any harm either—that the time
for that has gone as well. Anyhow you may
trust me, sir."

"I am sure of it," said Soulsby, in his courteous
manner, as he left the dwelling.

It was late in the evening when he entered it
again, with Dolores walking behind him. Julia
gave but a glance to the tall, spare woman, with
the simple garments and worn face; and then led
the way in silence.

As the door opened, Claverhouse started to his
feet, and put out his hands, as though to repel
approach, his ear turned to catch the footsteps on
the floor. As Dolores came towards him, some
words broke from his lips like a cry.

"Why did you leave me? Why could you
spare me nothing of all that you gave?"

As their hands met, Soulsby slipped from the
room, closing the door behind him. Julia gave
no sign of surprise, as she saw him enter the
passage. She moved from the door, placed a
chair for him in silence, and entered the
kitchen.

It was long that he sat in the darkness, with
his hands moving slowly against each other, and
his grey head bent as if in pondering. They fell
on his ear—filling him with emotions that held
thought in abeyance—the voices of these two
fellow-creatures of his reverence—the deep, harsh
sounds that were to him a prophet's utterance,
and the impressive, woman's tones which he had
thought to hear for his own hourly cheering.
When the hour grew late, and he rose and entered
the chamber, he found them sitting at the table
together; with their lips moving, and their faces
seeming to tell simply of long, unbroken friendship. For some moments he watched them
mutely; and then stepped forward, and stood
at hand, making no further sign.

With instant obedience, as if almost wearied
by the hour they had lived, they rose together.

"Ah!" said Claverhouse, with so much of the
old sudden vigour of the word, that Soulsby
was startled; "so we have had the hour I have
lived in. You know it all. It can be as if these
years had never been—even though they must
remain."

They clasped hands in silence ; taking their leave in the manner of the many partings of the older time ; and turned from each other with a quiet word of meeting on the morrow. Soulsby followed, as Dolores moved to the door ; believing, without the faintest bitterness, that his own presence was forgotten. But the sensitive ear of blindness was skilled in the subtlest inflections of the language of the sounds of movement.

"Soulsby, my friend !" said Claverhouse, with an utterance of the last word which gave it a burden of eloquence. "This is not the least of the services you have done me."

Soulsby turned, and grasped the hand that was held to him, and hastened after Dolores without a word.

They walked in silence through the streets. Dolores was living again with each pulse of her heart, the hour which seemed the undoing of the five hard years, whose every day was a day of bereavement ; and Soulsby shrank from breaking her musing, or seeming to seek her confidence. He felt all the natural wonder on that time of the past, when the lives of Dolores and the play- wright had mingled. He pondered with strong emotion and eagerness for fuller knowledge ; speaking much to himself that could not pass his lips.

He spoke to himself of a scene in a country churchyard—feeling no flush on his cheeks, or

quiver of personal pain at his heart—questioning
simply the troubled way of the woman he loved
with the love of a subject and a friend. So her
history was sadder and nobler yet. But why had
they suffered thus? Why had the years been
spent by them thus—by him with his blindness
forsaken, by her in the empty constraint of that
parsonage home? He could not tell. The part
played by the friend of his own youth—the slow-
worded father—in the drama held from his knowledge, was hidden from him; and he did not understand. But there was to come understanding.

One evening, when the Huttons' return to
Millfield was at hand, he went to fetch Dolores
from the playwright's dwelling, where she spent
many hours of each day; her father and sister
believing the intercourse to be that of teacher
and pupil. He was earlier than usual; and
entering the room unperceived, stood for some
moments watching.

Dolores was reading from the very manuscript
which had defied his efforts; and Claverhouse
was leaning towards her in eager listening, his
face so free from the familiar signs of trouble,
that the friend's heart misgave him for the
different future. He waited, listening, till the
full-toned voice was silent.

"Ah! there is nothing good in it," said Claverhouse, in his old vehement manner. "My time
for work was past; and my heart was heavy, so

that I lived too much in my own life. There is nothing good in it."

"There is great good in it," said Dolores, turning the pages with grave scrutiny. "You must give yourself to it again, and carry it on to its end. It is not like the work of your prime; but then it is not the work of your prime. It will have its own value for that."

"Ah! it is good to be talked to as a thinking man, even if an old blind one," said Claverhouse.

Soulsby's heart smote him, for every loyally-meant assurance, which had wanted his heart's sanction. He felt his spirit recoil before the coming time—the months of the failing life, with their burden of the old weariness, the old struggle to attain to gratitude, heavier for the knowledge of different days. That evening he sought a word with Dolores—a word long pondered, but postponed in trembling to the latest moment.

"Dolores," he said, with the tone of uttering a sacred word, which marked his speaking of her name. "You will let me say a word to you?"

Dolores raised her face in silent sanction, struggling for the courage she had long been fostering for this moment of trial.

"It is only—only a few words—only one thing I have to say. Could you—you will make your home with my wife and—will make your sister's

home your own, until Sigismund Claverhouse—
that is, as long as he is spared to us?"

Dolores' face grew set; but she answered without pause, in words which by daily, lonely effort
she had learned to utter for this answer.

"What of my father? I cannot leave him."

"But his is the lesser need," said Soulsby, with
a solemness undisguised.

"But the greater claim," said Dolores, her
voice not argumentative, but sadly resigned.

"It might be for such a little while," said
Soulsby, with pleading as simple as a child's.

"But it might be for years," said Dolores.

"Well, if you choose to leave him," said
Soulsby, his manner altering, and his tones holding threat and tears; "you will be parted till
his death — and wholly parted. You cannot
write to him; for he is blind, and would spurn
your words through another. You cannot see
him, when you come to Sophia; for the emotion
of meeting and parting would be dangerous in
the state of his heart. Your meeting when the
news of your going is broken, will be your last;
and your parting will be a parting for both your
lives. And you are to him—well, why should I
tell you what you are to him?"

"I *cannot* see it otherwise," said Dolores, in a
low voice that was almost a sob.

Soulsby took a step nearer.

"There would be nothing easier than for your

father to find some one else to keep his home; and whom could *he* find to fill your place? The injury to him is unspeakably greater than the good to your father. Remember what life it is that we speak of; and think of what is in your hands. And it might be for such a little while."

His tones again sank into the pathetic pleading; and Dolores turned her eyes from his, into the future—and wavered.

A footfall sounded in the passage, and passed up the staircase—a heavy, even footfall; which fell on Soulsby's ear unheeded. But it had done its work.

"No, I cannot," said Dolores, raising her eyes. "I cannot leave my father to strangers, while I give what I can give to one who is—who has no claim." Her voice broke, but she resumed at once. "My father has his best years behind, and he has been through much. I am the only creature he has left to care for him. I shall return home with him."

Soulsby was silent.

"You wonder at my strength?" said Dolores, sadly, interpreting his look. "You would not wonder if you knew my life. It has been a preparation for this."

He was still silent.

"And it might have been a preparation for better?" she said, as if quoting his thought.

" Does it seem to you, that I should think it seems otherwise ? "

He turned and left her without further word. There was a task before himself that needed strength. On himself could be taken the breaking to his friend that which was upon him. Thus far he could save her.

He did it that evening—with blunt, short words, and a blanched face ; feeling himself to be copying another courage.

The blind man heard him, and bowed his head. His first words were a shock to his friend. They were low and calm.

" How soon will she be with me ? "

It was very soon. The spare figure was then at the door ; and Soulsby found his steps were unsteady, as with averted eyes he hastened away. But a stranger might have witnessed that last meeting, and heard the words that were said. It was of the wonted length, and its words were quiet and few. Claverhouse sat without sign of emotion, and spoke of himself. He told of the feelings that would be his own, in the time that lay between that hour and the hour of death, seeming to feel he could bear to suffer what she knew. Dolores hardly moved her lips. She listened with all her powers yielded to the listening ; with no sense of being dazed, or struggling to comprehend how matters stood—simply a clear consciousness of what was being done and suffered.

When Soulsby appeared in the doorway, and stood silent and still, she did not hesitate to rise. He made a helpless gesture of wincing, and shrank into the passage, and closed the door. But there was nothing that his eyes might not have seen. There was simply a handclasp—long and strong, with the clasp of a parting till death ; but a handclasp simply — the farewell which carried most, from its being linked with so much of the past.

Then they turned from each other ; and Soulsby and Dolores walked through the streets in a silence broken by some words on the beauty of the night.

CHAPTER XX.

Two days later Dolores returned with her father to her childhood's home—to the parsonage with its fulness of memories, its emptiness of younger voices. Her three-and-thirty troubled years had taught her much; and nothing, if not to live a trivial life for a worthier within her grasp, in brave knowledge of their difference; but her spirit all but quailed before the seeing her service to her father so bitterly far from seeming essential and great. He seemed to be changing further from the silent, deeply-needing man; whose doings were always, and whose thoughts were never, open to his family's questioning; who craved for earnest fellowship, and cherished dying memories. He talked more freely and more lightly than of old; was often from home without accounting for his absence; and seemed to be in all things falling from the old, elusive personality, which was woven with the fibres of her tenderness. But with all the pain of seeing the change, she saw it only as one who, with eyes straining after a beloved, fading form, sees other things that render his vision vexed. Her inner sight could not waver from the life, beloved and fading, she had forsaken at its lonely close; and there were times when she felt sadly near the end of her power of accepting bitterness. For the times had to come, when she opened the letters from Sophia — always written to herself, and carrying the folded paper in the delicate, scholar's hand— with a touch that did not tremble; when she wrote the answers — with their message, with its bitter impotence, to be entrusted to the same faithfulness—with no sign of the inward passions; when she spoke of her sisters in their married life, as a woman content that love should not be for herself. So far was her life from what it seemed, that when a letter was brought her, some two months after her return, with the narrow border of the mourning of a friend, her heart gave a throb of thankfulness. It was over. There were no more days to awaken to living in the worn spirit's trouble. It was gone to its long home; and the future had the ease of unvexed grief.

She read the few restrained words, in which sorrow was given no place, as lending no meaning to sympathy for a bitterer, subtler form; and folded the letter calmly.

"Father, I must go to Oxford," she said, in

a quiet voice, but rising from her seat. "Claver-house, the dramatist, is dead; and it is my wish to be present at the burial."

Her father met her eyes for a moment; and then seemed to rouse himself as though for some effort; as if finding the moment meet for some difficult and needful words; but hesitating beyond the limit, answered in his usual, neutral manner.

"My daughter, I have neither the right nor the desire to put restraint on your actions. I fully understand a wish to attend the funeral of a man whose works and teaching you valued. If you feel you have lost a friend, you may feel sure of my sympathy."

Dolores made no response to the question in the last words. She went to the duty of en-suring her father's welfare in the days of her absence; and in two hours she was gone.

Two months! — the length of a visit or a journey! — and lived alone! The thankfulness had grown to fierce rebellion, before she reached her sister's home. Ah! that she had left her father for these empty days, while she cheered the path to the grave of the creature whose life she saw as dark and great! It was not until some sad hours were behind, that her nature reasserted its power; and she saw her actions with unshrinking survey, as her best with the knowledge that was hers; saw that, with the past to live again with the same understanding, she must do again as she had done.

Walking from the graveyard, with her sister and her sister's husband, she felt a further change. She felt come over her with the old force, the old tenderness for her kind. Looking forward, she looked on years, when personal griefs would be passive under the old flowing of feeling for her race. Sophia's sister's tenderness, given with sensitive forbearance of question as to one bereaved; and Soulsby's unworded sympathy, and shrinking from allusion to the truth of the cry of his own sorrow, "it might be such a little while;" and even the dumb devotion of Julia, who had fallen suddenly into aged feebleness, and been taken into Soulsby's household, to give nominal service while she lived, grew in her thought to things that called for gratefulness of heart; and the life of care for her father became an ennobling filial tendance.

When she reached the changeless village, and saw the grey-headed, slow-moving figure lonely in its waiting, a great wave of pitiful lovingness came over her.

She joined her father with words of tender thanks; and tried to brighten the walk to the parsonage, by telling of Sophia and her married content.

But he seemed uneasy and absent; and she found that in spite of herself her feelings were

becoming chilled. He looked away into the
hedges while she spoke; threw covert glances
at her face when she was silent; asked already-
answered questions; and seemed not to follow
words of inquiry or narrative.

When they were walking through the churchyard,—as if driven to the point by the approaching end of an hour sought with a purpose, he
suddenly spoke, in tones that came strangely
from his lips.

"Dolores, I expect what I have to say will
be something of a shock to you; but I know
you have nothing but welcome for what makes
for another's happiness; and this, I believe, will
be greatly for mine. I am going very soon to
be married. It was settled while you were
away; though of course I — we had had
thoughts of it before. I am sure you are
generous enough, to acknowledge that this does
not alter my gratitude for what you have done
for me, and been to me. I know it is always
your happiness to see the happiness of others;
and I am sure you will find little else in seeing
mine."

He broke off; and walked on rapidly, with his
eyes averted. There was something in his tone,
which betrayed that some of the convictions he
expressed were of a wavering quality. Dolores
followed in silence, finding that no words came,
until she saw, or rather felt, his glance drawn

to herself. Then she spoke in an earnestly sympathetic tone.

"Father, you are far too much to me, for me to feel regret over anything that will make your life fuller. You will understand anything that was the result of surprise? I shall find it easy to rejoice with you."

The Reverend Cleveland made an involuntary pause, and met his daughter's eyes. She read in his own the words he did not speak — the old pregnant words, "You are a good woman, Dolores." She spoke again, with no purpose but the easing of his task.

"Is it any one I can guess, father? Not that it makes any difference, who it is. There is no one I can think of whom we know, for whom I do not already feel friendship."

"It is Mrs Merton-Vane," said Mr Hutton, in a tone with a rather peculiar easiness.

They had reached the parsonage door. They looked into each other's faces. Their hands met; and Dolores gave her father an embrace of earnest wishing of good. Then she went to her room, and stood at the window.

No thoughts of her altered future or her father's came. One sentence seemed to be burning itself on her soul. "So it was for nothing that she had left him." Her father's cheering — for these two months! — was other than her own. Ah, that he had told her in time—that either had known — that both had known — what there was to know! Her face grew old and hard; and, as never before in her life, she felt her heart fail.

It was long before weeping came, to give the sad courage of looking forward. There was this left to her—to work, and pity, and be just.

When she sought her father, she found him sitting in his study, quiet and ponderous. A knowledge of the gulf between them came almost invincibly repelling, as she met his look and words, and read his belief that her time had been given to household dealings. She took the seat that faced him, and spoke with her hands laid out on the table clasped, and her eyes drooping.

"Father, it is better that I should leave your home for good before your marriage. I shall take up teaching again. I think of spending a time with Sophia and her husband; and looking for suitable work from there. So your way will be clear of all impediments. I was the last and the chief one, was I not?" She ended with a touch of playfulness, and met her father's eyes with a smile, unconscious of the look in her own.

But the Rev. Cleveland saw it; and, though its meaning was hidden from him, it pierced his heart with pain that was heavy with the past. As he rose and hastened from the room, a word came muttered and helpless in the voice of an old man — a word which his daughter heard, and knew as not uttered as her own name—" Dolores ! "

A few weeks later there was another mistress at the parsonage. The marriage took place at a neighbouring parish, where Mrs Merton-Vane was staying with some friends. Dolores came to witness it with her married sisters and their husbands, as a one-time member of the household returned for presence at its festival. Many times before the parting, she felt the wisdom of the course she had chosen. The new Mrs Hutton's manner to herself had a coldness that was absent from her words to the sisters, who had given up claim to their father's roof; and her father gave her the same unemotional greeting and parting that he yielded them all; having assumed the veil over his deeper feelings, which he was to wear for the remainder of his days.

The wedding was an hour of uneasiness for all who saw it, in spite of the countenance given it by the sons and daughters of the earlier marriages. The guests adapted their deportment to their common, unflattering sense, that the purpose of their presence was simply the disproving the occasion a ground for sensitive feelings. Dr Cassell hardly opened his lips ; and rested his eyes on the little gold cross, which Mr Hutton still saw reason for including in his

x

daily equipment, with a doubtful aspect of regarding ritualism and third marriages as having
some subtle and repellent connection; not so
much as moving his eyes, when Elsa nudged
him, and begged for the anecdote he had told
at the last wedding.   Mr Blackwood's "Well,
Vicar, good-bye.   You have every good wish
from us all for many years of happiness," had
a forced, unemphatic ring : and Elsa's words,
"Oh, Uncle Cleveland, I am sure you ought to
be quite ashamed of having three wives! It is
a good thing you did not live in the time, when
the clergy were not allowed to marry. I suppose
I ought not to call you uncle any longer?" had
the unwonted effect of provoking a less ready
smile on the face of Mr Hutton, than of any
other of her hearers.

When it was over, Dolores returned to Oxford
with Soulsby and Sophia. In the evening she
wandered alone in the graveyard, where there
stood the tombstone which drew her to read
its words : "In sorrowing remembrance of
'Perdita,' wife of Sigismund Claverhouse"; and
below the simple inscription, "Also of Sigismund
Claverhouse, husband of the above."   As she
wandered, she was startled by a touch and
voice at her elbow.

"Is it—— ? Yes it is. It is Dolores !"

"Felicia?" said Dolores, with surprise and
welcome. "After all this time?"

"More in name than in nature, after seven years of nurturing the youthful mind for daily bread," said the voice whose familiar qualities carried so much. "But in both at this moment. How pleasant to see you, Dolores ! Why have you kept me so long without your address ? "

"Because you have kept me for the same time without yours," said Dolores, finding herself with the old, light, student manner. "On your conscience be the guilt ; for you knew my father's address, which would have found me always."

"I knew it was some vicarage somewhere, but I forgot the rest. And I had some doubt whether 'The Vicarage' would reach you. I daresay 'The Hovel' would not have reached me. If it would have, why did you not write ? "

"I did write," said Dolores ; "but the letter was returned. It seems that your family moved soon after I saw you last."

"Oh yes ; no doubt. As often as the rent of one house is too large to be paid, we move to another. It is the series of steps to '*the* House.'"

"How little you have changed !" said Dolores, looking down at the merry face, as a tender woman might look at a child.

"And you have changed more than a little ? "

said Felicia, her tone betraying for the first time that she had grown older. "You look as if you had had trouble, Dolores. What have you been doing these last years ; and what made you give up your post at the college? To think of our meeting like this, at poor Perdita's grave! I am teaching here, and came to look at it. But what of yourself? You are not married or a widow, I suppose?"

"I have been at home," said Dolores. "I gave up the post, because my father needed me. No, I have not been married."

"My father needs me too," said Felicia. "But he needs my help with the rent more. He told me I was one of this world's heroines; and I see I am not a heroine in any more interesting world. But I can tell you of some one who is going to be married. Miss Butler!"

"Is that so?" said Dolores. "She said nothing of it in her last letter. I hear from her two or three times a year."

"It all came to pass very suddenly," said Felicia. "I suppose no one who recognised such worth, would waste time in making his position secure. I had always looked on Miss Butler as wedded to the classics. I wonder who will succeed to her post. But don't let us part as suddenly as we met. When can I see you again?"

"Will you come with me now?" said Dolores. "I am spending a time here with a married sister; and there is welcome for my friends."

They turned from the tombstone side by side — these women whose ways had met, and parted, and met.

CHAPTER XXI.

"Miss Butler has not asked any of us to be her bridesmaids," said Miss Greenlow. "Can it be regarded except as an omission?"

"No," said Miss Cliff. "To grudge us such crumbs as are available for us of matrimonial privileges! It is a sad example of friendship."

"Very sad," said Miss Dorrington. "A great blow to one's faith in things."

"And to one's hope and charity," said Miss Cliff; "the former especially."

"I undertake to act more tactfully, when I am in a similar position," said Miss Greenlow.

"A universal vote of thanks to Miss Greenlow," said Miss Cliff.

"Are you all going to leave my generosity isolated?" said Miss Greenlow, with her comical pathos.

"May I express myself of the same intentions?" said Miss Lemaître.

"Things seem strange without Miss Butler," said Miss Adam. "There seems quite a gap in our company."

"Very complimentary to Miss Hutton," said Miss Lemaître.

"Oh, people are not interchangeable," said Miss Cliff. "A different person in any place means loss and gain at the same time. We must feel the miss, as we feel the new advantages."

"I miss Miss Butler as much as any one, I expect," said Dolores. "I had never learned the value of her counsel, till I tried to fill her place."

"I expect you do," said Miss Cliff gently.

"Oh, one does not think of Miss Hutton as filling any one's place," said Miss Adam. "She was one of ourselves for so long, that it seems only natural to have her here."

"Yes, yes, of course," said Miss Cliff, with a note of apology.

"Miss Butler is the only member of the staff who has ever been married, is she not?" said Miss Adam.

"There was Miss Kingsford," said Miss Cliff.

"Yes, yes. Poor child!" said Miss Dorrington.

"Did you ever see her in the year she was

married, Miss Hutton?" said Miss Lemaître.
"You were the only one who used to hear
from her."

"No," said Dolores.

"She was happy, I suppose?" said Miss Cliff.
"It seemed a strange thing; but one must not
put faith in seeming. He was clearly content
himself in that year; and certainly if any one
ever sorrowed sincerely, he did."

"More than she would have sorrowed, I
suspect, had she been the widowed one," said
Miss Lemaître. "She could not really have been
happy with him. Honestly, Miss Hutton, though
I suspect you of a veneration for him, do you
think any one could have?"

"I think some people could have," said
Dolores.

"Oh, you are connected with his great friend
now, are you not, Miss Hutton?" said Miss Cliff.
"I suppose you know more about him than ever.
William Soulsby is a sort of cousin of mine; so
you and I may imagine ourselves connected.
I found I was ignorant of amazement, when
I heard of his marriage. I thought he was
incarnate bachelorhood. I cannot call up a
picture of him making an offer of his hand,
can you?"

"Certainly when I knew him first, I did not
think of him as a likely person to marry," said

Dolores. "But it is the unlikely that happens. In this case it was very unlikely. He is more than thirty years older than my sister."

"You are experienced in people's manners of offering their hands, then, Miss Cliff?" said Miss Greenlow, in tones of polite comment.

"Ah! The cat is out of the bag," said Miss Dorrington.

"No," said Miss Cliff, with easy laughter. "I have no right to speak as one having authority."

"Ah! That is all very well now," said Miss Dorrington. "You certainly spoke in an unguarded moment with no uncertain sound."

"How many of us have that right, I wonder," said Miss Lemaître.

"I suspect Miss Adam," said Miss Greenlow, shaking her head.

"Miss Adam, you are a marked character," said Miss Cliff.

"Clearly we are right, Miss Lemaître," said Miss Greenlow; as Miss Adam yielded without great unwillingness to the impulse to look conscious.

"Anyhow we are rude," said Miss Dorrington genially.

"Oh, we can surely talk to young people, as old women may," said Miss Cliff.

"If youth is the qualification, Miss Hutton is

the fittest mark for our elderly interest," said Miss Lemaître.

"Miss Hutton, can you meet our eyes?" said Miss Adam, not without suggestion that this was beyond herself.

"Oh, we will acquit Miss Hutton. She is the most sensible of us all," said Miss Cliff.

THE END.